REMEMBERING ELLIE

GILLIAN JACKSON

Chapter One

An unwelcome sense of fear washed over Ellie as slowly, almost reluctantly, she emerged from unconsciousness, instinctively aware of being in a hospital bed yet perplexed about why and utterly powerless to perform even the simple task of opening her eyes. Perhaps the sharp, clinical smell gave away her whereabouts, or the unfamiliar, tinny noises reverberating in her ears. Voices reached her – hollow sounds which seemed to come from the end of a long, dark tunnel, the words pitched low and indistinct, lacking the clarity to decipher them.

Ellie's eyes were dry and gritty, but the strength to reach out and rub them eluded her, and her hands stubbornly refused to do her bidding. The voices drifted near and then far away, all so very odd. Was it a dream? It must be, and soon she'd wake up in the safety of her own bed, not this scratchy, uncomfortable hospital cot with its rubber mattress irritating her skin.

Ellie floated again into the unknown, breathing in the warm, sterile air and relaxing, letting go of the awful bewilderment and succumbing to the dream once more, drifting back to a place which wasn't quite so confusing.

Someone moved closer, their breath warm on Ellie's cheek, stroking her forehead with a cool, welcome touch. 'I thought her fingers moved. Look, her eyes flickered too!' It was her mother, Grace, her voice anxious and heavy with emotion but so comforting to hear. Ellie willed herself to offer a smile of reassurance, not understanding why she felt it necessary, but even her face muscles refused to obey. The floating sensation washed over her again; she was drifting, meandering – returning to the dream, she supposed.

A sense of falling evoked sudden panic, and a tightness across Ellie's chest inhibited her breathing; someone was pushing at her body, lifting her, and a moan escaped her lips.

'Can you hear me, honey?' a brisk, confident voice asked, but she could offer little more than another moan in reply, and her weighty eyelids still refused to open.

'We're just cleaning you up a bit, sweetheart, to make you feel fresher, more comfortable.'

It must be a nurse, the pleasant, sing-song voice continued. 'Will you try to move for me, honey? Squeeze my hand if you can.'

Making an enormous effort, Ellie was rewarded by feeling a trembling finger rise a mere inch off the bed.

'Get Mr Samms,' the nurse ordered, 'I think our girl's coming round!'

The fluorescent light was dazzling, stinging her eyes, but she fought hard now, determined to wake up if only to discover why she was in hospital. Turning away from the white glare above, Ellie succeeded in opening her eyes a fraction. The first thing that came into focus was her mother, Grace, sitting beside the bed with an enormous smile and tears streaming down her cheeks. A bulky, white-coated doctor stood at the other side of the bed, with two pretty young nurses looking on. They were all grinning like monkeys, and Ellie wished they'd share the joke.

A modicum of strength was returning to her limp body, and her fingers, obedient now, exploring her face, discovering a tube plastered down and running from her nose. What on earth was going on? Panic once again seized Ellie, and she turned to her mother.

'Mum! What is it? Why am I here?' The hoarse and barely audible voice sounded like someone else, it was such an effort to speak, and her throat was sore and scratchy. Hot tears scalded her face as she struggled to make sense of everything while remembering nothing.

'It's okay, Ellie, love.' Her mother gently stroked her arm. 'You were in an accident, and you've been unconscious for a while, but you're back with us now. You're in hospital, in York, and they're taking excellent care of you. Try not to worry; I promise everything will be fine now.'

The bulky figure of the doctor stepped forward, introducing himself as Mr Samms, the consultant neurologist. He leaned his tall frame over the bed whilst gently lifting Ellie's drooping eyelids to peer into her eyes. Holding up three fingers, he asked how many there were.

'Good,' he said, and nodded, asking next if she was in pain.

'I feel stiff and weak, but no pain. I'm so thirsty. Could I have a drink?' Grace was there in a flash with a glass of water, helping raise Ellie's head from the pillow to sip the tepid liquid. The doctor instructed the nurses in muffled tones, and after asking his patient a few more questions, he left to continue his rounds, promising to return later in the afternoon. Ellie looked closely at her mother, noticing how tired she was and how much older than her fifty-one years she appeared to be.

'What day is it, Mum?'

'Thursday, love.'

'And how long have I been here?'

Grace took hold of her hand in both of hers, squeezing

gently. 'You've been in a coma for over four weeks.' She spoke almost apologetically as if it was somehow her fault.

'Four weeks! But how? I mean, what happened?'

'It was an accident; a car knocked you off your bike. Amazingly, you have no broken bones, only a few cuts and bruises, and they've all healed nicely, no scars, thank goodness.'

'But I can't remember, Mum. Why can't I remember?'

'Shh... Don't worry about it now; it'll all come back in time. The doctor said it's common for memory to be affected by head injuries. It'll just take time, that's all.'

Ellie lay back and drew in a deep breath, trying to relax and not worry about the accident. After all, did she really want to remember such a painful event? Yet the last month was completely lost to her, which was really scary.

Recent events had clearly affected her mother too. It was little wonder she looked so tired. Both she and her dad must have been worried out of their minds. Suddenly Ellie's exams popped into her mind.

'Mum. Have the exam results come through? Did I pass?'

'What exams, love?' Grace looked puzzled.

'My A levels, what grades did I get?'

Grace Watson frowned, squeezed her daughter's hand again and forced a smile. 'Don't worry about it now – you're still a little confused. Try to rest – we'll talk about it later. I've rung your dad and Phil. They're so excited to know you're awake and should be here anytime, and Phil's bringing Sam in too.'

Before Ellie could ask the next troubling question, Derek Watson appeared in the doorway next to a tall, grinning young man carrying a plump little baby in his arms. Her father stood back, allowing the younger man to approach the bed. In a sequence which appeared to play out in slow motion, Ellie's mother rose to take the infant while the young man, his soft brown eyes wide and glistening, leaned over the bed, placed his hands on her shoulders, and kissed her gently on the lips. If her reactions had been quicker, she'd have turned away; who did he think he was, kissing her like that?

'Ellie!' The young man's voice cracked with emotion. 'I've been so worried, and we've missed you so much.'

Turning to her mother, who was still holding the child, Ellie asked in a quiet, pleading voice,

'Mum, who's this?'

The colour drained from Grace's face as she looked from her daughter to her husband and then to the young man before replying, 'It's Phil, darling; he's been here every day with Sam...' Her words trailed off, and there was an awkward silence while she mouthed something to her husband which Ellie missed. Derek leaned over to kiss his daughter, unable to speak and patted her arm before leaving the little hospital room to find one of the nursing staff.

The tall, handsome man with a mop of sandy hair sat down next to the bed and took hold of Ellie's hand, a concerned expression on his face. She didn't possess enough strength to pull away. This was all so confusing and exhausting. *Surreal*, yes, she thought, that was the word for it, surreal, and she felt quite dizzy with the effort of trying to comprehend exactly what was going on. Perhaps it was a dream after all and one from which she'd soon awake. Looking into the young man's hopeful brown eyes, Ellie closed her own, sinking silently back into a place where things were not quite so strange.

Chapter Two

E llie was unaware of how long she'd been asleep – it could have been for another four weeks, although she doubted it. Her eyes, less gritty now, opened more readily, and a sense of relief washed over her as she realised no one was beside the bed. Sitting alone, Ellie welcomed the opportunity to remain still for several minutes, taking in her surroundings and trying to assemble her muddled thoughts.

The room was a side ward with one other bed, which thankfully was unoccupied. A window at the far end was black, with no daylight, so presumably, it was night-time, and a closed door in the corner probably led to a bathroom. The ward door stood open with the nurses' station in view a few yards away, where a solitary nurse sat frowning at a computer screen, her nose almost touching it. Several piles of dog-eared, brown folders cluttered the surface of the desk where she worked, and unsurprisingly, the nurse looked harassed.

Ellie didn't attempt to attract the woman's attention, craving a few minutes alone to try and remember what had happened, to recall the events which brought her to this point in time yet now escaped her. Closing her eyes, she focused on the incomplete scraps of memory floating around her brain, but it proved too challenging, like doing a jigsaw puzzle without a picture for guidance, and hindered by several missing key pieces.

Ellie's mother said she'd been knocked off her bike, but that particular memory eluded her completely. Maybe if she knew where the accident had happened or where she was going at the time, it might jog some recollection. However, the images remained stubbornly incomplete. The only memory hovering in her mind was of the last day of term at the sixth-form college that she and her best friends, Rosie and Fran, attended. Fran had surprised them all by sneaking in a bottle of wine, and Ellie remembered the three of them drinking in the students' common room at lunchtime, keeping the bottle secreted in a tote bag as if they were alcoholics.

Oh no! A sudden panic seized her. *Please, God, I wasn't knocked off my bike after drinking the wine.* But Ellie was sure she'd not drunk more than one glass – she would never be so stupid, surely? A throbbing headache pounded at her temples, and being unable to remember anything constructive was becoming increasingly frustrating.

It was no good. All attempts to trawl the recesses of her brain only exacerbated the headache and confused Ellie even more. Perhaps the nurse would know the circumstances of her admission; trying to remember it herself was like coming up against a solid and stubbornly unmovable brick wall.

In a voice barely more than a whisper and trying to sit up, calling out to the nurse was no easy task. Ellie's body appeared to be made of cotton wool, and she possessed very little strength to draw on to help herself. The nurse's attention shifted from the computer screen to her young patient, and she quickly entered the little room, her rubber soles squeaking on the polished floor and her round, plump face wearing a wide smile.

'Hello there.' The nurse, whom Ellie guessed to be in her forties, possessed an endearing dimple in her chin and an almost conspiratorial grin. 'They told me you'd come round yesterday. Welcome to the world of Ward 32!'

Ellie instantly liked this friendly woman with twinkling eyes and managed to return the smile.

'I'm Caroline,' the nurse half-hitched her ample bottom onto the side of the bed as if settling in for a chat. 'Night staff nurse and keeper of the kettle, not to mention the chocolate bickies.'

'So, what time is it?' Ellie asked.

'1.37am, and I think you and I are the only ones on this ward who are not sleeping.'

The nurse possessed a natural, relaxed manner. Ellie watched her pour a welcome glass of water as if she'd read her mind, and helped her patient to sit up and drink. When Caroline asked if she wanted to sleep some more or sit up for a while, she chose the latter option. Sleeping seemed to have been her only occupation for some considerable time. The nurse was gentle but strong in helping lift her, and soon Ellie was propped up with two fresh white pillows plumped behind her, supporting her frail body. As Caroline seemed in no hurry to get back to the computer, Ellie took the opportunity to find out what, if anything, she knew about the accident.

'Yes.' Caroline frowned in concentration. 'Four weeks is about right. I remember because you were admitted while I was away on holiday. The doctor will be doing his rounds in the morning, and I'm sure he'll be able to tell you more about your injuries than I can. All I know is that there were no internal injuries, a blessing, and no broken bones. Your head seems to have taken the entire trauma, hence the coma and confusion, but now you're back with us, the future's looking rosy. You might be a bit muddled for a while, which is quite normal. Things will fall into place in time, so don't worry about it. Mr Samms is your neurologist; he's great – a brilliant doctor – you couldn't be in more capable hands.'

'My parents,' Ellie asked. 'There was someone with them last evening who seemed to know me, a man… do you know who it was?'

'Sorry, I wasn't here then, love, but don't worry, your mum will be here in the morning. Such a lovely lady; she hasn't missed a day in visiting you.'

Ellie wished she could stop thinking; it only hurt her head, but she was wide awake now and readily accepted Caroline's offer of a cup of tea, hoping it might help her relax. It would be a long time until Grace Watson arrived, hopefully, to answer all the questions stacking up in Ellie's mind.

The early morning hours dragged, brightened only by Caroline, who brought the promised tea and a slice of toast. Ellie's throat was still dry and sore, but Caroline assured her it was to be expected and would soon pass. The nurse also removed the catheter, which had been in place and helped to support her first unsteady steps to the bathroom. Ellie felt incredibly weak and was sure she'd lost weight – perhaps not a bad thing but a drastic way to do it.

As the nurse helped her back into bed, she caught sight of the name written above the bed, which read, '*Eleanor Graham, known as Ellie*'.

'You've got my name wrong,' she remarked to Caroline. 'It's Eleanor Watson, not Graham.'

'Oh, sorry, love, we'll sort it out when sister comes on duty at eight. Now is there anything else I can get you, a couple of magazines perhaps, another cuppa?'

'I'd like a shower if it's possible?'

'Maybe later when the day staff are on, and there'll be more pairs of hands to help you.'

'Great, thanks. I think I'll try to rest for a while now. It feels like I've run a marathon, not just been to the loo.'

Caroline smiled before returning to the desk to make a few notes about her patient's confused state of mind, anticipating an even greater shock for this young woman in the morning.

Chapter Three

E llie slept remarkably soundly for a few more hours, then managed to eat a little breakfast, only orange juice and cereal but it made her feel considerably better and stronger. Grace Watson arrived earlier than usual, moving slowly down the corridor with a weary air. Ellie thought she too, appeared to have lost weight as she studied her mother who'd stopped briefly at the nurses' station to talk to the ward sister. Grace looked unwell too, which both shocked and saddened Ellie. Her mother growing older was something she'd never seriously considered; most children were blinkered regarding their parents, thinking them invincible, unlike other adults who aged and one day would no longer be there. Yet now it seemed the years were telling on Grace Watson, and Ellie was stung by guilt, assuming the stress of the accident had aged her. Even her hair held more streaks of grey than she'd previously noticed.

Ellie watched the two women deep in conversation from her vantage point, and from Grace's sagging shoulders and furrowed expression, it was clear she was anxious. Inadvertently Ellie had put her parents through quite an ordeal over the last few weeks. The thought of her mother's weary appearance being somehow her fault brought regret and a determination to make it up to Grace once she was well and home again. Ellie was aware of it being her last summer at home before leaving for university, and was determined to make every day count.

'Hi, there!' Grace entered the little side ward, her voice unnaturally high and chirpy as if she'd flicked on the 'pretence' switch, 'How are you feeling this morning, love?'

'Much better than yesterday, thanks. I've slept quite a bit, been up to go to the bathroom and even eaten a little breakfast.' Hopefully, this positive report would erase some of the worries from her mother's face and smooth out those new wrinkles on her brow.

'That's great, sweetheart.' She kissed her daughter's forehead.

'You're very early, Mum. Couldn't you sleep?'

'Oh, I'm fine. I don't need as much sleep as I used to. The sister tells me Mr Samms will be round this morning; he's the neurologist looking after you, the one you saw for a little while yesterday. We'll have a chance to ask him some questions then if you like, okay?'

'It's you I need to answer a few questions for me, Mum. Have you brought the results of my exams with you; they must have arrived by now. And who was the man with Dad last night – and the baby?'

Grace's face reverted to a solemn expression once again, her eyes clouded over, and Ellie took over the role of offering comfort.

'Hey, Mum, it's okay – I'm on the mend now. You'll soon have me back at home plaguing you as usual.' Ellie reached for her mother's hand and squeezed it gently. 'I'm sorry, I've really put you through the wringer with all of this, haven't I? But things will be fine once I get out of here and back home anyway.'

Grace took a tissue from her bag and blew her nose. 'I know you'll be all right, sweetheart, but you still seem slightly confused. The sister's called the doctor, and he's coming soon, then we can have a little talk.'

'But can't you tell me, Mum? Did I fail my exams, is that it? You don't have to protect me, you know, if I failed, I can always resit them in the autumn.'

'No, my love, you did really well; three A stars and a B. Dad and I are so proud of you.'

'Fantastic. I should get my first choice at uni with those grades!' Ellie was all smiles, really excited now, but it was evident her mother didn't share her exuberance.

'What is it, Mum? You don't seem very pleased for me, tell me what's wrong?'

As Grace was about to answer, a young police constable appeared in the doorway and coughed awkwardly to make his presence known. He looked somewhat nervous, holding his helmet in his hands and fiddling with the brim as he spoke.

'Ellie Graham? The nurse said I could see if you feel up to talking to me now?' He took a couple of steps nearer to the bed.

'Is this about the accident?' Grace replied for her daughter. 'Because if it is, it's a bit soon. She only regained consciousness yesterday.'

'It's okay, Mum, I'll be fine, but my name's Watson, not Graham.'

The young officer moved forward and introduced himself as PC Jason Green, showing his warrant card with more than a bit of pride. 'The hospital informed us you were awake. We've been waiting to speak to you to get your version of what happened on the day of the accident, so I'd like to take a statement, nothing too onerous, I assure you.' PC Green grinned and as Ellie returned his smile, she thought how young he looked, only about sixteen years old, fresh-faced and clean-shaven – he could have been one of her fellow students at college.

'Well, actually, I don't think I'll be able to give you a statement.'

'Oh, shall I come back tomorrow then?' His face reddened, embarrassed his visit might be premature.

'No, it's not that, you see, I appear to have lost my memory and can't remember anything at all about the accident. Apparently, it's not uncommon to forget such trauma, and I simply haven't a clue what happened. Perhaps you can tell me something about it. You must know more than I do?' Ellie was suddenly hopeful of learning some of the missing details.

'Umm, I'm not sure if I can… you do know we've found the driver who knocked you down, don't you?'

'No, I know absolutely nothing. Found him? Are you saying it was a hit and run?' Ellie was surprised and flashed a look of something like reproach towards her mother.

'We haven't had the opportunity to tell her much about it yet. There've been other priorities,' Grace interrupted, 'But we were going to tell her soon.'

Ellie's expression conveyed the sentiment that, in her opinion, her mother should have already told her the facts surrounding the accident.

'Oh, well, I suppose if you don't remember, I could go over some of the details… shall I?' the officer asked.

'Yes, please do!' She was keen to know more. PC Green opened his notebook and started his account.

'You were cycling along St James Street at 3.45pm on May 19th going through the traffic lights, on green, when a man in a Toyota ran a red light at speed and hit you full-on, knocking you from your bike. There were several witnesses, mothers who'd just picked their children up from school as well as other shoppers, and fortunately, a nurse, who administered first aid until the ambulance arrived. The driver didn't stop and made off south, down St James Street, but a few witnesses took photos of his vehicle, which enabled us to pick him up within the hour. It appeared he'd been drinking and was arrested immediately for, er – dangerous driving, running a red light and driving under the influence of alcohol. He admitted the charges and appeared quite remorseful at the time, so I'm sure he'll be glad to know you're out of the coma and on the mend.' The young officer snapped his notebook closed and smiled at both women, pleased with his account of the incident. Ellie rather cynically assumed the man's relief would probably have more to do with the charge not being one of manslaughter than any genuine concern for his victim.

'Will you need my statement to proceed?' she asked, 'Because quite honestly, I don't know how long it'll take for my memory to come back, and the doctors can't give me a timescale either. It seems to be a case of if I'll ever remember, not when?'

'It's certainly an unusual situation.' The young officer scratched his chin thoughtfully, clearly unsure of the protocol in a case like this. 'This is rather unprecedented in my experience, but I don't see why we shouldn't be able to proceed as he's pleaded guilty, and as I said, there are plenty of witnesses. Look, I'll leave my card and if you do remember anything in the next few days, give me a ring and I'll pop back to take the statement then.'

After saying goodbye and politely wishing her well, PC Green left and Ellie turned to her mother. 'Why didn't you tell me all this, Mum?'

'There's hardly been time, has there? Besides, you've enough to worry about without knowing it was a stupid drunk driver who caused it all.'

'I understand, Mum, but please, let me decide what to

worry about in future, will you? If I think you're keeping things from me it'll only make matters worse; I can handle the circumstances of the accident and anything else which has happened over the last four weeks.'

Ellie needed her mother to be honest with her, not to treat her like a child, but after her little speech, Grace barely seemed able to look her daughter in the eye. She made an excuse to leave for a few minutes to get some coffee, promising half-heartedly to answer all of Ellie's questions when she returned.

Chapter Four

M r Samms appeared in the doorway of Ellie's room, a big man with a big smile and, if Caroline was to be believed, a big heart to match. He must have been six foot five or six, with broad shoulders, close-cropped dark hair and round, deep-blue eyes. The neurologist was followed by Grace, who hurried behind carrying two coffees, one of which she placed on Ellie's bedside cabinet.

'Well, hello there.' The doctor's very presence filled the tiny room. 'I can finally get to meet you properly. Good morning, Ellie.'

Ellie couldn't help but return his smile; the man's whole nature was infectious. She'd been quite groggy and hardly remembered his brief examination of the previous day. Now, she watched him closely as he picked up the chart from the end of the bed and glanced through the notes.

'Everything seems to be in order. I see you've been up for a little walk, eating and drinking okay. Well done.' He drew up a chair on the opposite side of the bed to Grace and Ellie half expected him to pat her on the top of her head.

'Just a few quick questions for you this morning.' He spoke

kindly, in a soft voice for such a big man. 'Easy ones first, what's your full name?'

'Eleanor Grace Watson,' she replied.

'And do you know what day it is?'

'Well, Mum told me it was Thursday yesterday, so I reckon it's Friday today.' Ellie grinned at the simplicity of the questions.

'Very good, we'll try the hard ones now. Who's the Prime Minister?'

'David Cameron.'

'And what year is it?'

'2010.' The game was beginning to get tiresome.

'Ellie, can you remember anything at all about your accident?' Mr Samms' face took on a more earnest expression now.

'No, absolutely nothing. The last thing I remember is being in the common room at college with my friends, and then I woke up here. I seem to have completely lost the last four weeks of my life.' She sighed, glancing in the direction of her mother and was shocked to see Grace's grim expression. Suddenly Ellie was scared.

'What is it? What's wrong?'

'Just one more question.' The doctor placed his hand gently on her arm. 'How old are you, Ellie?'

'Eighteen. But something's wrong, isn't it? What is it you're not telling me?' Tears of frustration threatened to spill over.

'It's okay, no more questions for now.' Mr Samms held up his large hand in a quietening gesture. 'But I need you to listen carefully to what I'm going to tell you, Ellie, and I don't want you to worry because everything will be fine in time.'

Now Ellie was really panicking. When someone told you not to worry about what they were going to say, it most certainly wasn't going to be good news. The doctor continued in his soft bedside voice,

'When someone has an accident like yours, and the head suffers the kind of trauma yours did, there are all sorts of things which can happen. What I will say is that it's a good job you were wearing a helmet, otherwise I'm pretty sure we wouldn't be here today having this conversation. The brain is a very complicated and sensitive organ which doesn't take too kindly to being knocked about. One of the things which can happen with a trauma like this is memory loss. We know you've experienced this because you have no recollection of the actual event. But sometimes the memory loss is more than just a few hours prior to the accident and in some cases the patient has no recall of several years before the event. Do you understand what I'm saying, Ellie?'

A silent, solemn nod confirmed she did. Ellie was already putting two and two together and wasn't at all comfortable with the result.

Mr Samms continued. 'I'm afraid this is the case with you. Now, remember it's not an uncommon thing and in most cases, what is forgotten eventually comes back, so I don't want you to worry. It simply means it will take a little longer for you to get better, back to the old Ellie again. In many ways, you're an extremely lucky girl to have no other physical injuries and going forward from this, it would be better for you to dwell on the positives rather than the negatives.' Mr Samms watched his patient as she struggled to process his words. She was an intelligent young woman and he doubted she'd become hysterical when she learned the full extent of her memory loss. But this was, however, a complex case, and he'd prepared the ward sister to administer a sedative if necessary. It was time for him to leave his patient with her mother, time for Grace Watson to fill in the blanks of her daughter's lost years.

Biting her bottom lip, Ellie studied Mr Samms' broad back as he left the room, a nurse scurrying after him and closing the door behind them. Grace, finally alone with her daughter, swallowed hard. Ellie could see it was an effort for her mother to keep her emotions in check.

'Mum, I know something's terribly wrong. He was preparing me for something bad, wasn't he and it's scaring me, Mum, am I going to be all right?'

Grace wrapped her arms around her daughter, pulling her close and rubbing her back like she would an infant whilst quietly trying to reassure her. 'Yes, Ellie, you're going to be fine, my love. Don't worry, it's not that.'

Ellie released the breath she'd been holding and then pulled away, asking with urgency,

'Then will you please tell me what's wrong? I feel as if everyone knows something which I don't and if it's about me then I want to know too – I need to know!'

Grace stroked her daughter's arm and took hold of her hand, which trembled with fear and exasperation.

'It's okay. Don't get upset, I'll tell you.' Sitting up straight in the chair and pulling her shoulders back, she took a deep breath. 'You do understand you've been unconscious for almost a month, don't you?'

'Yes.' The reply was brief. Ellie wanted her mother to get straight to the point.

'Well, Mr Samms explained how some people lose their memories after a head trauma, and to some extent, that's what's happened to you.'

'To what extent, Mum? What's happened that I can't remember?'

'Ellie, sweetheart, your memory seems to have lost a few

years. But you mustn't get upset about it – it could come back at any time.'

'A few years! How many?'

'Nearly ten, it's not 2010, it's 2019.' Grace, biting her bottom lip, studied her daughter's face.

'2019, then I'm not eighteen, I'm... twenty-seven, twenty-eight?'

'Twenty-eight, it was your birthday while you were unconscious.' Grace looked sheepish as if it was all somehow her fault as Ellie sat rigid in the bed, her mind struggling to process what all of this meant.

'But what's happened to me in those ten years, Mum? Get me a mirror – I want to see what I look like.'

Grace fumbled in her bag and pulled out her compact mirror, hesitantly passing it to her daughter. Ellie stared in horror, moving the mirror around to examine every part of her face. It was like seeing someone else, someone familiar whom you couldn't quite place. She fingered her fair hair. It was still long, shoulder-length as she generally wore it, but with layers added and much lighter too; had she resorted to colouring it? Her green eyes appeared startled as Ellie frowned at the lines around them, lines she'd never noticed before, or more accurately, couldn't remember! Her heart-shaped face was much slimmer too, with cheek bones more pronounced, but it was a good thing, wasn't it?

Ellie's brain was working at speed, an abundance of questions swirling in her head – the answers slow to come. Turning to look at the name above her bed, she read aloud, 'Ellie Graham... I'm married, aren't I?' Her eyes were wide with the sudden fear of not knowing who she was anymore, but she could still think rationally. The young man, the baby! 'Mum, tell me; tell me everything.'

'Yes, Ellie, you're married. It was your husband, Phil, who came in with your son yesterday. But you're very happily married, and little Sam is such a beautiful child, the centre of your world. You have a good life, love, a truly great life!' There was anxiety and empathy in Grace's eyes, with tears threatening to spill.

'But how can it be such a good life if I can't remember it? That man, Phil, he was a stranger – and the little boy – surely I would remember having a baby?' The sobbing started. Ellie's mind swirled with questions for which there were no answers as her brain struggled to process this new and somewhat frightening information.

How long had she been married?
When was her son born?
Where did they live?
Were they really happy?
And why couldn't she remember?

At this moment in time, the happiness her mother spoke of eluded Ellie completely, and she allowed Grace to hold her while she cried, loud sobs racking her body as her mother rocked her to and fro as if Ellie was a child again.

Chapter Five

The side-room door was propped open as usual, and Ellie watched her mother talking to Mr Samms beside the nurses' station. His broad back blocked her view of Grace so she could neither see her face nor pick up on their conversation. Clearly, they'd be talking about her, not simply exchanging pleasantries about the weather, which was frustrating, to say the least. Surely, they should include her in their discussions, not treat her like a child.

When the doctor visited Ellie earlier in the day, checking the notes at the end of the bed and asking how she felt after learning of the amnesia, her answers were rather curt. Ellie had woken feeling inexplicably angry – with herself, her parents and even the doctor, who was only trying to do his best and who'd been so pleasant to both her and Grace. And now they were excluding her again, more fuel for her anger.

Learning the full extent of her memory loss yesterday was devastating, and Ellie sobbed bitterly on her poor mother's shoulder. Grace decided it was unwise to have visitors for the rest of the day, it would take time to process the recently learned facts about her life, and visitors would undoubtedly add pressure.

Unsettling thoughts invaded Ellie's mind at an alarming rate; she no longer knew who she was or what had happened to her parents during the last decade. Grace certainly appeared to have aged, but her mother was sixty-one, not fifty-one as Ellie initially thought. Yet worse still was the loss of her own memories when apparently so much had happened. Those precious university years were lost to her, the places she'd travelled to were forgotten, but by far the scariest loss was the memories of having fallen in love with this man, Phil, married him and having even given birth to a son. It was inconceivable! To the present Ellie, Phil and baby Sam were complete strangers.

During the afternoon, Ellie had been taken for a CT scan, a surreal experience in itself, and Mr Samms assured her this morning the scan was completely normal, but if so, why was there no memory of a whole decade of her life?

Watching the doctor talking earnestly with her mother, Ellie regretted being abrupt with him earlier and attempted to stifle future anger, resolving to apologise as soon as the opportunity arose. The situation wasn't his fault, or anyone's really; it simply was what it was.

Grace Watson stepped out from the shadow of the doctor and moved towards her daughter's room. Ellie noticed how her mother's expression once again changed from grave concern to a forced smile as she met her daughter's gaze. It didn't fool her one bit.

'Hi, love.' Grace bent to kiss her. 'Mr Samms is pleased with your progress, and the scan showed nothing at all to be concerned about.'

Ellie resisted bombarding her with more questions, being heartily sick of asking why and when. A slow acceptance that no one could answer the most important question; when would her memory return? Playing along with her mother's forced brightness seemed prudent – offering a smile of her own and feigning interest in Grace's chatter about minor problems with the buses.

But the small talk irritated her. When conversation ran dry, Ellie looked directly into her mother's eyes and asked, 'This is what, day three, Mum? What's going to happen to me?'

'You don't have to worry about the future yet – just get plenty of rest to build up your strength.'

'I'm getting all the rest I need. What was Mr Samms telling you just now?'

'I told you. He's pleased with your progress and the scan results were fine.'

'What else, Mum, what about tomorrow and the day after? He must have said more – please don't hold back on me. I need to know. I thought we'd decided on a policy of honesty yesterday?'

Grace's eyes dropped to earnestly study the pattern on her skirt while trying to form an acceptable reply, eventually deciding the best way forward was to be completely honest, as they'd agreed. 'The truth is we don't know what to do for the best. You can stay here for another couple of days until you're a little stronger, but then, as physically there's nothing wrong with you, we can't decide what the next step should be. There's simply no way of knowing when your memory will come back.'

'And don't I get a say in these decisions?' Ellie tried to sound calm, although some of the irritability from earlier bubbled to the surface again. Yes, she understood how hard this had been for her parents and had no desire to make matters worse, but she needed to know what would happen in the immediate future, what exactly was expected of her. The frustration gnawed at her as her mother tried to explain.

'Phil wants you to go home from here. He's missed you, and so has Sam. It's been a terrible time of worry for him. But your dad and I thought it might be best if you came to stay with us for a while until you feel a little better. Mr Samms suggested some kind of psychiatric help, or counselling perhaps, which could be residential or as a day patient.' Grace's face was drawn, pale from worry and lack of sleep. Ellie's mood softened as her heart went out to her mother. 'Oh, Mum. It's such a mess, isn't it? Is memory loss a psychiatric problem – does the doctor think I'm going insane or something?'

'No, sweetheart, not at all. I think he has a dilemma here; physically, you'll be ready for discharge in a couple of days, but we're unsure of the best course of action to take. Amnesia is a psychological thing, and he thinks treatment of some kind would be appropriate at some stage, although it's entirely up to you. It's still early days, and your memory could come back at any time. Have *you* thought about what you want to do next?'

Ellie rolled her eyes. 'I've thought of nothing else! I'm apparently a wife and mother, but I can't seem to come to terms with it.' She turned more fully to face her mother. 'I can't go and live with Phil, Mum – he might be my husband, but to me, he's a stranger! And Sam's a lovely little boy, but I don't even remember giving birth and don't feel like a mother should towards him. I wouldn't have a clue how to care for him. Surely Phil can't expect me to slot back into a life I can't remember?'

Ellie was exhausted. It felt like she was drifting in a thick fog which not only surrounded her but threatened to suffocate her as well. Grace grasped her daughter's hand. 'Phil's missed you terribly, but he's an understanding man who loves you and only wants the best for you. Look, he's coming in this after-noon and bringing Sam with him. We persuaded him to give you a little time in the circumstances, but he's desperate to see you and talk to you. Phil's hoping if you spend time together your memory will return and you can be a family again, which is only natural. I can't stop him coming in, Ellie – he needs to try, and who knows, he might be right?'

'But he's a stranger – and I know nothing about looking after babies, you know that. I'm amazed I have a child; being a mother wasn't something I ever thought I'd want to do.'

'I know, Ellie, but that was ten years ago. You've changed so much since then. You're a grown woman now, with a husband you love and a baby you chose to have. And if it's any comfort, you're a brilliant mother. Dad and I have been so proud of you...' Grace appeared to run out of words.

'But I don't feel twenty-eight at all – my brain thinks I'm eighteen. What on earth am I going to do, Mum?'

Chapter Six

P hil Graham changed his son's clothes for the second time in less than an hour. He desperately wanted their son to look his best, but a tooth was coming through and the constant dribbling had yet again soaked the front of his T-shirt.

'Here you are, Sam, the top with the giraffe on – Mummy loves this one.' He almost lost it then and swallowed back the tears. Phil promised himself at the very beginning of this nightmare he'd be strong for both Sam and Ellie, so the tears would have to wait until he was alone. He couldn't stop the flow then, when climbing into the big empty bed, missing Ellie's warm presence beside him – it was almost too much to bear. But during the day his son kept him occupied and gave him focus.

Sam was too young to understand what was happening but, with the resilience children so often display, he adapted, in many ways oblivious to the changes they were living with and the reality of his mother being cruelly absent from his life. Phil worked hard to keep his baby son happy, and as for himself, he tried not to dwell on the future.

After Ellie's accident, when it was touch and go whether she would survive, Phil hit rock bottom. Four of the most agonising weeks of his life followed with the awful uncertainty which accompanied each day. Then came the wonderful news she'd woken from the coma and spoken to Grace. But the excitement of taking Sam to see her was soon shattered, as Phil was plunged into the depths of despair once again when it became apparent his wife didn't know him. Ellie didn't recognise him or their son – a shock and unexpected complication which was so hard to bear – soul-destroying to say the least. It hadn't occurred to him that this might happen, but Phil's wife, his beautiful Ellie whom he loved so much, stiffened when he kissed her and looked at him with such horror that yet again his life appeared to be collapsing around him. He felt sidelined, forced to simply watch like an outsider and powerless to control what was happening to his family, his universe. Later, once Sam was asleep, Phil sobbed like a baby himself.

Mr Samms, although an excellent and understanding doctor in whom they all had complete confidence, couldn't predict how long it would take for Ellie's memory to return. It seemed for all his years of medical training and experience, the neurologist was no wiser than Phil in this matter and, hard though it was to accept, he couldn't rule out the possibility she might never recover her memory. To Phil, this was unthinkable. What if his wife never remembered him or their baby? Their marriage? The happy times they'd shared? How could he go on without her by his side, and how would it affect Sam in the long term to have a mother who couldn't remember him? Necessity forced Phil to push such thoughts to the dusty corners of his mind. Yet, they refused to remain there, haunting him in his weaker moments at night when he felt so alone, and when Sam cried and he felt inadequate to meet his son's needs without Ellie there to share the responsibility.

Phil was aware he would never have coped without the brilliant support of Grace and Derek. They were his rock during those horrendous weeks of uncertainty, even though they too were feeling as low as he was. Phil's parents lived in Spain, where they'd retired six years previously, and due to his father's failing health, were unable to return to England to offer any support. Keeping them in the loop about Ellie's progress became yet another duty to take on board, and he had yet to break the news to them about her amnesia.

At work, Phil's boss showed remarkable understanding and generosity, insisting he take extended leave for as long as necessary, and in return, Phil tried to work from home whenever Sam was asleep. Any work he could do remotely also helped to occupy his mind in those lonely, late hours and keep him sane. But he was aware his boss's generosity couldn't last forever, and he would need to return to some version of normality soon.

Now Ellie was awake, Phil wrestled with the immediate future and the next step to take. Without anticipating a complication such as amnesia, he'd assumed his wife would simply return home, and they'd pick up the threads of their life once more. But typically, fate threw up other notions, painful, unfair factors which railing against couldn't alter. While Ellie didn't remember Phil or their baby, the nightmare rolled on, but for how long? No one could provide answers, and it was so hard to keep hope alive when there seemed to be no end in sight.

Phil's biggest, yet so far unspoken fear, was that Ellie was somehow blocking the last ten years from her memory because she'd been unhappy with their life together. The idea was abhorrent, but one he couldn't shake off. As a couple, they appeared to have it all; a beautiful home, financial stability and Sam, who was very much a wanted baby. They'd been so happy when he was born, or at least Phil had been; did he really know Ellie's true feelings, her innermost thoughts? Was it even possible for one human being to know another so completely?

Phil constantly wrestled with his fears and insecurities – how could his wife not remember their wedding, the wonderful honeymoon they'd shared, the birth of their child? Could she subconsciously no longer want to be a wife and mother? These insidious thoughts constantly buzzed around his brain, yet Phil didn't dare to voice them, even to himself.

Sam's wet fist on his father's face reminded him it was time to set off for the hospital, and he picked up his chuckling son, almost envious of the child's oblivion to their predicament. If only Phil could close his eyes and wake up to his normal, wonderful world – if only Ellie had taken the car that fateful afternoon instead of deciding to take her bike. *If only* were two words Phil was beginning to loathe with a passion.

Chapter Seven

Although not asleep, Ellie's eyes were closed as she endeavoured yet again to remember the accident but still could recall nothing other than being at college with her friends, something she now knew to have been a decade ago. Squeezing her eyes tightly shut as if trying to see into the concealed recesses of her mind, only frustration rose within her. The answers must be there somewhere – surely memories couldn't be erased entirely without a trace? Well, perhaps in science-fiction movies, but this was reality, albeit an odd and frightening kind of reality.

The burbling sound of a baby startled Ellie. Opening her eyes, she saw Phil standing beside the bed with Sam, wriggling and reaching out his plump little arms towards her, making indistinguishable but happy noises. Although Ellie was expecting this visit, she was totally unprepared to see them standing there, and a sinking feeling threatened to make her cry out to ask this man to go away and leave her in peace. Reminding herself she was twenty-eight and not a child anymore, Ellie forced a smile; at least she could be civil, and they'd have to talk seriously sometime soon.

'Sorry,' Phil almost whispered, 'Did we wake you?'

'No, I wasn't asleep, just trying to remember.'

'Ah, right. I'm sure it'll all come back soon, perhaps when you get home and see the house and everything?' He balanced Sam on his hip whilst dragging a chair over to the bed. Ellie was pleased he'd made no effort to kiss her, it would have been an embarrassing moment for them both, but he'd mentioned home, so she decided to confront the situation straight away without any preamble.

'Look, Phil, I'm not sure about coming home. I mean – I don't know where home is anymore. I still think of Mum and Dad's place as home, and I think that's where I want to go, initially at least.' The look of disappointment on Phil's face spoke volumes. Ellie was saddened to be the cause of such pain but there was no way to avoid the issue.

'What I'm trying to say is... I can't slip back into some sort of life of which I have no recollection. You seem a nice man, and your baby is beautiful, but I don't know you. How can I possibly come and live with you?'

'Our baby,' he corrected. 'You said *your* baby, but Sam's *our* baby, and he needs his mother.'

Again, Ellie was conscious of his pain, evident in the distraught expression on his face, and she felt a weighty pang of guilt at being the source of it. Ellie reached up to take the child, an almost instinctive move and Phil's face softened as he released him into his mother's arms. It was a strange sensation for Ellie who couldn't remember ever having contact with such a young child, but when Sam patted her face and smiled up at her with his damp little mouth blowing bubbles, it felt unex-pectedly good.

'Hey, little fellow, how are you today?' she cooed. Sam made what seemed to be happy noises, then repeated, 'Da, da' as he reached again for his father.

'He's really missed you – he needs his mummy.' Phil appeared to be close to tears – it wasn't easy to meet his gaze.

'Tell me about our house.' Ellie wanted to divert Phil's attention but her curiosity about the place she'd lived in for the last ten years was genuine. Her sudden interest brought a flicker of a smile as Phil described their house in great detail, and his hope that a verbal tour of their home might jog a memory was undisguised.

He talked of the house where they'd been so happy and when he spoke of their large family room, asked, 'Do you remember choosing the colour for the walls in there? We had a shade specially mixed but you didn't like it when I put it on and made me change the colour three times before it was right! That little episode was the closest we came to a row in the first year of our marriage.'

Ellie lowered her head and, looking up at Phil with a twinkle in her eyes, asked, 'Should I apologise now, or did I do so at the time?'

'Well, you did eventually apologise, which of course, I accepted gracefully. What I didn't tell you was – you were right about the colour all along, it looked so much better the third time around, but I wasn't going to admit it.'

They both smiled. Phil at the memory and Ellie at the relaxed and amusing way he related the story. Phil was actually a very good-looking man with a strong jawline and a rather cute cleft in his chin. Sandy hair flopped into his eyes, causing him to flick it back with an unconscious head movement, or by running his hand through it. With his large, soft, brown eyes, Ellie could see why she'd fallen for him.

Oddly, their conversation flowed and there were none of the embarrassing silences which she'd both anticipated and dreaded. Phil chatted comfortably about their house and the work they were doing in the garden, which she found surprisingly absorbing, and which prompted her to ask questions, and the answers genuinely were interesting to hear. There were many things Ellie wanted to know, and without her memory, the only way to find out was to ask questions.

'What about your parents, Phil? Does Sam have a second set of grandparents?' It seemed another *safe* topic and would fill in another gap in her memory.

'He does, but they live in Spain on the south coast, somewhere between Marbella and Malaga. They retired there a few years ago, and love it. We've had some great holidays with them over the years, although Sam's only been once, last year in the autumn when he was just a few months old. They wanted to come over to see you but Dad's been diagnosed with cancer and is growing increasingly frail. They've kept in touch these last few weeks and are very concerned for you, Ellie.'

'Oh, Phil, I'm so sorry.' She almost regretted having asked, sorry for her husband but unsure she could take any more sadness on board just yet. 'How old is Sam?' Ellie watched the little boy as he snuggled into his daddy's arms, sucking his thumb, his eyelids drooping.

'Ten months, his birthday's not far away, in July. I was hoping perhaps you might be back with us by then?'

The suggestion came as a shock and there were a few moments of silence before Ellie could form an answer. 'It would be very strange for me to come home with you and Sam even then if my memory still hasn't returned. I don't think I can cope with the pressure of having a time limit. How would you feel if I went to my parents for a while to see how things work out and to give us both a bit of time?'

'I don't need any time, Ellie, I've been waiting four weeks for you to come back to me, and I'd rather you came home.' Phil looked visibly upset by her suggestion. 'But if it's what you want, then it's what we'll do. You will come and visit though, won't you? I'm sure if you see the house, you'll remember.' His face was pained, like a hurt little boy who was trying so hard to be brave.

'I hope so, but can we take it a day at a time... no timescales or anything?'

'A day at a time,' Phil repeated slowly, and in what Ellie thought to be a somewhat reluctant agreement.

Chapter Eight

Grace and Derek Watson arrived at the hospital early to collect Ellie, clearly delighted to finally be taking her home, a day Ellie knew they'd feared would never come. Behind their façade of delight, she could sense their anxiety as to what shape her future would take.

After considering the available options and mostly his patient's wishes, Mr Samms agreed it would be better for Ellie to be discharged into the care of her GP's practice rather than the alternative of moving to a residential facility. A follow-up appointment was made for her to attend his outpatients' clinic in a couple of weeks, when again she'd have the option of considering further treatment if her memory still hadn't returned. Ellie accepted her discharge letter as if it was an accolade and, with a smile on her face, said goodbye to the nurses, thanking them for their patience and kindness – they'd been brilliant and she was grateful.

'Hey, you were no trouble at all. I wish all our patients were as easy as you.' The staff nurse returned the smile and added, 'Try not to worry too much. I'm sure things will work out in time, and I'm sorry no one's been able to give you a definite prognosis but this manner of injury is almost impossible to predict. Take it one day at a time, eh?' Hugging Ellie, the nurse returned to the ward, leaving her patient in her parents' capable and willing hands.

Stepping through the door of her childhood home, everything appeared so much smaller than Ellie remembered and elicited the oddest feeling of being simultaneously familiar and strange. The furniture she expected to see was no longer there. The old, saggy three-piece suite of her childhood, a sometime castle, cave or palace, was replaced by two new sofas, and a glass-topped coffee table took pride of place in the centre of the room. The flowery wallpaper her mother once loved so much was gone and the walls were painted in a fashionable grey with modern shutters at the windows rather than curtains. The whole effect was elegant but rather disappointing to Ellie and not quite the home she'd anticipated entering.

The short journey and the exertion of packing her few belongings tired her more than Ellie expected, and she willingly flopped onto the sofa while her mother bustled away to the kitchen to make a pot of tea. Sitting with his daughter, Derek repeated, for about the tenth time, how pleased they were to have her home.

'I know, Dad, you've both been brilliant and I'm truly grateful but it's going to be strange for you as well as me. Having had the place to yourselves for the last ten years, you now have an unexpected lodger billeted with you.'

'We don't mind in the least and don't be thinking you're in the way. Your mum wouldn't settle if you were anywhere else but here, and neither would I. This is still your home, love, for as long as you need it to be.'

Ellie reached over to hug her father and kissed him on the rough stubble of his cheek. Derek Watson was a quiet man who didn't always express his feelings, but she knew how much both of her parents cared for her and was eternally grateful to belong to such a loving family. 'So, when did you change the room?' Ellie asked.

'Ah yes. It was only a couple of years ago when we retired. We decided to put our little lump sum into the house, get it just the way we wanted, and treat ourselves to some new bits and pieces. Do you approve?' Derek grinned.

'Yes, it's lovely but wasn't the plan to travel when you retired?'

'We've managed to do a little travelling as well. Your mum always wanted a safari holiday, and we went to Kenya on a guided tour, which was amazing and certainly the holiday of a lifetime, but we were glad to get back, we missed you and Sam.'

Ellie lowered her eyes, reminded again by her father's apparent affection for his grandson how much the little boy was part of her parents' world. It hadn't gone unnoticed that the photographs on the walls and coffee table were all of her son, a pictorial record of his life so far. It would be these little things which would take Ellie by surprise, but hopefully help her to learn more of her life.

Since her decision to move in with her parents, a sense of guilt hovered uncomfortably at the back of Ellie's mind. It was prompted by the knowledge of her distancing herself from her son when theoretically he was partly her responsibility, a responsibility which she was knowingly abdicating. Truthfully, life with Phil and the thought of being a mother scared her half to death and she couldn't imagine attempting to pick up the threads of a life about which she knew nothing. For the time being, she would stay with her parents and hope her memory returned soon but this decision gnawed at her conscience – was she choosing to ignore her son's needs in favour of her own? If so, what kind of a mother did this make her? With doubts and uncertainties crowding her mind, Ellie could almost feel herself pushing her head further into the sand. And then there was Phil; naturally he wanted her to visit their home, something she'd have to face up to soon but perhaps after the weekend when she felt a little stronger?

Grace entered the lounge with a tray of tea and what Ellie thought to be the most genuine smile since she came round in the hospital. Derek noticed too. 'Your mother's going to love having you at home. There's nothing she likes better than playing nursemaid and spoiling folk. I know I'm such a disappointment to her as I'm not ill often enough, so you'll get me off the hook for a while, that's for sure.'

After tea and biscuits, Ellie went upstairs to unpack the few things she'd brought from the hospital and found several items of clothing already stored neatly away. They were unfamiliar but Grace assured her these were hers; her mother had been to Phil's to fetch them the previous day.

It was a relief to find the bedroom hadn't changed as much as the rest of the house, fresh paint and new curtains were the backdrop for the same single bed and wooden furniture from her childhood, and for this, Ellie was grateful. Spending a few minutes reflecting and moving around, she handled the familiar objects, comforted by the three rather threadbare teddy bears squashed into a child's rocking chair in the corner. It didn't seem long ago that she too, fitted into the chair. It was a favourite place to curl up with a book after Ellie discovered Enid Blyton's *Famous Five* novels. She would rock furiously when reaching the climax of the story, unable to read quickly enough, then disappointed when the much-loved book was finished and she was swamped with a feeling akin to saying goodbye to an old friend.

Running her fingers over the satin pastel quilt, which she'd slept under for most of her young life, brought a rush of much needed comfort to Ellie. The muted pinks, mauves and yellows were faded with age, but it was still an item of familiarity and security, one which, as a very young child, she'd rubbed between her fingers each night to help her fall asleep.

The clothes which Grace brought from Phil's didn't seem to fit into this room. They were clothes for the unfamiliar adult Ellie, bought for someone she didn't know, and simply touching them felt like prying into another woman's life.

Picking out a pair of fitted jeans and a soft angora sweater to change into, the result was pleasing as she looked into the mirror. When her mother tapped on the door a few minutes later, Ellie joked she'd found the first positive aspect of memory loss. It appeared she'd acquired a whole new wardrobe of clothes.

———

Grace smiled, encouraged by Ellie's positive attitude. Perhaps being at home would be conducive to her daughter's recovery, and it was undoubtedly more relaxing for them than the endless visits to the hospital of late. Although she wouldn't readily admit it, the strain, compounded by their fears, had been immense.

When Ellie first woke from the coma, Grace's hopes soared, only to be dashed again when it became apparent she'd suffered such severe memory loss. Determined to be proactive in her efforts to help Ellie, she researched the condition and ordered a book online on the subject of amnesia. Reading anything other than a novel was a learning curve for Grace, yet she religiously applied herself to researching this unusual phenomenon in an effort to help her daughter's recovery in any way possible. Hopefully, the book would provide valuable insights into amnesia, enabling Grace to support her daughter with a more informed approach.

Much of the book's introduction dealt with the various types of memory loss – information Grace already knew from Mr Samms' patient explanation of how her daughter was suffering from retrograde amnesia. It appeared Ellie's case was typical for the kind of head trauma she'd suffered, but as each case varied greatly, it was impossible to predict how long the memory loss would continue. During her first reading, which lasted almost two hours, Grace felt no further forward with only a headache to show for her efforts. Ploughing through the section on how the brain makes and stores memories through a process of consolidation was all new material and quite interesting, but her conclusion was as she'd initially thought, the only way to help her daughter was to encourage her to live in the present, one day at a time.

From Grace's research, it became clear that any kind of stress would exacerbate the condition – which may be evident from an objective viewpoint, but putting herself in Ellie's shoes, stress avoidance was a pretty tall order, and she'd need to protect her daughter as much as possible. Retrograde amnesia is the loss of old memories. Sadly, Grace could find no statistics on the length of time before these memories returned, or any data on percentages of patients who never recovered at all. It was inconceivable, although entirely possible, that Ellie might never remember the last ten years of her life, but it was a bridge they'd cross together if it happened.

Everything considered, Grace supposed retrograde amnesia was only mildly preferable to anterograde amnesia when the sufferer could not retain new memories but was usually only a temporary form of amnesia. Swings and roundabouts, she decided.

However problematic the future might be, Grace and Derek were delighted to have Ellie home and well, physically at least. Later, after Ellie went to bed, the couple discussed the way forward. Their only conclusion was to proceed one day, or perhaps even one hour at a time. The future by its very nature was unpredictable but, in their case perhaps even more than most.

Chapter Nine

It seemed to take an age for Ellie to fall asleep even though she was physically exhausted and her body ached for rest. Thoughts and questions flooded her mind, primarily disturbing ones, but in the stillness of the night, she couldn't voice them and learn the answers – it would hardly be fair to keep her parents up all night.

As one question arose, it invariably prompted another, and Ellie anticipated the inevitable heartache to come in learning some of the answers and events of those lost years. Squeezing her eyes closed in an attempt to sleep, thoughts of Bess, their family dog, suddenly flashed into her mind. There'd been so much to take in on her arrival home, and initially, Bess's absence went unnoticed. In her childhood years, the spaniel was her constant companion, rarely leaving her side. But now, in the dark quietness of the night, Ellie did the maths. Bess was fourteen when she was at sixth-form college, and no dog lives to be twenty-four. The thought was painful. She must have grieved for her beloved pet when Bess died, but now the same loss was flooding her mind all over again. Ellie had no idea of the circumstances surrounding her dog's death. When the younger Ellie was sad or upset and had needed her, Bess invariably curled up beside her, instinctively sensing her mistress's feelings. How she longed for the comfort of her little dog now, for her warm, soft body and silky ears. The pain was tangible, even though she knew Bess must have died several years ago.

By the same logic and reasoning, Ellie wondered about her beloved grandmother. Vera Watson was the only grandparent she'd ever known, but the old lady would be well over ninety if she were still alive. Tears filled her eyes as thoughts of the gentle, white-haired old lady came to mind – a woman who always spoiled her only grandchild. Ellie remembered her as an old lady, as children do, but Vera was young and strong once. Of course, it was feasible she was still alive, perhaps in a residential facility somewhere, but it was doubtful. Her mother or father would surely have mentioned her if it was the case. Yet another question to add to the growing list of lost memories.

Tossing and turning in bed, Ellie's mind meandered back to her very first day of school, a massive step for any child and one she remembered vividly. Perhaps being back in her childhood home triggered the memory and again she experienced the genuine fear of that momentous day. Ellie was a shy only child, used to her parents' undivided attention and her mother's constant companionship. Starting school was a completely new experience and one which filled her with dread. She remembered holding on tightly to her mother's hand as they walked the short distance to school, and asking if Grace could stay with her.

'No,' came the gentle answer, 'but I'll be thinking about you all day, so in a way, part of me will be with you.' Ellie latched onto her mother's words, and the idea made the experience a much easier one to bear. It was typical of how her parents continually helped and guided her, which was even now apparent and ongoing. Their protection was a given, but sadly, they couldn't ease her current predicament as readily as they'd solved their little girl's growing-up problems.

Sleep claimed her eventually, a dreamless, sound sleep from which Ellie woke refreshed and feeling better until reality dawned as sure as daybreak, and the endless questions swirled around her mind once more. Today she would spend time with her parents and hopefully learn something of the gaps in her memory – the growing list of blanks niggling at the back of her mind. There would undoubtedly be opportunity – Derek and Grace were now both retired, which was another new concept to get used to. Ellie still thought of them as in their prime, her father a self-employed plumber running his own small company and her mother a primary-school teacher, but that was ten years ago. They were no longer those people, causing Ellie to wonder not only about her own forgotten life, but theirs too. Yes, today she'd learn of events from the last decade and perhaps knowing what had transpired might in some way jog her memory.

After showering and dressing, Ellie discovered she was the last one downstairs and her parents had already eaten breakfast. Grace almost pounced on her daughter, offering a tempting choice of food, but Ellie only wanted tea and toast. Her appetite hadn't quite returned.

With a mug of tea in hand and Ellie's legs tucked beneath her on the sofa opposite her parents, small talk seemed inappropriate, yet launching into a lengthy list of questions was hardly a better prospect. In the end, Derek opened the dialogue.

'We're expecting a flood of questions, Ellie.' He smiled. 'Don't hold back, love. There are things you need to know and we're quite prepared to answer everything we can. Who knows, it might even help you to remember?'

'Thanks, Dad, there's so much I don't know, but I'm scared to find out. Is that stupid?'

'Not at all. Fire away – we'll do the best we can.'

Grace nodded her agreement enthusiastically, she too appeared determined to help Ellie.

'Well, I was thinking about Gran last night.' Ellie was conscious of reopening painful wounds but her parents were pragmatic people and well prepared.

'Ah, yes, we should have told you. Gran died about seven years ago. Naturally, you were devastated, but she'd been poorly with cancer, so it was a blessing at the end and we all felt a sense of relief for her.' Derek smiled wistfully while remembering his much-loved mother. 'I don't suppose you remember losing Bess either?'

'No, I was thinking of her last night too.' Sudden tears halted Ellie's words and Grace moved over to hug her daughter. After a moment, she pulled herself together and blew her nose.

'I'm sorry, but it's like losing them all over again. It's a shock, yet logically I know I should be over the loss.' Ellie wasn't sure she could cope with suddenly having ten years' worth of bad news and pain to cope with, but that was exactly how it seemed to be.

'Well, let's think of some happier events to tell you, shall we?' Grace's smile was comforting. 'Can you remember anything about university?'

'No, Mum, I don't even know which one I went to eventually. Tell me?'

'You went to Nottingham, in the end, to study a BA in arts and humanities. Your A levels were three A stars and a B, so you got your first choice and came away with a first-class degree. We were so proud of you but perhaps we should celebrate it now as you can't remember?' She forced another smile.

'And did I come back to York to live after uni?'

'No, not initially, you stayed in Nottingham in the house you were renting with a couple of other girls, before going to Australia for four months with Karen, she was one of the friends you shared with, and then you came home. You met Phil in Australia, and as he too lived in York, you were keen to come home – and we were only too happy to have you.' Grace covered nearly four years of her daughter's life in a couple of sentences which raised dozens more questions. Ellie looked bemused, struggling to take in so much. Remembering her long-held dreams to visit Australia, she felt cheated. Apparently, that particular dream had been fulfilled, yet she had no recollections of any of it at all. What an absolute waste!

'So, I spent four months in Australia and can't remember a thing about it? And who's this Karen? Are we still friends?'

'Karen's a lovely girl and yes, you are still friends, but she lives in Australia. She met her husband there too and went back to marry him. I think you chat on social media but I'm not sure if Phil's been in touch to tell her what's happening. I never thought of Karen.'

The mention of social media reminded Ellie of her laptop, which she'd already discovered wasn't in her room. Phil must have it – of course it wouldn't be at her parents' home – why would it? If she could only log on to her Facebook page she'd probably learn much more of her present life. Ellie always loved posting photos of everything when she was younger. Did she even still use social media?

'Does Phil have my laptop, Mum? D'you think you could ring him and ask him for it?'

'Yes, he'll be at home today, so I'll give him a ring. I'm sure he'll be glad of the excuse to come round.'

'I'll go and ring now,' Derek offered and left the women alone.

'How's Phil been managing for work with Sam? Gosh, I don't even know what job he does.'

'His boss's been very good. Phil works for a software company but I haven't a clue as to exactly what he does, it's all beyond me. He's managed to work from home quite a bit and we've helped out as much as we could, fitting it in with visits to the hospital.'

'And what about me, Mum, what did I do after uni, apart from travel to the other side of the world and meet Phil?'

'You landed an excellent job in advertising, something to do with graphic design, I think. You know I'm not up on all this technology stuff, give me a pen and notebook any day. You work for an agency called Solutions and took a career break when Sam came along to spend time with him. I'm sure Phil will be able to tell you more about it than I can, love.'

'Oh, Mum, I've caused you so many problems, haven't I?'

'No, you mustn't think that, Ellie, it's not your fault. We visited you in the hospital because we wanted to, and we wanted to help with Sam too; it's been good to be useful when there wasn't much else we could do, you know I like to keep busy.'

Ellie looked closely at her mother, noticing the deepening lines around her eyes and the slight downturn of her mouth. Yes, Grace was ten years older than she remembered, Ellie knew, but some of those lines were probably from more recent stress. Her family had been through so much, and it wasn't over yet. Perhaps it was only beginning?

Derek entered the room with a smile on his face. 'Phil's bringing the laptop round with him and your phone too. I asked if they would like to stay for lunch, is that okay, love?'

'Fine by me, they're welcome anytime.' Grace seemed delighted to be having visitors but Ellie's heart sank. She'd hoped to have the first day at home alone with her parents, time to catch up with them and learn the answers to her endless questions. Everything seemed to be moving so fast – and although they'd talked easily enough in the hospital she was still a tad uncomfortable with Phil. There was so much to take in without having to be polite to him, to consider his feelings when she was so absorbed with her own. Phil might be her husband, but to Ellie, he was still a stranger.

Chapter Ten

In less than an hour, Phil rang the doorbell and walked into the house without waiting for an answer. Ellie's first instinct was to shrink back as he entered the room – his beaming smile and physical presence were strangely confusing. Inexplicably she wanted to see him but at the same time didn't; how utterly bewildering. Was it simply curiosity about the man she'd married, the man she'd shared a bed with and with whom she'd had a child?

Derek and Grace's delight at Phil's presence was natural and undisguised. Ellie watched, an observer, as her husband lowered Sam to the floor and the little boy crawled straight over to his grandmother, gurgling nonsensical sounds and dribbling on the carpet. Grace whisked him up and wiped his wet chin with the bib he wore, then kissed his forehead and grinned at him.

'Hello, little man! Have you come to see your grandma, then?' The two were so wrapped up in each other, causing Ellie to feel like an outsider. As if to underline this unwelcome sentiment, Phil planted a kiss on Grace's head and squeezed her shoulder, so much a part of the family – her family. Was it a pang of jealousy bubbling inside her while watching this little tableau play out? Ellie immediately scolded herself for being so immature. She was twenty-eight now, not eighteen, and she did actually like Phil – the whole situation was just so bizarre, so tricky to get her head around. It appeared the world was turning swiftly around her and Ellie was a spectator rather than a participant.

'I've brought your laptop, Ellie, and your phone. The screen was broken in the accident, but I've had it fixed and it seems to be working as good as new.' Phil handed the phone to his wife and placed the laptop on the side table. A sudden urge to grab both of them and run upstairs washed over Ellie, a desire to hide away and be alone, yet instead she mumbled a thank you and forced a polite smile.

'Right, well, I'll just go and get a few things ready for lunch.' Grace stood, attempting to extricate herself from Sam's grasp, and the little boy turned his attention to Ellie.

'Can I help, Mum?' Ellie asked, unsure if she wanted to escape to the kitchen or not, but her mother shook her head emphatically.

'You get to know Sam, love. Phil, get his toy box out from the cupboard, will you?' Grace disappeared into the kitchen and Phil dragged a large box from out of the hall cupboard, the sight of which excited Sam no end. He squealed as the box was opened and immediately pulled out a Snoopy dog on wheels, thrusting it towards his mother, almost giving her a black eye.

'I remember this!' Ellie turned towards her father.

'Yes, your old toys have got a new lease of life now, haven't they, Sam?' Derek grinned at the look on his daughter's face. 'I'm sure he'll share them with you though.' He laughed.

The little boy quickly pulled everything out of the box, presenting each item to his mummy for her approval, then just as swiftly snatched them away again. Several of the toys were from her childhood, and Ellie was touched her parents had kept them. Watching Sam playing with them now made them all smile.

Phil appeared to think it necessary to fill every silence with a commentary about their son, yet Ellie soon tuned him out as she became absorbed in playing with the little boy. It was a natural reaction to wipe his chin as her mother had done and once again that satisfying feeling of her son's presence was restored to her, as it had been in the hospital when she'd first held him. Perhaps spending time with Sam and Phil was the secret to making sense of this weird situation. Would it also serve to bring back her memory? Please God it would.

Grace presided over lunch and kept the conversation flowing, after which Sam rubbed his eyes, tired from the excitement of being the centre of attention. Grace took him upstairs to sleep where there was a cot in the spare bedroom; apparently, they often looked after their grandson. When she returned, Ellie started asking questions again, directed at her mother when Phil could have answered equally as well.

'What's happened to Fran and Rosie, Mum? Do I still see them?' She remembered them as her two best friends throughout school and sixth-form days, but her parents had talked more about Karen and not mentioned any other friends.

'Rosie lives somewhere in Norfolk, I think, married to a doctor and with twin sons about the same age as Sam. Fran's still in York, but I don't think you've been in touch with her since your wedding.'

'Rosie knows about your accident,' Phil chipped in. 'I sent her an email, and she's been very concerned.'

'And what about Fran? Perhaps I could see her sometime if she still lives locally?'

'I don't think you have an address for her.' Phil was frowning; he didn't seem keen for her to contact Fran, but Ellie could do with seeing an old friend, someone familiar whom she could actually remember.

'I'll probably be able to find her on Facebook later and I'll send an email to Rosie too.' She let the subject drop, sensing his discomfort with the talk of old friends. Ellie hoped he didn't expect to make all her decisions for her. Surely recovery from this accident would be at her own pace. Phil had agreed not to put any pressure on her.

It was almost a relief when Sam woke an hour later and once again became the focus of attention. Ellie played happily with him and he appeared to enjoy having both his parents' attention.

Knowing how hard the last few weeks had been on Phil and Sam, Ellie braced herself and agreed to visit their home the following day, after lunch. If she was honest, it was more to please everyone else than a burning desire to see her house as the thought of this new life of hers still terrified Ellie. But she committed herself to it for whatever reason and it was arranged for Derek Watson to drive his daughter there the following day. Phil couldn't hide his delight at this arrangement, and the look of hope in his eyes almost frightened her. When he stood to leave, Sam surprised them all by clinging onto his mother's neck, reluctant to leave her, an unexpected reaction which left Ellie with mixed feelings of her own.

Finally, the opportunity of being alone and logging on to her laptop was presented to Ellie. She was keen to search her Facebook account in the hope of learning more about this complicated mystery which was seemingly her life. It was an unfamiliar laptop, slimmer than the one she remembered as hers, but she took it up to her bedroom almost greedily, on the pretext of needing to rest. Her parents offered no argument – they too were feeling somewhat jaded by the morning's activities.

Logging on, Ellie clicked the Facebook icon and was taken

straight to her page where an unfamiliar image of herself smiled up at her, cheek to cheek with a younger version of Sam. The profile picture must only have been a few months old and took her by surprise. Struck by the expression on her face, one of such complete and utter joy, Ellie almost cried. So, her parents were right when they told her that her life was happy. So, why then could she not remember it? An overwhelming sadness at all the lost happiness suddenly washed over Ellie. For a few moments, she stared at the screen, unable for a while to proceed with her intended search.

Pulling herself together and driven by curiosity, Ellie clicked into her Facebook photograph file, feeling almost voyeuristic, as if snooping into someone else's life. Several images of 'friends' were prominent on her page, but most of these were strangers to her. Some of them, her parents said, had been in touch, wanting to visit while she was in the hospital, but Grace and Derek politely declined on her behalf, knowing how inappropriate such visits would be. There were pictures of Phil, handsome and relaxed, of the two of them together arms entwined and faces full of joy and laughter, the perfect happy couple. Ellie scrolled past several other images of unrecognisable people who she assumed to be more recent friends. Most of the settings were unfamiliar too – a barbecue in a garden, could it be her marital home? An unknown park with Sam and Phil – and then she scrolled down to a selection of her wedding photographs.

Being unable to remember her wedding struck Ellie as incredible. Surely it was every girl's dream, the most important day of their life? Although most of the faces were familiar, her parents and her beloved gran, many were unknown, or more accurately, forgotten.

Three bridesmaids smiled up from the page, Rosie, Fran, and a girl whom she supposed to be Karen. Ellie found these images difficult to look at, almost painful and quickly scrolled down to older photos of her time in Australia. There were several with the girl she assumed to be Karen and more of herself with a much younger Phil, which must have been taken when they met. Ellie hadn't exactly doubted the things she'd been told about her life but seeing them recorded here brought them more sharply into focus. It was a stark reality now rather than a story she'd been told, but still a forgotten truth.

Growing increasingly upset and frustrated at the unfamiliar Facebook profile which was supposedly hers, Ellie searched for her friend Fran, hoping she still had the same surname. Immediately a smiling, familiar face appeared on the screen, Fran! She was pulling a goofy face, and even with ten years of change recorded in that face, Ellie would have known her anywhere. Fran was always the most outspoken of her friends, her direct manner often getting her into trouble at school, but a trait which endeared her to Ellie, who at times envied her friend's devil-may-care attitude.

Perhaps she should send Fran a message? It seemed they'd had no contact on Facebook recently, yet she could do with a friend, someone who knew her from the past and who could help her get her head around the present. Without further thought, her fingers quickly tapped in a message to her old school friend.

> Hey, Fran, we seem to have lost touch lately.
> How about a catch-up? There's so much odd
> stuff happening in my life, and I could do with
> a friend.

Hitting the send icon, Ellie smiled; it would be good to connect with Fran again. She'd been such fun when they were younger and hopefully wouldn't have changed too much over the years.

Ellie returned to her profile page with a consuming desire to know everything about the last ten years, whilst simultaneously finding it challenging to accept the proof of what was clearly before her. Once again, her mind reeled with frustration and even anger at the unfairness of knowing nothing. After a few more minutes of being immersed in this stranger's life, Ellie gave up and switched off the laptop. Confronted with what was undeniably her own life, it was not the one she knew. Although the clarity of the evidence before her went some way to alleviating her curiosity, it also served to heap upon her a new level of distress. Ellie turned in to her pillow and, giving way to her pent-up emotions, sobbed bitterly.

Chapter Eleven

I t was teeming with rain as Ellie set off with her father the following afternoon, a complete contrast from the beautiful June weather they'd experienced of late. While she briefly wondered if this was a harbinger of a disastrous visit to her marital home, Derek greeted the change in weather as good news, chatting about his beloved garden and how much the soil needed the rain. The rhythmic motion of the windscreen wipers marked time as they drew nearer to their destination, and Ellie's heart raced with them.

The house looked exactly like any other from the outside, an ordinary suburban dwelling, perhaps a little larger than average, on a tidy, well-maintained, modern estate. Ellie made no move to get out of the car, and Derek Watson wisely allowed his daughter to take her time, remaining silent as she stared at the dark-blue front door, lost in thought. The door was shielded from the elements by a tiny porch, where a clematis plant clung resolutely to the wooden trellis, battered by the rain which still fell steadily, and in need of a little TLC. The drive was neatly block-paved, the windows double-glazed – all in all, the house's appearance was inviting, or it would have been if there hadn't been two strangers waiting inside who knew Ellie intimately, whereas she knew nothing at all about them.

'Do you want me to come inside with you, love?' Derek offered.

'No, this is something I have to do by myself.' Smiling at her father to reassure him seemed somewhat ironic when she felt anything but reassured herself. Since coming round in the hospital, her parents had done a fantastic job of protecting her from well-meaning friends, who simply didn't understand how difficult this was for Ellie, and yes, the friends could wait. But it was unfair to keep her husband and son waiting any longer.

'Just a couple of hours, Dad, no more, right?'

'Okay, love, I'll not be late, and you can always ring if you want me to come back any sooner.' Derek leaned over to kiss his daughter on the cheek, hearing her drawing in a deep breath before opening the car door.

When Ellie was five years old, a little boy in the reception class at her school told her that every house had monsters living under the beds, monsters who only came out at night to nibble the toes of little girls while they slept. Convinced this was true, a terrified Ellie insisted her daddy went into her bedroom first every night to check beneath the bed before she would go to sleep. Derek faithfully did this every night for several months, a routine which reassured her it was safe enough to go to bed – Ellie knew with certainty her father wouldn't let anything bad happen to her. Sadly, however, Derek Watson couldn't banish the monsters which lurked in her mind today as she stepped from the car to enter this house – her house.

With no expectations as to how she might feel or how the next two hours would go, Ellie's legs trembled on approaching the door and her face and hands felt clammy. Would she remember anything? Would it all come flooding back and her world once more make sense, or was that too much to hope for? Ellie concentrated on keeping her expectations low, for her own sake and Phil's, but she couldn't begin to imagine what her husband must be going through.

Phil would surely have seen her arrive, an assumption which was confirmed as the door opened before she rang the bell, Phil's face a picture of expectation, like an excited child at Christmas.

'Hi, come in out of the rain!' Phil waved to Derek in the car, who pulled away now his daughter was safely handed over.

'Coffee?' he asked, almost too soon.

'Hmm, please.'

'Come on through to the kitchen while I make it and we can chat.'

Ellie dutifully followed Phil into the kitchen, desperately trying to think of something to say.

'Where's Sam?' was her best offering.

'Upstairs, he still has a little sleep after lunch.'

'Yes... of course.'

Looking around the kitchen while Phil's attention was turned to the coffee machine, Ellie was impressed. She observed how beautifully it was designed, with plenty of storage cupboards and one of those central islands with a hob and a feature stainless-steel hood suspended above it. It almost appeared futuristic – an up-to-date, good quality space finished to a high specification. Silly questions crowded her thinking; were they wealthy? It all looked costly. Did they choose this style, or was it here when they bought the house? But what was still uppermost in her mind was what Phil hoped to gain from this first visit.

Taking the proffered coffee, Ellie followed him back into the lounge and they sat on the L-shaped sofa, not too close yet not quite at opposite ends. Phil looked directly at her, his eyes almost pleading.

'So, do you remember anything?' He paused and then jumped in again when she seemed to hesitate.

'Damn it! I'm sorry, I wasn't going to ask that question but it's all I've been thinking about since you agreed to come over. Please ignore my stupidity. Tell me how you've been, how are you coping?'

Ellie was at a loss, not knowing how to reply and acutely aware of how desperate he was for some sign of her memory returning. Yet there was absolutely nothing she could say to give him the hope he craved. Zilch, nothing. It was all a complete blank, as if she was visiting this house for the first time. Aware this wasn't what Phil wanted to hear, Ellie sipped her coffee, surprised when it was just how she liked it and played for time to find the right words to say. Eventually she admitted, 'I wish I could say yes, but the truth is I still don't remember anything. I'd hoped seeing the house would bring something back, and I'm disappointed too. I do want to remember.' She offered a benign smile; it was all she had.

It was Phil's turn to sip coffee and procrastinate. Ellie sensed how much this visit meant to him. If only she could give him the miracle he wanted – Ellie wanted it too – but there was no earth-shattering memories to offer them even the slightest hope.

'Are those photographs?' Ellie tried to turn the mood around. 'Can I see?'

'Yes, please do, I thought they might... you know...'

Ellie smiled. 'It is okay to talk about it. It's not a disease, and hopefully, not a permanent condition either, so, let me have a look.' Gaining in confidence and with an unexpected and strong desire to put him at ease, she picked up the album from the coffee table, and Phil moved a little closer to look at it with her.

The first photograph was of them both when she was heavily pregnant. Instinctively Ellie put a hand on her stomach, wondering how on earth she could have had a new life growing within her own body for nine months and not recall a single moment of it. In the darkest hours since waking from the coma, Ellie thought this whole situation was one awful sick joke at her expense – a stupid idea – one rooted somewhere deep in her subconscious mind as she struggled to rationalise her position. But common sense told her it was all true, supported by the stretch marks and her unfamiliar, more rounded stomach and fuller breasts.

The rest of the photos were mainly of Sam, a careful chronological record of his first year of life. As Ellie studied them, many of which included her, it was surreal, bringing the reality of this unknown life sharply into focus. Phil kept up a running commentary as she turned the pages, but it was more like seeing someone else's family photos than her own, although there was no doubt they were hers.

'I've printed these off the computer, there are loads more, but I thought you might like to take some away with you?'

'That's very thoughtful, thank you, I'd like that.'

Phil smiled, clearly pleased to have done something right, and then instinctively jumped up at the sound of Sam crying upstairs. Moving to go to his son, he paused to ask, 'Would you like to come?'

Ellie smiled and silently followed him up the stairs into a room at the back of the house. Sam was chattering now in his sing-song baby way, standing up in his cot and watching as his daddy opened the curtains. Light flooded the room, the rain had stopped and sharp rays of sunshine revealed a well thought out, charming nursery. The walls were painted pale blue with a border of tractors chugging around the room. Prettily patterned curtains hung at the window and the plush carpet was a darker shade of blue. Purpose-made children's furniture completed the room, and a musical mobile hung above the cot which Phil turned on, causing Sam to clap his chubby hands together and smile, revealing the beginnings of two tiny white teeth. The little boy was in no way perturbed at Ellie being in the room and raised his arms to be lifted out, knowing the routine far better than his mother.

Downstairs again, they sat in the same places, this time with their son strategically in the middle. Phil had collected several toys on his way back to the lounge, and the baby explored them with both his fingers and mouth. He giggled at those which made noises and his daddy was quick to encourage this by tickling his son until the child was laughing, a deep, throaty chuckle which made Ellie laugh too. Sam's presence provided a welcome focus. Neither adult felt the time was right to open up a serious dialogue about Ellie's amnesia and their uncertain future; it was too soon – it became the elephant sleeping in the room.

When Sam grew tired of the tickling game, his daddy picked him up and suggested they look around the rest of the house. Ellie agreed, curious to see her home and followed her husband and son, aware of Phil watching her for the slightest reaction in each room they entered. It was understandable he should want signs of recognition and his commentary was so obviously designed to jog some veiled memory. He narrated a verbal history of nearly every item of furniture they possessed, recounting stories of incidents which happened while decorating some of the rooms and choosing the carpets and curtains. All Ellie could do was smile and nod, longing, as much as Phil, to be able to say, '*Yes, I remember buying that!*' But in all honesty, she couldn't and felt the disappointment as keenly as he did.

Once back in the lounge, Phil stood Sam on the floor where the little boy held himself up against the sofa, managing to shuffle his feet along the carpet towards his mother. Ellie instinctively reached out for him, marvelling at his sturdy little body and determined independence in attempting to walk.

When he stumbled slightly, she happily gathered him up to sit on her knee.

'He'll probably be walking before his first birthday, and his teeth are through early too,' Phil boasted. As if to prove a point, Sam bestowed one of his toothy smiles upon her and reached for her hair, grasping and pulling, making both his parents laugh. It was a strange sensation for Ellie – the distinctive baby smell sparked a desire to hug the little boy closer, which she did, kissing the top of his soft downy head before untangling her hair from his fingers. Sam appeared content to sit there and although still hardly believing this child was hers, Ellie was delighted to hold him.

Derek Watson, true to his word, arrived well within the promised two hours. As soon as he entered the house, Sam patted the sofa with his little starfish hands, excited to see his grandfather who eagerly whisked him up in the air, bringing the laughter back to fill the emptiness of the room. It was a happy note on which to end the visit. Although there were no flickers of memory, or recognition of the home Ellie once shared with Phil and Sam, it was encouraging, a cornerstone upon which to build, giving them all a seed of hope to grasp and begin to nurture.

Chapter Twelve

'How did it go, love?' Grace was a bundle of nerves and anxious to know what had transpired on Ellie's first visit home.

'Better than expected, Mum. I like Phil and Sam's delightful, isn't he?'

'Yes, I certainly think so, but then I'm biased. I'm his grandma!' Grace grinned. 'Dare I ask if the visit prompted any memories?'

'Sadly no, although Phil was hoping for that outcome too. He seemed very much on edge at first and watched me for any reaction, but there was nothing. It was like looking around a stranger's house. I suppose I'd hoped to remember something too, so in a way, it was disappointing for us both but I did enjoy playing with Sam.'

'But that's a positive, isn't it? Perhaps we need to slow things down and not have too many expectations – difficult, I know, but it looks as if it could take a while for your memory to return.'

Ellie nodded in agreement; she desperately wanted to

remember everything, but her mother was right and putting pressure on herself wasn't helping.

'Oh, Mum, I meant to tell you Fran's coming round to see me this evening. I hope that's okay?' Ellie's old school friend had replied to her message of the night before and they'd arranged to meet and catch up on old times.

'Fran? But you've hardly seen her since your wedding.'

'Well, I can't even remember that. To my mind, Fran's one of the closest friends I have, and I just thought it would be good to see her.'

'Fine, let's hope seeing her will cheer you up, bring you out of yourself a bit, love. Did you explain the situation?'

'Not really. I thought it would be easier to explain face to face. Fran thinks she's coming round for a catch-up.'

'Oh, right, well, it'll be nice for you to see her again, I suppose. Do you want me to make anything special?'

'No, we'll just grab a coffee when she gets here, but it won't be until 8pm.'

Fran arrived precisely on time, and as Ellie let her in and hugged her friend, she secretly took in her appearance. Fran was always the one to differ from the crowd, which included favouring a rather bohemian dress style, and it appeared her tastes hadn't changed. She wore a full-length, cotton, multi-coloured skirt with a gypsy blouse and a heavily embroidered jacket. Bracelets jangled on her wrist, and her ears were pierced several times. Fran's long, straight hair was braided, with streaks of red in the long plaits, and her eyes were heavily made up; as always Fran hadn't spared the kohl. It was comforting to see her friend hadn't altered much, although, under the make-up, Ellie detected that Fran's face was lacking some of the firmness of youth, and a few lines hinted at her age.

Grace and Derek tactfully left the two alone, retreating to the dining room to read, and once coffee was made, Ellie and

Fran settled in the lounge and looked at one another. Fran was the first to speak. 'Well, your message certainly came out of the blue and seemed somewhat cryptic. Is there a particular reason for this catch-up?' Her smile softened the words, and Ellie knew an explanation was in order.

'Actually, yes. I've not long been out of hospital after being involved in an accident which left me in a coma for four weeks.' She paused, noticing the look of surprise on Fran's face, then continued, 'But that's not the worst of it. I'm suffering from retrograde amnesia, which means I've lost a whole chunk of my memory – ten whole years of it, actually.'

'Wow. Ten years – that's weird!' Fran's eyes widened.

'So, you see, if we haven't been in touch for a while, I'm not exactly sure why. You're actually in my very last memory, which is of the last day at sixth form when we smuggled a bottle of wine into the common room, do you remember? The next thing I know, I woke up in hospital, and now I'm back here with Mum and Dad, feeling like an eighteen-year-old when the reality is I'm twenty-eight.'

'But what about Phil… and didn't you have a baby?'

'Yes, we do. But I have absolutely no memory of Phil, our wedding day, or having a baby, whose name is Sam. Goodness, Fran, how on earth can I not remember my wedding day and giving birth to a baby?' Ellie bit her tongue in an effort to halt the tears which threatened to spill.

'Oh, you poor thing, how bloody awful! How on earth are you coping?'

'I'm not sure if I am. Today, I went round to Phil's house, well it's my house too I suppose, but it was so strange, and there was nothing I recognised. Phil was disappointed – he wanted me to move back there when I came out of hospital, but how can I when he's virtually a stranger?'

'This is crazy stuff, Ellie. What about your university years?

Don't you remember anything about those either?' Fran looked stunned as she absorbed the details of the story.

'No, nothing. Apparently, I spent four months in Australia after uni, where I met Phil, but it's all a blank. I've woken up thinking I'm eighteen years old and preparing for university, but the reality is I'm twenty-eight and have done all of it! I want to scream at the world that it's not fair. But by far the biggest problem is having a husband and a child who are total strangers to me!'

'Hell, Ellie, I wondered at this sudden contact after so long, but would never have imagined this scenario. You must be so confused – to have lived a whole ten years and yet have absolutely no recollection – it's bloody scary. It can't be easy on Phil either.'

Ellie continued with her story, suddenly feeling the need to talk, and Fran seemed willing to listen. 'It's difficult to explain how I feel. When I came round from the coma, my first thoughts were of my A levels and if the results were good enough to get into university. When I learned the full extent of my amnesia, I suppose I felt cheated and more than a little afraid. I've done the university course, got married and even given birth to a baby, yet can't remember any of it! Initially, it seemed like some kind of sick joke, but the reality dawned on me very quickly, and it's not only me who's suffering. Phil's devastated, naturally, as are my parents. They all desperately want to help but have no idea where to begin. It's nothing short of a huge, complicated mess, and now feelings of guilt are creeping in when logically I know it's not my fault.' Ellie looked at her friend and suddenly felt selfish for burdening her with these problems. 'Look, I'm sorry to prattle on like this, Fran, but it's not always easy to talk to Mum and Dad. They're too close to the situation and have expectations too; although they say not, I've caused them all so much pain.'

'But your parents are devoted to you, Ellie. I'm sure they'll do everything they can to help you. So, have you decided what you're going to do?'

'To be honest, I haven't a clue. I don't have any goals or plans, except for the glaringly obvious one of remembering my life. In losing those ten years, it feels like I've also lost being in control of my life – the past is nothing more than a puzzle to me. Do you know, I even had a career working for an advertising company called Solutions, yet can't remember anything about it, which rather rules out going back to work as well.'

'Do you mean you're thinking of starting again – of not going back to Phil?' Fran's eyes held Ellie's, apparently keen to learn how her friend's dilemma would play out.

'I don't honestly know, Fran, I can't possibly make any decisions yet – the very thought scares me. I suppose the right thing to do would be to pick up my life as Ellie Graham, Phil's wife, but it would be like living with a stranger. How can I even sleep with a man who I don't know, although I'm sure he wouldn't push that side of things. And I have a responsibility towards Sam too – after all, I am his mother.'

'You shouldn't and mustn't do anything you don't want to do, Ellie!' Fran was suddenly quite empathic. 'Be yourself and take time to get used to your life again. It's such a bloody awful situation to be in, like something from a horror movie, and I feel so sorry for you. Look, we've drifted apart over the years, but I want you to know I'm here for you now if you need me, all right?'

'Thanks, Fran, I appreciate that. Why did we drift apart, we didn't fall out, or anything, did we? And when did we last see each other?' Ellie knew there must be a reason, but had no idea what it was, like everything else in her life at the moment.

'There was nothing in particular unless, of course, you count the hen party? Rosie and I were your bridesmaids together with a girl called Karen, your friend from uni?'

'Yes, I've seen the photographs, but I don't remember Karen at all.'

'We never met her until the wedding, and I think she's living in Australia now. I took on the task of organising the hen night, and well, perhaps the male stripper was a bit too much, and you were a bit cross with me, but Phil went ballistic. He never really liked me, you know, but I think the stripper sealed it as far as he was concerned. He wasn't pleased about our friendship continuing after that.' Fran had the good grace to look sheepish as she told the tale and Ellie thought it was precisely the type of thing her crazy friend would do, perhaps only meaning it as a joke.

'We wouldn't have fallen out over that, surely? I was used to your pranks at school, you were always the one to get us into trouble, but we never really fell out, did we?'

'No, I suppose life just got in the way; you were a married woman and I was still single. We did meet up a few times for coffee, but with our work commitments, it never quite worked out and then Sam came along and I haven't seen you since.'

'And what about you, are you still single?'

'Naturally! It wouldn't be fair on the male population for me to tie myself down to just one man, would it? There've been a few boyfriends over the years, but it's all about the fun of it for me. I have no desire whatsoever to enter the domesticity scene.' She pulled a face as if it was the worst possible fate for anyone to suffer.

'No yearning to become a mother at all? I mean, you don't need a man these days, apart from for the obvious, but your biological clock's not spurring you on, is it?' Ellie smiled. She couldn't imagine Fran as the motherly type.

'You're joking! I have enough trouble looking after myself – I'd never cope with a baby!' Fran rolled her eyes in the familiar way Ellie remembered; she hadn't changed a bit. 'I have a smart little flat near the river, close to York centre and convenient for the nightlife. My job's a bit dull, but the money's okay. Perhaps I'll get tired of my life in the future, but things are just great for now. Maybe you'd like to come for a night out with me sometime, let your hair down again and forget all these problems?' Fran looked eager for Ellie to agree, but her friend shook her head.

'Sorry, but I'm not ready for going out yet. There's so much on my mind, and socialising isn't easy at the moment. But I do appreciate your visit today and the offer. Can we keep in touch, Fran? I don't want to lose you again.'

'Course we can. Anytime you need a shoulder to cry on, I'm your girl.' Fran smiled and patted her friend's hand, but there was a strange light in her eyes which puzzled Ellie.

Chapter Thirteen

With Grace's careful nurturing, Ellie took only a few days to begin to feel much stronger, physically if not mentally. Eating well and getting plenty of rest, combined with religiously sticking to the exercise plan the physio had given her, was beginning to pay off, and she silently blessed her mother's ministrations.

Grace was also the one to solve the dilemma of Sam's care. Having lost so much time off work while his wife was in hospital, Phil was keen to get back to some kind of normality, no longer wishing to take advantage of his boss's kindness and understanding, but childcare remained a problem. For Ellie, the thought of having sole charge of her son in a house she no longer recognised was understandably a scary prospect. Grace, with her quiet unassuming wisdom, suggested her grandson should spend his days at their house where she and Ellie could care for him together, a compromise which would allow Phil to return to work and keep Sam happy too.

Ellie jumped at her mother's suggestion, finding it the ideal solution, and the compromise it offered went a long way to alleviating the guilt she felt at not caring for Sam in his own home. Although he was a placid, cheerful baby, she had no experience of looking after such a young child, or none which she could remember at least, and was fearful of not being up to the task. Having her mother on hand to help was the perfect resolution to the immediate problem.

Phil arrived at 8am sharp the following Monday, juggling two bags in one hand and steadying his son, who was balanced precariously on his hip, with the other, Phil's cheerfulness incongruous so early in the morning. Sam was eager to be on his feet, so his daddy propped him against the sofa, allowing him a moment to steady himself, and the little boy very soon and unwittingly had everyone in the room smiling. Grace and Derek chattered to their grandson, completely smitten with him, while Ellie was left to see Phil out. An awkward moment occurred at the door when he moved forward to kiss her goodbye, an automatic gesture, but he stopped himself in time and handed over a key to their house instead.

'You should have this in case you decide to take Sam home.' He looked solemnly into Ellie's eyes, yet she didn't commit to doing so. It would feel like intruding, although she silently acknowledged she'd have to go there again at some point in the future, and not simply to visit.

'How about a shopping trip?' Grace suggested after Phil left, thinking Ellie needed cheering up. 'Sam loves to be out and about and it's such a lovely day. Phil's left the car seat and we've got the buggy, so what do you say?'

'Yes, why not?' It seemed preferable to staying in the house for the whole day.

A little over an hour later, mother, daughter, and son walked down The Shambles in York city centre. It was still early and the shops were relatively quiet, so pushing the buggy was an easy enough exercise, although not always the case on such narrow pavements and cobbled streets. Derek had declined the offer to accompany them, citing jobs which couldn't wait in his beloved garden.

Ellie loved York city, the atmospheric buildings and eclectic mix of old and new made it a place she never tired of. Pushing Sam was an unfamiliar experience or at least one she couldn't remember. Still, he appeared not to notice a novice was in charge and was happy enough, enjoying the attention of both his mother and grandmother. Sam chattered incessantly, burbling indistinguishable words and pointing at the bright shop windows. Later, he enjoyed a bowl of pasta when they decided to go into the Spurriergate Centre on Coney Street for a sandwich.

'It's a treat to be out shopping with nothing in particular to buy, just a good old browse around,' Grace said. Ellie nodded, aware of the many hours her mother must have spent at the hospital over the last month and the inevitable anxiety they would have' presented. Shopping would have been the last thing on her mind.

'Then let's treat ourselves to something nice, Marks and Spencer's, do you think?'

'Why not?' Grace grinned at the mention of her favourite shop.

The day turned out to be both relaxing and enjoyable, with the two women treating themselves to some of the new season's fashions and Grace unable to resist a cute little jacket and a sunhat for her grandson.

Sam, more used to his grandma's company than his mother's over the last few weeks, chose to reach out to his mummy when he wanted to be picked up, which surprised and delighted Ellie. It was a good feeling and confirmation of the bond which she and Sam were rediscovering. The little boy must have found it strange to visit the hospital and see his mother prone and unresponsive, but she was back, and their relationship was on track to being restored.

By early afternoon, Ellie was waning and ready to head home, where Derek waited with the kettle on to make afternoon coffee and express mock horror at the number of purchases they'd accumulated. Sam slept on the short journey home and was now ready to play again, demanding his mother's attention which she gladly gave. Grace, ever mindful of practicalities, disappeared into the kitchen to prepare a meal for them all, Phil included.

If anything, the day, although undoubtedly enjoyable, served to confuse Ellie. The recent visit from Fran had implanted all sorts of thoughts into her head – did she really want to be a wife and mother, or could this be her opportunity to carve out a new life for herself? Fran was single by choice; unencumbered would probably be how she'd describe it, but was this what Ellie wanted? On waking from the coma, learning she was a wife and mother came as a huge shock, and the responsibility of both roles weighed heavily on her mind. Did she want to step back into Ellie Graham's life? But then, this first day with Sam, caring for his needs and seeing the trust in his eyes, melted her heart. Perhaps with Fran, she'd been thinking like the eighteen-year-old she'd initially thought herself to be, and now the more mature Ellie was emerging. Which one did she identify with, which one did she want to be? It was too soon to know – too soon to decide.

After a relaxed family meal, when it was time for Phil to take their son home, Ellie felt a pang of something she couldn't quite describe, an almost physical pain at the separation from Sam which quite took her breath away. Later, tired but unable to sleep, she anticipated seeing her son again the following day and silently acknowledged to herself which Ellie she wanted to be.

Chapter Fourteen

The following morning, Ellie had an early hospital appointment which she insisted on attending alone, declining offers to accompany her from both Phil and Grace, and remaining determined not to be mollycoddled by those who loved her, well-intentioned though they might be.

Ellie did, however, allow her dad to drive her there – getting behind the wheel of a car was something she couldn't yet contemplate and was low on the list of Ellie's priorities. Grace happily remained at home with Sam, who, to Ellie's surprise started to cry when she left the house with her father.

There was very little for Ellie to report to Mr Samms and certainly no progress regarding recovering her memory. Wondering if the doctor would have any suggestions to move her progress along, Ellie tried to remain hopeful for a breakthrough.

Mr Samms' office was warm and comforting, not as clinical as Ellie expected it to be. A bookshelf crammed with hefty tomes of medical books filled one wall while a desk beneath the window held more personal items. A photograph of a pretty woman with two children, presumably his family, took pride of place on the green leather surface, and a flip-over calendar made by a child with crayoned images of a house and stick trees brought a smile to her face. Ellie already liked Mr Samms, and these personal items endeared him to her even more, somehow portraying him as profoundly human and approachable. The neurologist's big personality was engaging too, and his physical bulk, which somehow suited him, elicited a feeling of safety. The doctor greeted her warmly.

'How are you doing, Ellie?' His smile held genuine concern and brought a lump to her throat.

'I'd love to say I'm doing well, but that's not the case. I still can't remember a thing about the last ten years, and I'm beginning to wonder if I ever will.' Her look of utter dismay appeared to touch Richard Samms.

'You have to give yourself time, you know, it's not long since you left hospital and far too early to jump to such conclusions. Anyway, isn't it the doctor who should be offering a prognosis? Now, tell me what you've been doing since we last saw you.'

'Well, I moved in with my parents, which we thought was for the best at the time and I'm still there. I've visited my own home, but there were no memories triggered by the house, my husband or my son. It's got to the point where I honestly don't know what to do next and I'm beginning to lose sleep over it. I can't go on hiding at my parents' home forever but facing up to the reality of my life is rather scary – it's all so odd.'

'Try not to look at it as hiding, Ellie, but recuperating. You're still very much in recovery and the brain is such an unpredictable, sensitive organ. I can certainly prescribe something to help you sleep, not a sleeping pill as such but a muscle relaxant; it's completely non-addictive so there's nothing to worry about in the longer term. If you manage to sleep better, the days may not seem so stressful.'

'Thank you, that sounds good.'

Mr Samms turned away and tapped on his computer keyboard. 'I'll give you a short-run prescription. It's only a low dose so you can take two if one doesn't have the desired effect, and if they suit you, you can get a repeat prescription from your GP.' He swung his chair back to face her. 'Other than that, there's always the counselling option which I mentioned before, or we could try hypnosis?'

'Hypnosis?' Ellie was surprised. 'Would it help me to get my memory back?'

'It's occasionally used as a tool to assist in the recovery of forgotten experiences, but because a traumatic event caused your amnesia, your brain may still block the memory of the accident and may be unable to process memories from before that time too. There's also a risk of hypnosis implanting false memories and therefore not being reliable.' Richard Samms paused, allowing his patient to take in his words. 'Another option we could try is something called Eye Movement Desensitisation and Reprocessing, or EMDR. This aims to integrate the two hemispheres of the brain in an attempt to assist recalling events and would be undertaken during a series of sessions.' Mr Samms paused again. 'It's entirely up to you, Ellie. You don't have to commit to anything yet, it's still very early. You have a good grasp of your situation and I wouldn't want to press you to try anything with which you were uncomfortable.'

'Hypnosis appeals on one level, to be able to go into a trance of some sort and wake up remembering everything sounds fantastic, but I shouldn't think it's that simple, is it?' she asked hopefully.

'Not really, there are no guarantees with any treatment we might try,' Mr Samms confirmed.

'To me,' Ellie continued, 'the downside of hypnosis is that it would be like being unconscious again, and I need to be fully conscious and in charge of the present. The past is a mystery to me, so being in control of the present is important. Does that make sense?'

'Absolutely. The best outcome would be to remember naturally and given time it still could happen. I understand how difficult it must be to live a life which is unfamiliar but I know you have great support from your parents so make use of that. Avoid stress where possible and get plenty of rest. Hopefully, the Trazadone will help you to sleep and come to see me again in six weeks.'

Derek Watson was waiting in the car park, studying the latest edition of *The York Press*. He smiled when he saw Ellie approach the car and leaned over to open the passenger door for her.

'Everything okay?' he asked.

'As expected,' she grimaced, 'it's early days to embark on any treatment, and I'm not sure I fancy the suggestions he made anyway, but he's given me something to help me sleep.'

'Well, you haven't been long, so do you want to go straight home or would you like dropping off somewhere else?'

'No, let's get home, shall we? I'm sure Sam's settled by now but I don't like to think of him missing me.' It would have been more truthful for Ellie to admit she was missing her son.

Chapter Fifteen

Wednesday followed much the same pattern as Monday and Tuesday, with Phil bringing Sam to Ellie before work, and it turned out to be equally as pleasant. Ellie took her son out in the buggy in an effort to give Grace and Derek some time and space to themselves, something which had become a rarity for them during the last couple of months. Mother and son headed to the park, where Ellie used to play as a child.

Long-ago images of happy times with her mother brought a smile to her lips; Grace was a stay-at-home mum for most of Ellie's early years, only returning to work herself when she felt her daughter was ready. Being a teacher offered Grace the advantage of being around for the school holidays with Ellie, who remembered long, sunny days here in this park. Picnics at the river and many other simple pleasures which served to draw mother and daughter together, a close bond which remained strong throughout her childhood.

And now Ellie was a mother herself, which seemed almost unbelievable in the confusing times through which she was presently living. Watching Sam enjoying the swings and hearing his deep throaty laugh delighted her so much she wondered about the other joys of motherhood which were now lost to her. There was the birth itself, those precious early days of holding a newborn baby and introducing him to family and friends. The tender, quiet moments of feeding him herself were forgotten, of holding him to her breast and the special bond it would have brought to them both. Ellie didn't even know when Sam's first tooth came through, although Phil insisted it was early, or when he started to crawl. She even regretted those broken nights and feelings of exhaustion – there was so much she may never remember – it didn't seem at all fair. For a few moments, Ellie silently railed at the injustice, but being angry was never productive, and soon her pragmatic side took over.

Leaving the park, Ellie determined to dwell on the more positive aspects of her present life and top of the list was being with her son. There was no denying that she was overwhelmed by a powerful feeling of love towards him which must indeed have come from the time before the accident, a bond which more than a few days of being together would develop.

With these thoughts rattling around in her mind on the way home, and as Sam slept happily in the buggy, Ellie was encouraged about her relationship with Phil. Perhaps, if she could feel like this about their son, there was hope for her marriage too? Turning into the drive of her parents' home, she made a decision, one she knew would certainly please Phil and one she felt was right, the next step forward. From tomorrow she would look after Sam in his own home, in their home. It would certainly be better for Sam, and she was surprised at how good making this decision felt. Could it be a sign of turning some sort of corner? And if she could feel like this about her son, would it simply be a matter of time before it was the same with Phil?

Again, Ellie experienced an awful wrench when it was time to say goodbye to Sam and surrender him into his father's care for the night, a feeling which confirmed her decision that looking after her son in his own home was the right one. As expected, Phil was ecstatic at the suggestion, and her parents were pleased too, viewing it as a positive step. Perhaps, Ellie conjectured, she could even at some point pick up her 'new' life even if her memory didn't return? The thought wasn't as abhorrent to her as it had been a couple of weeks ago when she couldn't even have entertained such an idea.

On Thursday morning, Ellie woke with a seed of doubt in her mind; had she done the right thing in offering to look after Sam at home? Was it still too early? But by the time she'd showered and dressed, those intrusive, negative thoughts had dispelled and her confidence was restored. Applying her make-up with a little more care than usual, Ellie wondered if the effort was for Sam or Phil. Whatever, she went downstairs with a light heart, the tablets Mr Samms had prescribed were working well and she felt refreshed and happy at the thought of the day ahead with her son.

Another thing Ellie would need to tackle soon was driving. Phil assured her she'd been driving for years but her eighteen-year-old mind couldn't remember being in control of a car. Her only memories were of a few driving lessons as a teenager; taking her test and driving daily were lost entirely in the fog of her brain. Phil offered to take her out in her car – she apparently owned a Mini Cooper, which she'd seen and admired in the garage on her visit, but for now, there were more important matters on which to concentrate. Yet not driving meant relying on others for lifts, and this morning, Derek was going to drive her to her home.

'Hi, handsome boy!' Ellie scooped Sam into her arms as he crawled towards her at the door. His excitement was all the welcome she needed but it was also evident how pleased Phil was to see her. He seemed in no hurry to get off to work.

'There's plenty of food in the fridge, but if you fancy

anything different, there's a convenience store on the edge of the estate – look, I've drawn you a map.' And he had too. Ellie smiled at the scrawled diagram where he'd marked the path to the shop in one direction and the park in the other. What more could a girl need?

'If you want to know anything else, just ring me at work, okay?' Phil ran out of ways to procrastinate, and Ellie picked up Sam and walked towards the door to open it for him.

'We'll be fine, don't worry. I'm not sure I'll go far today, if anywhere. I'll probably feel a little uncomfortable meeting any of the neighbours and not recognising them, but it's a lovely day. We'll be able to amuse ourselves in the garden, I'm sure.'

Phil kissed his son and smiled wistfully at his wife before reluctantly climbing into his car and setting off for work.

The day passed quickly and pleasantly without any of the imagined hiccups she'd dreaded. Sam grew tired and grizzly after lunch but settled quickly in his cot. Ellie found herself reluctant to leave him, standing beside his sleeping form and gazing at his soft, chubby face as his breathing deepened and his little body relaxed into inactivity. Eventually, she went downstairs and searched around, looking for something to do. Perhaps a bit of cleaning, she thought, but would Phil interpret this as her assuming he wasn't coping? Ellie settled for making a coffee in the kitchen but rummaging in the drawers for biscuits made her feel like a sneak, an intruder, although common sense told her this was her house too, her *home*.

When Sam woke, they played in the garden where there was a small sandpit and a wheeled tractor which her son loved. Other toys claimed his attention and the time passed swiftly with Ellie taking dozens of photographs on her phone; at least these images would be ones she remembered taking when she looked at them in the future.

Ellie rang her mother, knowing both she and Derek would be wondering how things were going and Sam gurgled into the phone, delighting them all. She told Grace she intended to stay and make a meal for herself and Phil that evening, a decision which pleased her mother more than Ellie could know. It would prolong her day but oddly enough, she was keen to spend a little time with her husband as well as Sam and they could always discuss the day's events and the rest of the week too. Surprisingly, Ellie was keen to succeed and make this arrangement a permanent one.

Digging out some frozen salmon from the freezer, she put together a simple meal of salmon and salad, which, as expected, surprised Phil. Later, when Sam was bathed and settled in bed, his parents discussed his care for the coming days, and Ellie had no hesitation in offering to repeat the day's arrangement, which had gone so well.

'It's not just that I've nothing else to do,' she reassured Phil, 'I've loved today and although I didn't feel confident enough to go out, I'm sure that'll come in time, and I've always got Mum and Dad to call on if I need them.'

By the time Derek arrived to take her home, Ellie was both tired and happy. Phil even dared to plant a friendly kiss on her cheek as she left, which didn't bother her at all. She'd have been disappointed if he hadn't.

Lying in bed that night and anticipating the following day, Ellie wondered about asking Phil out on a date. The mental image of the expression on his face if she dared to do so made her laugh out loud – he'd love it, and surprisingly, so would she.

Chapter Sixteen

Life was going well for Ellie and was once again enjoyable. There were even times when she could see the funny side of amnesia, and it was no longer the frightening black hole it appeared to be on first waking up in hospital. Her baby son had effortlessly wormed his way back into her heart and she loved him with a passion which at times took her breath away – a passion she acknowledged to be a mother's love, strong and enduring.

Ellie had been looking after Sam at home for over two weeks, not venturing far but re-familiarising herself with the house and where everything was kept. Surprisingly she enjoyed being a mother and even relished the domestic chores involved in caring for Sam and their home. At the end of the week, buoyed by how successfully things were going, she decided to take the plunge and ask Phil out on a date. Astounded, he nearly choked on the coffee he was drinking, causing Ellie to burst into fits of laughter, with Sam joining in as if he too understood the joke. The couple were becoming increasingly relaxed in each other's company. Phil appeared happier than he'd done for weeks, and Ellie couldn't help but notice he was rather handsome too. The lines around his eyes were less noticeable, and the haunted expression had disappeared completely. Grace and Derek took no persuading to babysit for their date, viewing this as a significant step forward for their daughter and son-in-law which triggered some much-needed hope for the future.

Getting ready for the date, Ellie took extra care with her clothes and make-up, deciding after much deliberating on a short, green dress which, although unfamiliar, suited her well. A nervous feeling swirled in the pit of her stomach, taking her by surprise. She felt like a young girl on a first date, which her head told her it wasn't, but with no memories of any other date with Phil, it seemed exactly so.

Her efforts were rewarded by the appreciative look on Phil's face as Ellie arrived with her parents on Saturday night, ready for their date. Her husband looked handsome and relaxed, and an unusual, though not unpleasant, sensation flooded throughout her body. After kissing Sam goodnight, the couple set off to enjoy a meal at a restaurant which Phil assured her was her all-time favourite.

It was a balmy evening with the scent of stocks perfuming the air as they parked the car and walked through a traditional walled garden to the old country pub. Ellie was struck by the idyllic setting, from the bright summer blooms in the borders to the gentle sound of running water from the stream, hidden from sight somewhere behind the high red-brick wall. She felt relaxed, exchanging smiles with Phil and leaning in close to hear what he was saying. Already she didn't want this evening to end.

The pub, one Phil told her they'd visited many times before, was apparently the venue where they'd celebrated their last wedding anniversary and it suddenly struck Ellie she had no idea of when it was, or when Phil's birthday was either. There was so much to relearn, but tonight was not the time to worry. It was a time to enjoy herself and the company of this handsome, attentive man by her side.

After studying the menu, her choice was the medallions of beef with Cumberland sauce. Phil grinned.

'What? What's so funny?' She smiled; her head tilted quizzically to one side.

'You always choose the beef when we come here.' He laughed, and Ellie thought how relaxed he seemed, a more mellow expression now replaced his default anxious look; her husband was undoubtedly a very handsome man. A bottle of red wine was ordered, although Phil was careful to drink only one glass as he was driving, and the meal lived up to expectations; conversation was easy and light. It was a time to forget their problems and enjoy the moment, which Ellie was most certainly doing. At times she even found herself flirting with Phil, enjoying his light-hearted mood and the apparent pleasure which the evening was giving him.

'We should do this again,' she suggested.

'We do, or rather we did. Every month we made a point of having a "date night", just the two of us. Grace and Derek were always happy to babysit, and it was good to be alone together, but I have to confess, it was your idea.'

'Ah, so I've always been the sensible one, or so it seems.' Ellie reached across the table and squeezed Phil's hand. It felt so natural and their fingers fitted comfortably together. Phil lifted her hand and kissed it, she didn't pull away, and this simple act filled her with a warm glow of hope, an anticipation of a happy future, rather than the awful fear of what might be around the next corner which had dogged her of late.

Phil was almost on the point of suggesting his wife might like to stay the night, but stopped himself from doing so, knowing such a momentous decision must be made by Ellie alone. The evening went so well, better than he could have imagined, and he'd be content with that. It could have been any one of the many dates they'd been on in the past, and for the first time in months, he felt a positive, inward sense of expectancy and was able to relax and let time work its healing magic.

Over the last couple of weeks, since his wife had begun looking after Sam again, her growing love for their son was evident, and Phil marvelled at how quickly the bond had returned. He took this as a good sign – if her love for their child was still somewhere in Ellie's subconscious mind, then surely their love must be there too. If only he knew how to bring it all back to her, how to make her love him again. Yet Phil acknowledged it was still early days. Even before she left the hospital, Mr Samms had cautioned him to be patient, to give her time, which he was working so hard to do. But their night out was undoubtedly a step in the right direction, and to Phil, it was a gift, something positive to cling on to, an almost tangible hope he would at some point have his wife back again.

———

The date was over, and Derek and Grace drove a somewhat reluctant Ellie home. On too much of a high to sleep, she made cocoa for herself and her mother before attempting to go to bed, while Derek excused himself and went upstairs. Ellie, however, was in the mood for talking, and her mother was keen to listen.

'You know, I could have stayed tonight, with Phil I mean, but perhaps it's a little too soon.'

'Only you can decide that, love. It's the next big step, but you need to be sure you're ready first. It is going well though, isn't it, with Sam and everything?'

'Oh yes, brilliantly. I'm besotted by him – one grin, and

he's got me right where he wants me. I couldn't bear to be without him now.' She beamed at the thought of her baby son.

'That's great. Your dad and I are so pleased things are going well. You know I've been doing a little research into amnesia, and there's just no way to know how this is all going to work out. In films and books, the memory always comes back – in fact, I think in everything I've seen or read, another head trauma has brought the memory back. Now I'm not suggesting I whack you over the head with a blunt instrument, that's pure fiction, but I have been toying with an idea.' Grace was silent, looking to her daughter for permission to continue, and as Ellie's expression was open and interested, she went on.

'I thought perhaps you should try to forget about the amnesia.' Grace realised the pun when her daughter laughed out loud. 'I know, it sounds ridiculous, but let me explain my thinking. When you first came round, you were distressed and confused, which isn't in the least surprising. But I've watched you change in a relatively short space of time. What you've achieved already is remarkable, and I'm proud of your progress so far. However, I think you know amnesia has no guaranteed outcome – realistically, we don't know if you will ever recover your memory.'

Ellie's smile faded as her mother's words sank in. She didn't need a reminder of the uncertainty of her condition. Grace looked for a moment as if she regretted beginning this conversation, but it must be finished now.

'You understand there is no definitive prognosis, we all do, so rather than letting this hang over you, or consume your whole life, what I wondered is if you could try to live your life from now on, like that saying on plaques and fridge magnets: *'Today is the first day of the rest of your life.'* It seems to me you've been doing remarkably well. I know your love for Sam has returned, and hopefully, your feelings for Phil will come back too. Maybe it's worth a try? Let Phil court you all over again. It rather sounds as if you could be falling in love with him for the second time already, and why not? Yes, there'll be practical things to consider, things you may have to relearn, but we're here to support you. Don't worry about those lost years. If they come back, then great, but if not, you still have a lifetime ahead of you to make hundreds of new memories.' Grace studied her daughter's face, biting her bottom lip. Ellie was silent for a few moments but then slowly smiled at her mother, nodding her head.

'You're a genius, Mum. I rather like the idea, whacky though it may be.' The animation returned to Ellie's face as she continued enthusiastically, 'Do you know, I think to some extent I've already started to do that. Tonight felt like a first date, and Phil is pretty good company, I can certainly see why I fell for him!'

'You'll still need to take things slowly. If you're treating this like a new relationship, there's no need to rush things. Enjoy the experience, love. Not many people get the chance to fall in love with their partner all over again, so take your time. Naturally, Sam has to be considered too, but it sounds as if he's already got his loving mummy back.'

'He sure has, he's adorable, and I love him to bits!' Ellie smiled and finished her cocoa. 'You're brilliant, Mum. What would I do without you?'

'Well, my darling girl, let's hope you don't have to find out for a very long time.'

Chapter Seventeen

E llie was registered with a GP surgery situated on the edge of the estate where she and Phil lived and had an early appointment the following morning with Dr Carol Hudson. She had no memory of her GP but needed to see her for a prescription for Trazadone as the small amount Mr Samms prescribed were nearly all gone. Phil would be working from home and looking after Sam, so Derek offered to give her a driving lesson after the appointment; they all agreed driving again would make life easier. Ellie was ambivalent as to which of the morning's events troubled her the most.

Dr Hudson was a smiley, forty-something lady with a reputation for having time to listen to her patients and never rushing them. The downside of this being that her appointment times often ran over, and a long wait was the norm, so Ellie had purposefully booked the earliest time available to avoid delay. Phil told her not to hurry – but he was keen for her to begin driving lessons. Derek was again acting as chauffeur and happily waited in the car with his newspaper.

When her name flashed up on the waiting-room screen, Ellie followed the signs to Dr Hudson's room.

'Hi, Ellie, how are you?' the doctor greeted her with a smile.

'All things considered I think I'm doing okay.'

'I've been reading up on your notes from Mr Samms. He's given you a prescription for Trazadone? How have you found it?'

'Good, it helps me to sleep, so I'm here for another prescription if it's okay to continue with them.'

'No problem. I'll put them on repeat so you can ring and order them next time you run out, but I'd also like to see you every few weeks, or more if you need to.' Dr Hudson tapped away on her computer, and a prescription spewed out of the printer beneath her desk. 'Tell me, Ellie, have you had any recollections of the last ten years yet?'

'Sadly no, but I'm trying not to get anxious about it.'

'Always a good idea.' Carol Hudson smiled again. 'You won't remember me, but I shared care with the hospital during your pregnancy. Your little boy will be what, about a year now?'

'Almost, it's his birthday in a few weeks, and I'm afraid you're right, I don't remember anything yet.'

'Your notes say you were discharged to your parents' address. Are you still there?'

'Yes, but things have moved on a little since then. Initially, I needed my parents' support. With no memory of Phil or Sam, it was almost frightening to think of going there to live. But I started looking after Sam, with Mum's help at first, while Phil went back to work and eventually to his... no, to *our* house and I've continued to look after him there. He's such a lovely baby and we have such a great time together. I've grown incredibly fond of him, and caring for him is quite magical. Sam occupies all of my time and thoughts, which thankfully gives me little time to dwell on my situation.'

'That's great, Ellie. And are you going to continue looking after him?'

'Yes. I'm surprised at how much I want to. Do you think this must be some kind of bond which was there from before the accident? It can't simply have happened overnight, can it?'

The doctor looked thoughtful, pausing for a moment before replying. 'I really wouldn't know the definitive answer to your question, but common sense would support the theory that there is an existing bond somewhere in your subconscious mind. You know how strong your feelings for him are. What do you think?'

'I honestly feel like his mother now, which I didn't at the beginning. I'm protective of him, I hurt when he hurts, and I couldn't imagine life without him, so I think you're right. Surely this type of bond can't form in only a few days or weeks? Yes, we'll go with common sense and say the feelings are from somewhere inside, from the times I've spent with him in the past, even if I can't remember them.' Ellie felt relaxed and comfortable in this lady's presence.

'And what about your husband? Have you experienced the same kind of feelings for him?'

Ellie was one step ahead of her and nodded. 'Now you're thinking what I've been thinking! I keep telling myself that if I can love Sam, perhaps I can love Phil again too. It's your common-sense theory again, isn't it?'

Dr Hudson smiled. 'It is somewhat different,' she cautioned. 'But it seems quite feasible, and perhaps with time you'll rediscover your feelings for your husband as you have with Sam. It's important though to take things slowly. From what you've said, he's not putting you under any pressure, which is great but you mustn't put yourself under pressure either. Phil loves you and I'm sure he'll give you the time you need, don't you?'

'Oh yes, he's been patient when I know it's not easy for

him. In many ways we're already like a married couple; I go around each morning to look after Sam and cook a meal for us after work before going back to my parents. I've seriously thought about staying overnight, yet I've chickened out, I'm afraid.'

'It's probably still too early. This is what I mean about putting pressure on yourself – there are no timescales here, Ellie. Take a small step at a time and only go ahead with what you're comfortable with.'

'We did have a meal out together, which went well. Phil is rather handsome, so perhaps I could fall for him a second time.'

'You did once, so I would think that's quite a likely possibility.' Dr Hudson smiled at her patient. 'There will of course be things about those lost years which you'll need to know. Your own medical history and Sam's too, that sort of thing.'

'What would be the best way to do that? Will it be okay for others to fill me in on all the events I've forgotten, or is it better to wait for the memories to resurface naturally?'

'I'd have to say a bit of both. As I said, you need to know certain facts about your health, but I can happily tell you that you've had no significant health problems over the last ten years. And Sam, well, I can do you a printout of his notes, immunisations and the like, if it would help?'

'Oh, yes, please, that would be great. I'm assuming from the stretch marks that it was a natural birth?'

'Absolutely, no problems there, and he went to full term. I suppose you feel rather cheated having the stretch marks and no memory of the birth?' Dr Hudson grinned again.

'Yes, but I'm still hopeful of one day remembering everything.'

'Good for you, Ellie. Now, I understand you've declined the offer of hypnosis and EMDR, which is fine, but I want you to feel you can come and see me anytime you need to. If you have trouble booking an appointment, ask to speak to me on the phone and if I'm with a patient, I'll ring you back. You seem to have great support at home but sometimes you can be too close to someone and complete honesty becomes difficult, so remember, my door is always open.' Another of the doctor's reassuring smiles brought the appointment to a close and Ellie left the surgery to find her father, eager to embark on her driving lesson, after which she'd return to her role of caring for her son.

Chapter Eighteen

Ellie reluctantly swapped places in the car with her father and sat in the driving seat, unsure of the wisdom in doing so and with a knot of nerves in her stomach. They'd driven to a quiet suburb not far from where the Watsons lived, but it appeared Derek possessed more confidence than his daughter.

'It's not as if you need lessons,' he assured her, 'it's just a matter of getting the feel of a car again and then I'm sure muscle memory will take over.'

'Muscle memory, is that even a real thing?'

'Course it is, trust your old dad and switch on the ignition, will you?'

For their daughter's eighteenth birthday, Grace and Derek Watson bought her a block of twelve driving lessons, and the excitement of the gift remained vivid in her memory. Ellie had taken out a provisional licence a few months earlier but hadn't felt confident enough to begin lessons, therefore the gift was unexpected and not something she'd hankered after like so many of her friends did. Perhaps the reason they'd given her such an extravagant gift was because Ellie hadn't nagged them for it. The younger Ellie imagined passing her test, and the possibility of her father adding her to his car's insurance or even buying another car – one for her and her mother to share – would be perfect.

Her very first lesson was anticipated with great excitement and didn't disappoint. Ellie still remembered the warm glow of pride when her instructor said she was a natural, and he had every confidence that if her progress remained steady, she could pass her test first time around. Derek commented that perhaps they should have only purchased ten lessons.

The lessons continued weekly, and after only five sessions behind the wheel, the instructor encouraged her to apply for a test, a date which would take several weeks to come through. Full of the confidence of youth, Ellie didn't need telling twice and sent in her application that very night. But fate was to intervene, and Ellie's hopes of passing her test in record time were dashed when she broke her ankle while playing netball at college. She couldn't remember taking control of a car since then.

Derek had filled in the blanks in Ellie's memory, explaining that when her ankle healed, she'd resumed lessons and, as predicted, passed her driving test first time. Since then, she'd been driving regularly and her own much-loved Mini Cooper was sitting in the garage waiting for her to feel confident enough to drive again. Despite her father's reassurances that she was a good driver, it was a strangely unfamiliar sensation to sit behind the wheel, and she was hesitant to press the accelerator more than a fraction while releasing the clutch.

The car lurched forward and Ellie panicked and braked hard.

'Come on, love. You can do it.' Derek offered no other advice, so Ellie tried again. This time something connected, in her mind and with the pedals, and she manoeuvred the car a short distance down the street. Her father remained silent, no instructions or directions as Ellie turned left into a cul-de-sac. Derek smiled as she drove to the top of the road and attempted a three-point turn which turned into a five-point turn. He later praised her, saying the manoeuvre was well executed. An hour later, her confidence was high as she drove to Phil's, taking the car onto a dual carriageway to get there.

'Well done!' Derek beamed. 'It must all be in there somewhere, you did brilliantly, as if you've been driving for years, which of course you have. You'll do even better in your own car, I'm sure.'

Being able to drive again would give Ellie a sense of freedom and relieve the pressure on her parents, who must be feeling like a taxi service. She hated to depend on them, yet true to form, neither spoke a word of complaint.

Phil opened the door, a wriggling Sam in his arms. 'How did it go?' he asked rather too anxiously. Derek answered for her.

'The girl was great, a natural. I can confidently say she's ready to drive, eh, love?'

'Yes, it did seem to come back to me and after a couple of hiccups I felt quite relaxed.'

Derek left the little family, anxious to get home and tell Grace the good news. Phil and Ellie took their son inside.

Aware of being much later than usual, Ellie asked, 'Do you need to get to work now?'

'No, I can continue working at home today if you'll occupy Sam and then I thought we might go out for a late lunch somewhere to celebrate your success at driving.'

'Sounds great to me.' Ellie's face warmed – thoughts of their date were still fresh in her mind. Another outing, and this time with Sam, was more than welcome.

Phil disappeared upstairs into his office while Ellie flopped down on the carpet with her son, giving him her full attention. 'What shall we do now, little man, tickles?' She tickled Sam, a game he loved and was rewarded with the deep, throaty chuckle she so adored. Next, they made a brick tower and the little boy took delight in knocking it down again. A feeling of contentment settled comfortably in her heart. Ellie was precisely where she wanted to be, with her child and her hand-some husband upstairs, and a dreamy smile crossed her face. Life was looking hopeful.

'I thought we might go to The Balloon Tree Farm Shop? You'll love it, Ellie. There's a café, an organic farm shop and an animal corner which Sam loves. The café's quite bright and spacious but as it's such a lovely day we'll probably be able to eat outside.' Phil had finished work for the day and ran down-stairs, clearly keen to get out.

'And do we often go there?' Sometimes, it was frustrating when Ellie needed to rely on others to fill her in on such trivia.

'Yes, it's a favourite which I think you love more than Sam, especially the animals.'

'Ooh, what animals do they have?'

'Goats, pigs, chickens… you love them all! Hey, little man, how about we go to feed the goats?'

Sam clapped his hands, leaving Ellie wondering how much he understood; their son certainly seemed up for an outing, as was she.

Phil was right, the relaxed atmosphere at The Balloon Tree was perfect and the weather held sufficiently for them to enjoy eating outside. The menu suited them all. Sam was happy with spaghetti bolognaise while she and Phil chose the filled baguettes. The animal corner lived up to his recommendation too, and Sam could get close enough to the goats to feed them from the packet of seeds they'd bought in the shop. The afternoon was bursting with laughter and Ellie found herself wishing it didn't have to end.

An exhausted Sam slept in the car on the way home as his parents chatted comfortably, mainly about their son's exceptional qualities. As they neared home and lapsed into silence, Ellie's thoughts turned to Fran, who'd kept her word and been in touch on several occasions. They'd arranged to meet on Saturday, and as Ellie knew Phil wouldn't be working, she assumed having some time to herself wouldn't present a problem – every day for the last two weeks had been spent with Phil and Sam, and a break might be good for her.

Once they were home, much later than they'd expected, Derek was waiting outside for Ellie, so she quickly told Phil she wouldn't be coming round the following day as she was going into the city and would ring him later in the day.

'But it's Saturday. I thought we'd take Sam to the Railway Museum.'

'Oh, you should have said sooner. I've arranged to meet Fran now and I can hardly put her off.'

'Fran?' Phil sounded surprised and perhaps even a little angry. 'But you don't see Fran these days. You haven't seen her for years, so why on earth do you want to meet her now?'

Ellie was taken aback by the sharpness of his tone – could he have a temper she'd so far not witnessed?

'I'm sorry, I didn't think it would be a problem.' Her reply was almost as sharp.

'Where are you meeting her?' he asked.

'In York, in the city centre.'

'Well, I hope you don't intend to take the car.' Again, his somewhat petulant tone took Ellie by surprise.

'Of course not, it's too early to drive to the city, and I didn't realise I needed permission to go out with friends!' Almost as soon as the words left her lips, she regretted them, but it was too late to take them back.

'Don't be silly, of course you don't need permission – but Fran? She's not part of your life these days and I have to say she's not a good influence on you.'

'Oh, so you pick and choose who I see, do you? And I hadn't realised you thought of me as silly!'

'Ellie, that's not what I meant. I'm sorry.' Phil's tone softened and a look of hurt clouded his eyes. But she didn't give him time to finish as she dashed from the house and ran to the car where her father waited to take her home.

All evening Ellie replayed the conversation in her mind, or was it an argument? How dare he tell her who she should and shouldn't see – and was his anger something which was a regular feature of their marriage? Refusing to tell her parents why she was so upset, Ellie went straight to her room, only coming down when Grace called to say dinner was ready. When Phil rang later that evening, Ellie declined to speak to him, claiming a headache and needing an early night.

Chapter Nineteen

When Ellie turned fifteen, her parents allowed her to travel alone into York city centre, where she usually met up with Fran and Rosie. The freedom of doing so and the feeling of being at last grown-up enough to travel alone was a heady experience. After trawling the shops together, they would splash out on a coffee, or occasionally meet up with boys – a prior arrangement which they invariably neglected to mention to their parents.

Wandering the strangely named streets – Low Ousegate, Finkle Street, Coppergate and Ellie's personal favourite, Lady Peckett's Yard – she would imagine the people who'd lived there centuries ago, their simple lifestyles, their hopes and dreams. Her love for York had never diminished – the streets filled with bustling tourists, and street performers in the summer months, captured and held her attention on each new visit. It was a city of which she would never tire.

But all that was when she was a girl. Now the grown Ellie once again sat on the bus heading for York city centre, her thoughts whirring and doubt creeping into her mind, threatening to undo the fragile progress of the last few days.

The date night with Phil surpassed Ellie's expectations. It was nothing short of incredible and was followed immediately by her mother's remarkable idea, the absurdity of which she loved and was more than happy to embrace. More days of looking after Sam in their home reinforced her burgeoning optimism, days crammed with fun and even laughter, something which a few weeks before Ellie feared would not be possible again. Even her parents appeared so much more relaxed than they'd been for an age, easing her guilt and encouraging the belief that they could get through this challenging time and return to some semblance of normal life.

Yesterday, her mind was filled with thoughts of returning to live with Phil and Sam, heady thoughts of such a significant step, of intimacy and love, but now Ellie was losing it again – the uncertainty was returning to trouble her fragile mind.

Ellie regretted her sharp words and childish behaviour towards Phil. So much for her mother's bold new idea! It sounded pretty feasible at the time to simply 'forget' about her amnesia and begin a new life – but today, doubts were creeping in. Were there things she should know about Phil before taking that next big step of moving in with him? It was an impossible situation and Ellie longed to turn away from it all. Perhaps some time with Fran would be good for her. At least Fran was a familiar, trusted old friend.

The address of the wine bar was one Ellie remembered as a rather run-down traditional pub. The façade of the building was the same, yet stepping inside was quite a surprise. Glass and chrome ruled the day, with the wall behind the long bar covered entirely with large mirrored tiles, reflecting the bright lights and creating the impression of space. Ellie blinked, startled by the stark brightness and temporarily blinded. Then she heard Fran's familiar voice.

'Hey, why the long face?' Fran sat on a bar stool with a

glass of red wine already in her hand as she swivelled round to greet her friend.

'Oh, nothing, take no notice, I'm just feeling sorry for myself.' Ellie forced a smile and ordered a glass of wine for herself, 'A large one,' she added. They paid for the drink and headed for a quiet table in the corner.

'Come on then, tell Auntie Fran all about it.'

'Oh, Fran!' Ellie sighed. She hadn't intended saying anything about her troubles but relief at seeing a friendly, familiar face loosened her tongue. 'I was beginning to think things were going so well and now I'm not so sure.' Ellie related the events of the last few days, starting with how much she'd enjoyed looking after Sam and the date with Phil. She repeated their conversation of the previous evening when Phil seemed almost angry that she wasn't going to spend the day with them.

'What a bloody cheek! But I wondered if this might happen, I can't say I'm surprised.' Fran looked thoughtful.

'What do you mean?' Ellie's curiosity was piqued.

'Well, you're convenient, aren't you? A babysitter and a housekeeper rolled into one with a few extra benefits on the side...' Fran grinned wickedly.

'That's not true! I want to look after Sam and miss him terribly when I don't see him – and Phil hasn't so much as pushed me into lifting a duster, never mind anything more intimate.'

'Okay, but you have to admit Phil's benefiting from your compliance. Did you ever wonder why you'd taken a career break; was it for your sake or his?'

'I would imagine it was a joint decision. Sam's my son, and I want to look after him.' Ellie bristled slightly at Fran's implications, feeling suddenly defensive of her husband. The expression on her friend's face was difficult to interpret, a sort of 'I *told you so'* look. 'Why are you looking like that, Fran? Is there something I should know?'

'Oh, Els, you're such an innocent sometimes, but if you really can't remember, then perhaps there are things I should tell you.'

'What do you mean, if I really can't remember, do you think I'm faking this?' Ellie was growing uncomfortable and a little annoyed. 'If you've got something to say, Fran, then you should just say it!'

'Okay, okay, but calm down first. While you were engaged to Phil, there were several instances when it appeared he was controlling you and it grew worse over time. I tried to warn you, to help you see what he was doing, but you were blinded by love and wouldn't listen.' Fran kept her voice low, which alarmed Ellie even more.

'In what way was he controlling?' Surely, she thought, this couldn't be true?

'Mainly little things, like when you should go out and who you could see, just like today, and I'm pretty sure he made all the decisions about how you spent your money. I know you opened a joint account and put your salary into it – and buying that house seemed to be more Phil's choice than yours.'

'But lots of married couples have joint accounts, my parents do, and if Phil chose the house, he certainly got it right. I love it!' Again, defensiveness was creeping in.

Fran shrugged. 'Look, you asked, so I'm telling you. Rosie thought he was controlling too and isn't this the kind of behaviour you've just described? I don't know why Phil doesn't like me but he's the reason we stopped seeing each other. He disapproves of me, okay?'

'Oh, Fran, I don't know what to say. Up until now, he's been so patient and kind. This is so hard to believe.'

'Well then forget it, or at least let's change the subject and not spoil our time together. Another glass of wine?' Fran grinned and Ellie decided to let the matter drop although it wouldn't be easy to banish her friend's words from her mind.

A second and third glass of wine went some way to easing Ellie's confusion but she decided to slow down on the drinking rather than add a different type of fog to her mind. 'Let's grab a sandwich somewhere?' she suggested to Fran, who was at least one glass ahead of her.

'Why not? We'll get a take-out one and go back to my flat, shall we?' Fran draped her arm around her friend's shoulders and as they left the bar, Ellie was relieved to be outside, to gulp in some fresh, cooler air.

Fran's flat was only a short walk from the wine bar, a new development, close to the river, which Ellie couldn't recall being built. They took the lift to the seventh floor, talking now about nothing of importance, and Fran let them into the flat, instructing her friend to make herself at home. It was an impressive, open-plan space with a fantastic view over the River Ouse through a huge picture window.

'Wow, this is amazing!' Ellie moved to stare from the window.

'Oh, you get used to it, I suppose, but it's handy for the nightlife.' Fran chuckled and moved to the kitchen area. 'Coffee?' she asked.

'Black and strong, please.'

A quick look around the room and kitchen area suggested Fran was certainly not house-proud. Empty mugs littered several surfaces and magazines and papers were strewn everywhere. Ellie remembered her untidiness from their teen years and it appeared she hadn't changed – the flat was exactly like her bedroom had been when she was seventeen, messy. Fran handed her a steaming mug and moved a pile of papers so they could sit down.

'Els, I'm sorry if I upset you by talking about Phil, but that's just the way he is and perhaps you need to know it before

making any major decisions about moving back in with him.'
Fran looked quite serious now.

'But what else will I do except move back in – he's my
husband – and we have Sam to consider.' Ellie was close to
tears, reluctant to reopen their earlier conversation yet having a
morbid desire to hear more of Fran's opinions. The wine was
beginning to take effect on her too, and her head felt fuzzy.

'Well, you could look upon this as a second chance. I don't
know if you've been happy with Phil all these years but suppose
you haven't? You've been given another shot at life here, Els.
You could reinvent yourself, do anything you want, it's worth
thinking about, isn't it?' Fran looked excited at the thought, as
if they were planning something *on the edge* like they had when
they were teenagers.

Ellie didn't want to think of anything just then. Fran was
confusing her – she wanted to get away, to be alone somewhere
for a while. She told her friend she had a headache and needed
to go.

'But I thought we could hit the town tonight, the two of us
on the pull, just like old times?' Fran was quite serious, but the
idea was almost sickening to Ellie. Draining the last of her
coffee, she made her excuses to leave, promising to be in touch
soon.

The fresh air did little to alleviate her flagging spirits. Ellie
needed to think, to be on her own somewhere, to consider
Fran's words. As well as the bustling city centre, Ellie loved
York Minster and it was there she headed after leaving Fran's
flat, earlier than she'd expected and with the atmosphere
between them somewhat strained. Walking the short distance
to the Minster, she knew she'd find peace and tranquillity
within its cool stone walls. Ellie loved every aspect of this beautiful, ancient building, from the exquisite, hand-crafted
stonework to the magnificent collection of medieval stained
glass. Sure enough, after a few minutes seated in a quiet corner,

Ellie relaxed, and a calmer spirit washed over her. It wasn't that she was a particularly religious person, although she did believe in a higher power, and here in this building, she felt closer to God than anywhere else. The peace and serenity soothed her mind and she sat alone with her thoughts for half an hour until deciding it was time to return to Phil and Sam.

During the return journey, Ellie's thoughts became more balanced and her reasoning rational. It was entirely possible, natural even that Phil had a temper; didn't she fly off the handle occasionally? And what did Fran actually know? Their friendship had apparently been disbanded during the years since her marriage, although Ellie was still unsure why, knowing only her friend's version of events. As for Fran's preposterous suggestion of leaving her husband, it was almost laughable. Maybe Fran could still live like a teenager but that kind of lifestyle didn't appeal to Ellie, who was a wife and mother now and certainly didn't want to reinvent herself.

As Ellie relaxed, she found herself anticipating seeing Sam with pure pleasure, making everything else pale into insignificance. It would be good to make up with Phil too – she hated confrontation of any kind and it would be tragic to ruin the progress they'd been making.

Chapter Twenty

Ellie found it wasn't as easy to forget her friend's words by simply deciding to do so. The day out had been marred by Fran's revelations, or were they merely opinions? She attempted to keep an open mind but the conversation with Fran proved difficult to shake off. At no time had her parents ever suggested Phil was in any way controlling, although she knew how much they adored her husband, and anyway, would they even notice? As promised, Ellie went to see Phil and Sam after her trip to the city and spent a couple of hours with them, leaving only when their son was in bed.

Phil apologised profusely and tried his best to make things right between them, but the trouble with words is they can't be taken back once they're spoken. Attempting to explain, he claimed to have been surprised at her meeting Fran, not angry, but Fran's suggestion had taken root in Ellie's mind and sadly she now found herself weighing up Phil's motive for every word and action. There was a perceptible shift in their relationship, and things were again strained, a backwards step she regretted yet was unable to alter.

Once back at her parents' home, Ellie gave herself a good

talking to and the stark realisation that the progress she'd made could be in jeopardy seemed to do the trick. Persuading herself she was making a mountain from a molehill, Ellie decided to give Phil the benefit of the doubt and let the issue drop. Saturday hadn't been the best of days for her, but she'd endeavour to put it behind her and start afresh.

Sunday was spent with her parents, who'd invited Phil and Sam for lunch. Grace cooked one of her wonderful roast dinners and everyone appeared happy and relaxed. Once again, Ellie was able to anticipate the coming week with pleasure and looked forward to settling back into the routine of caring for her son in their own home.

The weather continued to be almost perfect with hardly a cloud in sight in the endless blue-washed sky, allowing the better part of each day to be spent outdoors. Each morning, mother and son now ventured to the park, a time they enjoyed and the part of the day when Sam was at his most active. Feeding the ducks and playing on the swing made him chuckle, a noise his mother never tired of hearing.

On Wednesday, Ellie returned from the park feeling quite weary. Sweat was beginning to trickle down the inside of her shirt, and she anticipated a long cool drink and perhaps a quick shower while Sam slept. The heat of the sun, which seemed to be getting stronger each day to the point of almost being relentless, sapped her energy, and if her son remained asleep as he was then, perhaps Ellie would take the opportunity to lie on the sofa herself after her shower.

Unlocking the door and turning to assess the best way of getting the buggy over the step without disturbing her sleeping child, Ellie's attention was drawn to the figure of a man hurrying across the street towards the house, obviously trying to catch her attention before she went inside. He waved as he drew closer, giving her no alternative except to stay and see what he wanted.

'Can I help?' the man offered, bending down to grasp the wheels of the buggy. Ellie somewhat reluctantly allowed him to help lift the sleeping baby over the doorstep but then swiftly wheeled Sam inside, away from the door and stood blocking the entrance to keep this stranger out. She was still somewhat uncomfortable about meeting new people.

'Ellie, don't you remember me?' He had the advantage in knowing her name at least. 'It's Dave. I live at number 40, see, just over there.'

Ellie looked in the direction he was pointing. So far, she'd avoided any contact with their neighbours, anticipating how embarrassing it would be to explain she no longer knew who they were. Half smiling to make light of the situation, she replied, 'Hi, Dave, I'm sorry, but actually, I don't remember you. I've not been too well lately.' Ellie attempted to retreat, taking a couple of steps backwards into the house.

'So, it's true then, the amnesia, I mean.'

'Yes, it is and I'm sorry, but I must go in and see to Sam.' She tried to close the front door but Dave deftly shoved his foot inside, pushing her back until she almost toppled over.

'Hey, don't do that! Please go. I'm busy.' Fear was rising in her chest, but Dave only moved further into the hall.

'Come on, Ellie, don't try to tell me you've forgotten our little arrangement; Thursday mornings, as soon as Phil's off to work. Surely you remember that, don't you?' Standing way too close, she could feel his breath on her face and see his smug expression as he reached out and held both of her arms, pinning her back against the wall. Fear prevented the scream which remained stifled inside her – fear for herself and Sam, but mostly of what this man, Dave, was implying. Could she have had some kind of arrangement with him? Surely not? Tears were threatening to fall but the only thing Ellie could do was to hold her body rigid and hope and pray he would go away. Dave touched her face, making her skin crawl.

'Hey, don't get sentimental with me now. This amnesia thing might fool everyone else, but I know you better than that. How about we get reacquainted while the little man's asleep?'

Pulling her right hand free, Ellie slapped him hard across the face and was shocked to see a trickle of blood run down from the corner of his mouth.

'You bitch!' he shouted, waking Sam who started to cry at the sudden noise. Dave released his grasp, glaring at her with dark, angry eyes.

'Okay, if that's the way you want to play it, I'll go, but I'll be back tomorrow... Thursday, as usual? And don't think you can get out of it by not being here, or I might just have to tell that doting husband of yours what his precious little wife is really like. You've never turned me down before. In fact, you're the one who made the first move, so don't think you can go all righteous and goody-goody on me now! Until tomorrow then.' Dave's face contorted into a tight smirk as he turned and walked out, deliberately slamming the door, causing Sam to wail even louder.

Ellie shivered, suddenly icy cold even though the sun was streaming through the windows and the room was warm. With trembling fingers, she struggled to unfasten the straps and lift her son from the buggy, then, collapsing onto the sofa, she held him close and rocked to and fro as they both cried. Sleep was no longer an option for Sam or her.

Their tears dried and the little boy was soon busily shuffling around the room from chair to sofa, using anything he could to help steady his still wobbly legs, the cause of his tears forgotten. But Ellie barely moved, frozen with fear from the unpleasant and unexpected encounter and terrified even to consider if there could be any truth in this man's accusations. Surely not, why would there be, when, as everyone kept telling her, she was so happily married? Well, almost everyone.

The next few hours proved an effort for Ellie to get

through. Sam needed feeding, after which he thankfully settled down for a sleep. However, his mother couldn't eat or rest, disturbed by the unwelcome and fearful thoughts crowding into her mind. When Sam woke, Ellie rang her parents asking them to come over, claiming she felt unwell – not entirely a lie. Grace and Derek readily came to take charge of their grandson, always a pleasure for them, and naturally concerned for their daughter but accepting it was just a nasty headache. Derek drove her home with instructions from her mother to go to bed and leave everything to them.

Ellie did go to bed yet knew sleep wouldn't come. Even the comfort of her warm bed, usually a place of refuge, couldn't erase the dreadful thoughts surging through her mind. Dave was a horrible man, that much was obvious even from such a short meeting, and she was certain, well almost certain she would never embark on a relationship with a man like him, or with any other man! She had morals, didn't she? She was a faithful wife, wasn't she? But the stark truth was that in losing those ten years, Ellie didn't know who she was anymore. Was she right to question her own moral fibre? Was there any truth in what Dave had said? His words stung, setting her world spinning yet again, and even thinking about them made her feel sick to her stomach.

Ellie was once more afraid. Having so recently begun to rediscover her life and enjoying every aspect of being a mother, it was now suddenly in jeopardy, and all could be lost – Sam, Phil and even the respect of her parents. But what could she do? Telling anyone was inconceivable. What would she say – what would they think? Ellie was only just coming to terms with the incalculable implications of her memory loss. She'd been on the brink of embracing a new life, no longer fretting over the amnesia, but now all that happiness was snatched away, and she was again plunged into a frightening uncertainty. Now it was even more important for Ellie to remember those missing years, not only for the positive things she'd forgotten but for anything which might make her ashamed. Could she really have been cheating on Phil? The thought was abhorrent, but there was simply no way of knowing. And there was very little time to think through these developments. Tomorrow was Thursday and Dave had made it perfectly clear what was expected of her.

Chapter Twenty-One

Ellie didn't sleep at all that night even after taking two Trazadone, and was in the kitchen making coffee when her mother came in and glanced in her direction with concern.

'Do you think you should see the doctor, love? You're looking very peaky, not well at all.'

'I'll be fine, Mum. I didn't sleep much, that's all.'

'But what about your headache yesterday? It came on quite suddenly, didn't it?'

Forcing herself to smile in a vain attempt to reassure her mother, Ellie poured coffee and offered some to Grace. The women sat at the little pine table in the kitchen, the early morning quiet almost tangible, broken only by the sound of birds chirping outside, until her mother spoke again.

'If you're still not feeling well, I could take Sam for the day. It would be no trouble.'

'Thanks, Mum, that's kind of you but we're in a routine now. I'd best keep to what he knows.'

'Then I'll come with you and can at least take him out for a while so you can have a break.'

Ellie studied her mother's kind, pleasant face – she'd

caused her parents so much anxiety lately, albeit unintentionally, but was she about to cause more? She made a sudden decision – her mother's presence might be just the right thing if Dave did come round as he'd threatened.

'I'd like that, Mum, thank you.' The silence descended again, mother and daughter content with the quiet, a precursor before plunging into the day ahead.

'Hey, good morning. Two for the price of one, I see!' Phil was in high spirits and the very sight of him made Ellie shudder with cold fear. Would his happiness be shattered yet again, and all because of something she couldn't even remember? Sam excitedly patted the sofa where he stood, his chubby round face beaming with pleasure, ready for another fun-packed day. Grace was the first to pick him up, bringing him to his mother, saying, 'Have you got a kiss for Mummy, Sam?' The answer was yes and the little boy almost leapt from his grandmother's arms to squash his face into Ellie's cheek. She took him gladly, burying her face into his soft sweet neck and breathing in the scent of soap and talcum powder.

Phil's happy-go-lucky mood softened and his brow furrowed as he asked Ellie if her headache had gone.

'I'll be fine. I didn't sleep too well so I'm still a little tired and headachy, that's all.' She forced a smile; the last thing she wanted was for them both to begin questioning her – her emotions were all over the place as it was. Her biggest fear was if Dave would call again and if she refused him he might become angry and tell Phil they'd been having an affair. Strangely it was her husband whose comfort Ellie craved even though so far there'd been very little physical contact between them, the odd peck on the cheek and a brief hug at most. The closest they'd been was in the restaurant when Ellie reached out for his hand and Phil kissed hers. How she longed for his physical comfort now – another sign perhaps of the old feelings towards him being rekindled? It was time for Phil to leave for work and after kissing Sam he gave Ellie a concerned squeeze on the shoulder.

'Take it easy today, love. You're still not up to full strength you know, so don't overdo things.'

'I won't.' Standing at the door to watch him go, she instinctively looked across to number 40 and was sure the curtains were falling back into place – as if someone had been watching.

For the first hour of their day, Grace insisted her daughter sat down to watch Sam play while she found a small pile of ironing to do. Sam wanted a hundred per cent attention, which generally would be no problem but today Ellie's mind was elsewhere, straining to hear any portentous noises from outside. When Grace went into the kitchen to put the kettle on, the doorbell eventually did ring. A feeling of dread almost froze Ellie to the spot, but she forced herself to go to the door – if it was Dave, he would know she was inside.

'Hello, you're looking rather sexy today!'

His words charged her with a new emotion as she glared at him and hissed, 'Shut up.' With a force which surprised even herself, she said, 'My mother's in the kitchen and Sam's awake, there is no way you are coming in here, so go; just go away and leave me alone!'

Dave, visibly surprised at this response, gathered his wits enough to retort, 'Don't think I can be dismissed so easily, my lovely, we have a history, you and I, and there are things we need to discuss. Now, will you agree to meet me next Thursday when I'm off, or shall I come in and begin by telling your mother what her precious daughter gets up to when she's bored?'

Ellie's heart pounded so much she felt sure it could be heard outside her body. Feeling trapped, she needed time to think, to work out how to get rid of this vile man. 'All right, I'll be in the park at ten thirty on Thursday morning, with Sam, at the swings.' She glanced round to see if her mother was within hearing distance, which fortunately was not the case. Dave grinned again, moving his eyes slowly up and down her body, making her flesh crawl. Turning to leave, he had the audacity to blow a kiss, at which point Ellie firmly closed the door.

'Who was that, dear?' Grace asked, coming from the kitchen with two steaming cups of coffee.

'It was a neighbour wanting to see Phil about something. I told him he was at work.'

'Odd, you'd think he would know that.'

'Hmm.' Ellie felt only mild relief at having managed to stall Dave today. As he seemed persistent, she'd have to think up some way to deal with this awful man. Perhaps she could explain to him that if they had been having an affair, it was a mistake and would have to end. But would that be tantamount to admitting an affair, and Ellie wasn't wholly convinced he was telling the truth. Having Grace around bought a few days' reprieve, but on the flip side, there was more time to worry about what might, or might not have been going on before the accident. It would be a long week – could she handle the pressure?

By mid-afternoon, Ellie decided she needed some help and the only person she could think of to confide in was her GP, Carol Hudson. 'Mum, I think I will make an appointment to see the doctor. Will you look after Sam if I can get one?'

'Of course, love, but it might not be for a few days, the doctors are always in great demand.'

Ellie rang all the same and managed to get a cancellation for early the following morning, and knowing she'd be able to speak to someone eased her anxiety to some degree.

After lunch, Grace insisted her daughter went upstairs to lie down and surprisingly, Ellie fell into a deep sleep. On waking, she heard Phil's voice downstairs and a quick look at her watch told her he was home early. Dashing downstairs, the scene she then witnessed nearly broke her heart.

Phil and Sam were down on the rug on all fours, heads swaying from side to side with a pile of cushions in between them. To anyone watching this impromptu game of peek-a-boo between father and son, it would have raised a smile, if not all-out laughter. But to Ellie, the scene playing out before her tugged at something deeper within, causing her to gasp and swallow hard to stem the threatening tears. It was a bittersweet cocktail of emotions, fear, self-loathing, but also love. Love for her son, who'd stolen her heart in such a short space of time, but also for Phil.

I love him. The words, although not spoken aloud, brought with them such a tangle of emotions that Ellie felt weak.

How could I have risked hurting these two beautiful people? I must have been mad.

The thought elicited such pain. Ellie turned away, making some feeble excuse to leave the room. Phil had come home early, concerned about his wife, yet not picking up on the anguish she felt, he continued with the game, delighting in his son's laughter and evident joy.

Ellie busied herself in the kitchen. Grace had brought a dish of chicken casserole, enough for three days – or a small army – and Ellie lifted it into the oven and proceeded to set the table for their meal. Inevitably, thoughts of Dave intruded into her mind and a sickening feeling of disgust, not only for him but for herself too, washed over her. Whatever had caused her to enter into a relationship with another man was now unfathomable. Was her marriage not a happy one? If not, then her parents and even Phil himself had undoubtedly not picked up on it. Or had she actually had feelings for Dave, which led her down the disastrous path of an affair?

If one thing was clear it was that it needed sorting out, and quickly too. Rightly or wrongly, Ellie had agreed to meet Dave on the following Thursday, a meeting she dreaded but must go through with, or risk the alternative of her husband finding out. Ellie was at a loss to know how the meeting would go or what on earth she would say to Dave. Could he be reasoned with and accept that whatever had transpired between them was in the past and she had absolutely no desire to continue any kind of relationship? Or would he insist on carrying on their illicit affair, forcing her to choose him, or letting Phil find out how badly she'd behaved?

There were too many questions without a single answer. If Dave felt anything at all for her, perhaps he would leave her in peace? Yet judging from their last encounter, she could expect nothing as chivalrous from him. It was a mess, a complete and utter disaster, apparently of her own making, and now there was so little time to find a solution to a problem which Ellie didn't fully understand.

Chapter Twenty-Two

'Make sure you tell the doctor about these headaches you're getting,' Grace reminded Ellie as she prepared for her visit to the surgery the following morning. Ellie opted to take a taxi, declining her father's offer of a lift as it was so early and hoping for a bit of time to herself to allow her to put things into perspective and decide precisely what to tell her GP. She didn't relish telling the doctor the real reason for her anxiety but the knowledge that Carol Hudson was bound by confidentiality was a comfort, meaning she wouldn't need to be too guarded in what she said.

Ellie had warmed to the doctor on her previous visit; the woman's friendly, open demeanour relaxed her, and surely in her profession, she'd be unshockable by now. A doctor must hear all sorts of weird tales. It would be good to discuss her unsettling feelings with someone who didn't know her well and therefore had no expectations of her, but, more importantly, someone she didn't have to be afraid of hurting. Inside, Ellie's mind was in turmoil. She felt utterly wrecked.

Carol Hudson was a little surprised to see Ellie again and it didn't go unnoticed that the younger woman had lost some of the sparkle and positivity evident at their last meeting. Wearing no make-up and with eyes framed by dark circles, Ellie's expression was melancholy.

'Hi there, it's good to see you again.' Carol's smile received little response but she let the silence hang between them for a moment; sometimes quiet can be soothing, and Ellie certainly looked as if she needed a little tranquillity. After a few moments, Carol asked softly, 'What can I do for you today, Ellie?'

For the first time, Ellie looked up, a brief moment of eye contact before turning away to draw in a deep breath.

'Perhaps you could tell me how you're feeling?' Carol tried again.

'To be honest, I wish I was dead!'

This edgy, almost angry voice was so different from the Ellie of her last appointment, but Carol simply asked, 'Can you tell me why?' A few more moments of silence stretched out between them, which the doctor felt could become a wedge separating them, yet still, she waited until Ellie was ready to talk.

'I don't know who I am anymore.' Ellie's voice was quieter, laden with grief. More silence filled the little room.

Carol was the one to speak next. 'Is this to do with the amnesia, or has something else happened more recently to make you feel this way?'

Ellie's eyes widened, and as she lifted her head there was an expression almost approaching fear etched on her face. 'I'm sorry, perhaps I shouldn't have come. This is hardly a medical issue.'

'As I said before, if I can help, I'll be happy to do so and I assume your dip in mood has something to do with the amnesia?'

'In a way, yes. I've been confronted with something – something awful which makes me feel the "me" before my accident may not have been a very nice person. It appears I've done things which I now feel ashamed of but apparently didn't at the time. I was beginning to like my life too – my baby, my husband.' The tears began to fall and great sobs shook Ellie's whole body. Carol moved beside her patient and slid an arm around the younger woman's shoulder, a spontaneous gesture of comfort. Although unable to guess what had happened to set Ellie back like this, it wasn't entirely unexpected. Her improvement seemed to the doctor to be too swift, and now whatever Ellie had learned about her past was threatening to reverse the progress achieved.

It was one thing to learn, or relearn, things about others and be tolerant and accepting of them, but to find out something distasteful about herself appeared to be unforgivable to Ellie. Carol often found people could accept faults in others which would be wholly unacceptable in themselves. This seemed to be the case now.

'Don't be hard on yourself, Ellie. I'm assuming this is something you've learned from someone else and not something you've remembered?'

Ellie nodded, blowing her nose in an effort of composure. Dr Hudson waited, not wanting to rush or make her patient feel obliged to explain. Moving back to her seat, Carol wished there was some way of taking away this young woman's pain. The temptation in such situations was to offer advice or try to make the problem seem less of a stumbling block than it was. But this was Ellie's life and she must find her own answers.

Finally, Ellie spoke. 'It's been a terrible week. I met someone I didn't like, but apparently, I… spent time with him before the accident. I've learned things about myself, things I've done which, well… which I find appalling.' She looked directly at Carol with something akin to hope in her eyes, perhaps a longing for her doctor to take away the problems, to make everything right again. Carol saw this many times and ached to wave a magic wand, but that was impossible. There was very little she could do other than listen and explore all the options of how to deal with each situation and emotion. Carol could not and would not want to tell her client to take a particular course of action; this wasn't her role in psychological problems.

'Have the things you've learned come from one person or several people?'

'Just one,' Ellie whispered.

'Then maybe you should be looking at why this person has told you this and what kind of person he is. Someone told me several years ago that when I received criticism, I should look at the person offering it. If it was someone whom I held in high regard and respected, then I should ask myself if the remarks were valid and, if they were, take them on board. If the comments came from someone whom I knew to be unreliable, envious perhaps, or even a gossip, then I should take the remarks with quite a liberal pinch of salt. I don't know if this would apply to your situation, but perhaps you could somehow verify these things you're supposed to have done and discuss them with someone whose judgement you do respect?'

Ellie listened intently, taking in the doctor's quietly spoken words as if they presented a lifeline. She wondered if she could confide fully in her and relate all the details but wavered. Carol would almost certainly not be shocked but Ellie was so embarrassed her face flushed even thinking about it. Verbalising it simply wasn't an option. Words would give the situation life and make it real, so she remained silent. To try and confirm Dave's claims was almost impossible. The only people she trusted and had respect for at the moment were her parents and Phil, and these were the very people she would not want to know such things.

Remaining pensive and withdrawn yet aware that the doctor had a waiting room full of patients who needed her every bit as much as she did, Ellie thanked Carol.

'Don't get yourself into a state, Ellie. I'm always here for you if you need my help.' Carol Hudson's parting words, although welcome, did little to ease her burden.

By then, Grace and Derek would be at Phil's looking after Sam, so Ellie took the opportunity of going back to her parents' house to be alone until they returned. It meant she wouldn't see Sam and Phil until the next day, Saturday, which she'd agreed to spend with them, but perhaps the solitude of her own company would help her decide what her next move should be.

Chapter Twenty-Three

The weekend was looking grim and proved to be an arduous one for Ellie. Sunday would be Sam's first birthday and a family party was planned, an event she'd looked forward to for weeks. So much of her son's life was lost in the fog of amnesia, and the opportunity of making new memories was exciting. But that was before Dave soured everything, and it was now proving to be a bittersweet experience, marred by the agony and constant turmoil of her mind and haunted by thoughts she couldn't shake off. Doing her best Ellie knew wasn't good enough, but it was all she could offer, and so she made her best effort to enter into the celebratory mood for Sam's sake, knowing he deserved better.

Saturday was spent preparing for the party, shopping with Phil and Sam in the morning and then food preparation in the afternoon, although Grace insisted on doing the bulk of the catering. Phil wrapped presents after lunch while Sam slept, and blew up balloons, hiding them in the cloakroom, ready for the following day. Ellie made jellies and cakes and forced herself to enter into the spirit of the weekend; it was a milestone to observe even if the little boy would probably forget.

When Derek arrived to take her home that evening, Ellie was reluctant to leave her son and experienced a burning desire to be with him when he woke on his birthday – such strength of feeling brought tears to her eyes.

After a fitful night, Ellie was the first to rise in the Watson house, willing her parents to wake so they could set off to see Sam. When Grace did appear in the kitchen, she smiled at the sight of her anxious daughter, taking her impatience as a good sign. Derek wasn't far behind his wife, and soon breakfast was over and they were setting off on what was a glorious sunny day. The plan was to spend the whole day together, and as Grace had prepared enough food for a siege and the weather was fine, most of it could be spent in the garden.

Ellie scooped up her son and buried her face into his warm neck, holding him so close he wriggled to be put down. Sam didn't fully understand what was happening but entered into the joy of the occasion wholeheartedly, delighted to have those he loved the most around him. The present opening was an unmitigated success with exciting new toys to widen his eyes, toys that played music when buttons were pressed and others which felt good to put in his mouth and chew. A new wooden train captured his interest for quite some time until he turned back to tearing at more of the brightly coloured wrapping paper, crunching it in his fists before exploring the next new present.

Sam could now manage two or three steps unaided and was keen to show off this new skill. His speech was developing well too, and as 'Dada' and 'Mama' pleased the grown-ups, Sam gleefully burbled the words repeatedly. Countless photographs were taken, a record of a happy day, and Ellie tried her best to play her part, to manufacture a joy she didn't feel and grateful that the photographs couldn't capture the turmoil in her heart.

When his grandma brought in a cake with a single candle

burning brightly in the middle, Sam clapped his chubby hands, a gesture he'd learned made everyone around him smile and join in. And he loved the singing, even this unfamiliar song which was not one of his favourite nursery rhymes. The candle was blown out with a bit of help from Daddy, and soon a slice of chocolate cake was set before him on the tray of his high chair. A grinning Sam poked it once or twice before picking it up in his fist and pushing as much as he could into his mouth. More laughter ensued, and after he'd demolished the cake, Grandma wiped his hands and face and lifted him down to play again.

Phil was both delighted and relieved to have Ellie and her parents sharing in Sam's birthday celebrations. There'd been a time, not too long ago when he was dreading this occasion, a time when he was unsure if his wife would even live. Then, when the miracle occurred, and it appeared she would, another blow came from out of the blue, a cruel setback when the extent of her amnesia became known.

Phil still worried constantly about the future. Ellie's memory hadn't returned, with no guarantee it ever would, yet they'd begun a new relationship which in itself raised his hopes. He knew without a doubt she loved their son, a love which was rekindled in such a short space of time and gave him hope that Ellie's feelings for him could return too. They appeared to feel comfortable with each other and when they spent time together, he hoped and even dared to believe it was because she wanted to, not out of any sense of duty.

In his heart, Phil knew he hadn't imagined the progress they were making but these last few days dashed his hopes again as Ellie once more seemed to be withdrawing into her shell. Phil was at a loss to know why or what to do to regain their recent closeness. Subtle changes had crept into their relationship, which he struggled to make sense of, but as his wife insisted nothing was wrong, he felt it unwise to labour the point.

Catching Grace alone in the kitchen, washing up, Phil managed a brief conversation with her, asking if she too had noticed this sudden change in Ellie. The answer was yes, but Grace was just as bewildered as to the reason why as he was. Eventually, he decided the recovery process must have been too fast, too soon, and now a melancholy had crept back into his wife's demeanour, nullifying the progress they'd made. Yet Phil remained convinced her growing feelings for him were real. She was even taking the initiative at times – hadn't their date been Ellie's idea? Was it perhaps his clumsiness about her contact with Fran which had driven this new wedge between them? How he wished they'd never had that conversation.

Watching his wife now, he studied her smile. It was the duty smile again, the one which didn't quite reach her eyes. There was something on her mind, something troubling Ellie and he was being left out of her confidence. If only she would trust him enough to allow him in, he was sure they could still become a happy family. Phil would do anything for her if only she would allow him to.

Chapter Twenty-Four

With the birthday celebrations over, Monday morning rolled around again. Despite the way she was feeling, Ellie remained determined to continue the routine they'd so recently established and bravely declined her mother's offer of help with Sam. Her parents needed to return to the pattern of their own lives; she couldn't lean on them indefinitely for support. Had Ellie been truthful with her mother she'd have admitted to feeling low in mood.

The thought of being with Sam spurred her on and Ellie arrived in good time to take over his care from Phil. The weekend's excitement was well and truly over although Sam still clung to his new toys as if they might be whisked away from him as quickly as they'd appeared. To welcome his mother, Sam crawled over to the corner to fetch her a saggy balloon from the sad-looking pile that was still partially inflated.

It was a relief when Phil left for work and Ellie could concentrate solely on her son, his need for attention occupying her mind and bringing respite from the painful thoughts which constantly plagued her.

The week dragged interminably, perhaps the longest week

Ellie could remember but she steadfastly kept to her routine. Thursday inevitably came around and she shuddered, wishing the day to be over while simultaneously dreading what it might hold – and no wiser as to how to handle the situation with Dave.

Ellie didn't seem to notice when Phil kissed her on the cheek before leaving for work on Thursday morning; she was somewhere else entirely, a distant place that he or anyone else couldn't reach. Sam was unusually fractious, fighting against his mother, who struggled to get him into his jacket.

'Please, Sam, Mummy doesn't need this today,' she begged, but the little boy seemed to have picked up on his mother's tension and started crying, the only way he knew to get attention. Finally, they were ready and the ride to the park in his buggy seemed to soothe him, but not Ellie, whose legs felt like jelly as she clung to the handles of the buggy for support.

By the time they arrived, Sam was thankfully asleep. Ellie's thoughts had centred on this meeting all week, yet she was still no wiser as to how to approach the problem. She'd considered challenging Dave, telling him she didn't believe they'd had any kind of relationship. Pleading and trying to reach his humanity was another option, but it was doubtful whether this awful man had any humanity in him at all. No matter how many words she played with in her mind or how many phrases she put together, nothing sounded right. Ellie would simply have to wait and see how any kind of conversation might play out.

It was a pleasant day, warm with the promise of another scorching afternoon, the kind of day which made people smile at strangers. Stunning displays of begonias flanked by the majestic spears of red lupins greeted visitors at the entrance to the park, but Ellie didn't notice them. She was gripping the handles of Sam's buggy so tightly her knuckles were white; her teeth were clenched and her head ached.

Dave was already there – waiting. Sitting on a bench at the

far side of the swings, his eyes following her every step. Walking slowly, Ellie willed her heart rate to slow, yet it did quite the opposite as Dave's smug smile came into focus. Ellie interpreted his expression as an acknowledgement of the victory he had won by her very presence.

Stopping, she turned the buggy around so Sam faced away from Dave, who patted the space on the bench beside him with another satisfied smirk. Ellie reluctantly sat down, perching as close to the edge as possible.

Dave spoke first. 'I knew you'd come. You couldn't resist, could you?'

Turning to look at him with disgust, Ellie's eyes narrowed. 'You didn't leave me much choice, did you?'

'Aw, come on, be nice. You always used to be nice to me. I'm sure you haven't forgotten.'

'Sorry to disappoint you but I have no memories of you whatsoever – and I would like to keep it that way.' Ellie was feeling a little bolder now. Being out in the open brought a sense of safety – what could this man do to her in broad daylight? Perhaps escape from this nightmare was feasible after all.

Dave smiled and snaked an arm around her shoulders, making her recoil, feeling physically sick at the contact. Moving as far away from him as possible on the bench, Ellie mustered the courage to challenge him. 'For all I know you could be making this all up. How do I know what you're telling me is the truth? You certainly don't act like a trustworthy person, threatening and issuing ultimatums!' Ellie's voice was raised, the emotion threatening to choke her, but aware of Sam, she lowered it again and continued, 'I don't like you, Dave, and if that's true now then I'm pretty sure I wouldn't have liked you before. I don't believe what you say is true and it's probably best if I go now and have nothing more to do with you again.'

'Hey, don't be in such a hurry and don't come the Little

Miss Righteous with me either! We have a history whether you like it or not. If you want your grubby little secrets to become public, then fine, walk away! But if you do, I can guarantee you'll regret it!' Dave was so smug. Ellie was desperate to get up and go, but could she risk it?

The joyful sound of toddlers playing with their mothers on the swings filled her ears. She should be over there with Sam, carefree and having fun, not here with this loathsome man giving rise to fears about the past and what she might or might not have done. Dave spoke again, this time lifting the hair at the back of her neck and running his forefinger along her hairline.

'If we weren't having an affair, how would I know about this birthmark here on your neck? Kissing that spot always got you going...'

'Don't!' Ellie pulled herself away, angry and repulsed. How on earth could he know about that? 'It must have all been a terrible mistake... and I want to end it, now!'

'But what if I don't?' His self-satisfied expression made her feel sick to her stomach. 'You think you're too good for me now, do you? Well, let me tell you what's going to happen next. You can go now, straight home while the kid's asleep, and then in ten minutes, I'll come round. Leave the door unlocked, like you always used to, so there's less chance of us being seen, and we'll see if I can remind you of the fun we used to have.'

'No!' She mouthed a silent scream but Dave laughed and patted her knee.

'Off you go and get yourself ready for me like a good little girl.'

It was a relief to stand up and put space between herself and Dave, and Ellie almost ran back to the park gates, unaware of the darkening sky and the rain, which was starting to fall in huge drops.

Instead of turning left into the road which would take her

home, Ellie turned right and hurried towards the local primary school. The laughter of children dancing in the welcome rain barely registered as she quickened her step, passing the school and the local shops until eventually, she turned into the safety of the grounds of the health centre.

Sam was warm and snug in his buggy, but Ellie was now soaked to the skin as she pushed open the glass doors. Only then did she wonder what Dave would do when he discovered she wasn't at home waiting for him as he'd instructed. But she was reasonably confident he wouldn't stand for long on her doorstep; presumably he'd not wish to draw attention to his presence at her home.

Chapter Twenty-Five

'I need to see Dr Hudson. Please... it's an emergency.' Ellie was clearly distressed although Sam slept peacefully in his buggy.

'She has a patient with her at the moment, then she'll be breaking for lunch. I could have a word then?' The receptionist spoke softly. 'It'll be another ten or fifteen minutes if you'd like to wait?'

'Yes, thank you, I'll do that.'

June, the receptionist, asked her name and if the emergency appointment was for herself or the child.

'It's for me.' Ellie almost sobbed. Her legs were still trembling from almost running the whole distance from the park to the surgery, and she sat on the end of an empty row of seats to catch her breath. Sam, oblivious to his mother's anxiety, slept on but had been so for nearly an hour and would probably wake soon.

Even as Ellie silently told herself to calm down, take deep breaths, and relax, the ten-minute wait seemed like an eternity. She picked up a magazine that held no interest for her and put it down again. Eventually, a woman came out of the doctor's office, and the receptionist went in.

Almost immediately Carol Hudson's energetic figure was out of her room and striding towards Ellie, putting a hand on her shoulder to guide her into the little room she looked upon as a haven.

'I didn't know where else to go.' The tears flowed and Ellie took out a tissue to muffle the sound of her sobs.

'It's okay. I said I was here to help and I meant it.' Dr Hudson lapsed into silence, allowing her unexpected visitor to compose herself enough to speak, but Sam chose that very moment to wake up with a grizzly cry.

'June, my receptionist, could take him for a few minutes if that's okay with you?' the doctor offered. Ellie nodded her consent, and Carol pushed the buggy out to reception, catching the receptionist as she was finishing for lunch. June smiled and took charge of the buggy.

'I need the practice.' She grinned, putting her hand on her swollen belly as she pushed Sam to the corner of the waiting room where several toys were set out for babies and children. The little boy was easily distracted and reached out for the toys, forgetting whatever had caused him to cry. His mother too, ceased her tears for the moment and turned, ready with an apology for Carol.

'There's no need to apologise, Ellie. Has something happened?'

'Yes, and I have to tell someone, or I'll go mad! It's related to what I told you last time, do you remember? About finding out something about my past?'

'I remember.'

'Well, it's horrible – there's a man, a neighbour, who keeps pestering me – saying we were having an affair – and I don't know if it's true or not. How on earth can I tell? He's pressurising me into meeting him. I should be at home now; he said he would come from the park where I met him – but I came here instead. What shall I do?'

'The park? Were you with him in the park?'

'Yes, he made me promise to meet him there, to talk, but then he wanted more and told me to go home and wait for him. Please tell me what to do!' Ellie was talking quickly, upset and angry, but the doctor seemed to understand her dilemma.

'Well, you certainly don't have to do what he says.' Dr Hudson was emphatic. 'You have a choice here, Ellie.'

'No, I don't! He said he'd tell Phil and my parents!'

'Tell them what?'

'That I've slept with him! They'll hate me if they find out...' Tears were flowing freely again and Carol pushed the box of tissues nearer to her young patient.

'This man is blackmailing you, Ellie. Do you want him to get away with this?'

'No, of course not, but I don't want Phil to know what I've done.'

'Yet you're not sure you have done anything, are you?'

'I wasn't, until today... He mentioned a birthmark I have on the back of my neck. I've always been sensitive about it and keep it hidden. How would he have known about it if we hadn't been intimate?'

'I should think there are several ways he could have learned about it. Knowing about your birthmark is hardly conclusive proof of a relationship. When we last met and you told me you'd learned something from your past – if you remember I asked if you respected and trusted this person. I'm assuming it was this man?'

'Yes.' Ellie dropped her head with shame.

'Do you respect him or trust him?'

'No! From what I've seen and learned about him in the last couple of weeks, certainly not.'

'You're obviously feeling afraid of the consequences, but

couldn't you talk to Phil or your parents, perhaps? The not knowing seems to be weighing equally as heavily on you as bringing it all out into the open would.'

'But I don't think I could! I'm frightened. I've only really just started to appreciate my marriage and family again. I can't risk losing them.'

'Ellie, it's entirely up to you, but perhaps you should take a long look at all the possible scenarios before deciding. Put your thoughts down on paper if it helps, then weigh up the options, or we could chat about it now if you like. You're the only one who can decide what to do, as you're the one who has to live with the decision. To state the obvious here, you have a son and husband whose lives will also be affected. Look, I have the time now if you're up to a little brainstorming, and I can pop out to check on Sam if you like?'

'Would you? I need to make some sort of decision – I can't go back in case Dave's there. If Sam's okay and your recep-tionist doesn't mind, there's a bottle in his bag, some rusks and a clean nappy.'

Dr Hudson left her room to see how June was coping with her little charge.

'We're fine, getting to know each other really well. Tell his mummy to take as long as she needs. I'll feed and change him now.' June was clearly enjoying herself and Sam seemed happy enough with an assortment of new toys to amuse him.

Carol returned to Ellie with assurances that everything was under control. Her patient nodded a brief thank-you and visibly relaxed, then taking a deep breath, attempted to view her problem objectively.

'I suppose there are three things I could do. Firstly, I could do nothing and see what happens. Or secondly, I could go along with Dave and continue to see him, or the third option is to tell Phil and take the chance he'll forgive me.' Ellie was able to pull herself together sufficiently to look at her predicament more dispassionately and express the options concisely.

She continued, 'How awful! It's a choice of the lesser evil, but honestly, I don't relish any of them. To do nothing is risky. Dave might do as he says and tell Phil, my parents and anyone else who will listen. But the second option – agreeing to a secret relationship, I think would make me ill in the longer term. I can't bear the man; he makes me sick! No, I really couldn't do that! Which leaves the third option, telling my husband and throwing myself on his mercy; sounds rather melodramatic, doesn't it?'

'They're certainly not easy choices, but it sounds as if you've at least ruled out the second option?'

'Absolutely. I couldn't possibly go there!' Ellie was determined on that point at least.

'So, you're left with two options; do nothing, which if this man is making it all up will call his bluff, or confide in Phil.' Carol looked into her patient's eyes. 'You've been through so much lately, Ellie, and could do without this complication. Living with amnesia is frightening in itself; losing your past must cause confusion and unimaginable pain. Could this man be taking advantage of your vulnerability? Or do you think you really did embark on some kind of relationship with him?'

Ellie shrugged. She didn't know the answer any more than Carol did. 'I honestly don't know but I suppose it's progress having just two options instead of three?'

'And you have time to consider the two,' Carol reminded her.

Before Ellie left the surgery, Dr Hudson insisted she made an appointment for the following Wednesday, the day before she expected to see Dave again. Ellie thanked her and the receptionist. June had kept Sam so happy and he was reluctant to leave his new friend.

It would be a long week, but there was always her son to focus on – Ellie would put his needs before her own.

Chapter Twenty-Six

E llie's parents and husband couldn't fail to notice this new dip in her spirits but tactfully remained silent. Her frequent claims of suffering a headache were an attempt to stave off her family's enquiries, yet in reality, it gave rise to concern that her accident might have caused more damage than they'd been initially aware of.

Each day Ellie tried to look on the positive side of things and rid herself of the awful doubts she was experiencing about her behaviour. It proved hopeless and she could rarely find any positive aspects to dwell on. Perhaps the only one was her son, for whom Ellie willingly continued to care. The strength of her love for Sam pulled her back to their home day after day, even though seeing Phil brought such a kaleidoscope of emotions, with pain, guilt and an almost tangible, ever-present fear for the future. Each evening, when Sam was in bed, Ellie, now driving herself, made excuses to go back to her parents' home, ignoring the hurt in Phil's eyes as he assumed she no longer craved his company.

At home, Ellie locked herself away in the bedroom as often as was politely possible, passing the hours logged into her Facebook account, trawling through posts from people she didn't remember in a futile attempt to regain her lost memories. If only she had the certainty of what had transpired during the last ten years of her life – surely regaining her memory was the key to everything, but so much was still locked away, unreachable and exasperating.

Ellie rarely checked her emails. When Phil first brought her computer to her, she'd been almost overwhelmed by the volume of messages on her account and unable to bring herself to open and read them. Over the weeks, she'd deleted many unopened but tried to read the few which were from senders whose names she recognised. Looking once again at the build-up of mail, she started sifting, deleting dozens from unfamiliar addresses. Left with only a handful, Ellie opened them to determine if they required a reply.

One of the emails which had been sitting unopened in the inbox was from Rosie. Fran's version of Rosie's life made their old friend sound boring, leading a vacuous existence as a doctor's wife and mother of twins. Fran assumed such an existence to be dull beyond measure, but now Ellie had experienced the joy of motherhood for herself, she wondered if Fran's opinion was biased. She opened the email and read with renewed curiosity.

Hi Ellie!

I am so sorry for your present troubles. Phil emailed to let me know of your accident about a week after it happened and I simply couldn't believe it! Your husband's been an angel in keeping me updated during what must have been an absolutely horrendous time for you both. The last I heard, you were out of the coma and still in hospital but

I'm assuming you're home by now, hence this email.

It's times like this when being so far away from home is such a pain. I'd love to be there with you, helping out with anything you need, but I'm stuck here in Cromer with my two lovely boys, unable to offer anything except a shoulder to cry on, should you need it!

I'm writing on the assumption you still haven't regained your memory, sure that Phil or yourself would have let me know if the situation had changed. I asked Tom about amnesia (he's my gorgeous doctor husband) and he said it's so unpredictable and every case is different. You poor thing, I can't imagine how you must be feeling, scared and alone perhaps?

In case it helps, I'm attaching a couple of photos; one from our sixth-form days, which I don't know if you remember, and one of me with my brood. Tom and I are blessed with two gorgeous boys, just a couple of months older than your Sam, so you can see them and wonder at the old lady holding them who used to be me!

We've always kept in touch over the years, Ellie, especially since we both embarked on motherhood, and we usually speak on Skype when one of us is tearing our hair out and the other one trying to offer sage advice. Naturally, there've been many times when we were both tearing our hair out and we simply commiserated with each other until we ended up laughing.

I want you to know I'm still here for you, Ellie, my dear, dear friend. You can call on me anytime, even if you don't know me as the wife and mother I am now, I'm still the same Rosie I was at school. If you feel up to it and want to visit us here, it would be amazing, we have stacks of room, not five stars but comfortable enough. I'm sure Sam would love the sea. We're literally two minutes' walk from it. I won't, however, keep pestering you — if it's easier not to reply until your memory returns, then that's fine by me, no pressure, honestly!

With love to you, Phil and Sam

Rosie xx

Ellie couldn't help but smile at the warmth conveyed in her friend's email. She downloaded the photographs, eager to see how much Rosie had changed but opened first the ten-year-old picture of the three 'best friends'. They were all grinning like the proverbial Cheshire Cat, and she instantly remembered the photo being taken when a group of students took an unscheduled day off college. The river in the background was a local beauty spot where they would swim and hold impromptu parties. Carl had taken the photograph; he was one of their classmates whose ambition was to be a professional photographer, hence he was never seen without his camera. It was the day when he and Fran became an item, one of many boyfriends she always seemed to have in tow but who she changed as frequently as she changed her hair colour. Ellie was sure she had a copy of this picture too, but where was anybody's guess.

Eagerly she opened the next image and found herself face to face with a magazine-perfect family. Clearly, it was Rosie but a more mature woman than the girl she remembered. Rosie was always a plain girl during their school days, not a stunner like Fran and somewhat on the plump side, but not anymore; in this image, she was positively beautiful and glowing with pride at her family. As she'd said, Tom was handsome in a rugged, mussed-up sort of way, a tall, dark-haired man with a broad, friendly smile. Ellie gazed at the image for several minutes with a mixture of joy that her friend was so happy but also a tinge of jealousy. Rosie knew who she was, and Ellie was envious of her certainty. Surely the worst thing about amnesia was not knowing who you were.

Unsure whether Rosie's email had helped her mood or not, Ellie turned to another from someone else she recognised, Fran.

```
Hi Ellie,
    Is it time for another catch-up? I
know last time wasn't so brilliant but I
promise to keep off dodgy subjects,
namely husbands! So how about another
girls' trip out, perhaps one evening
this time— there are some great night-
clubs in the city — a few drinks and
letting your hair down could be just
what you need.
    Give me a ring and we'll fix a date,
    Fran x
```

How different from Rosie's email but so typically Fran. Yet the last thing Ellie needed now was a night out clubbing. Surely her friend knew this? Still, she was pleased Fran had made contact again and not taken the huff about their time together in York, which had been a little awkward to say the least. On impulse, she took out her phone and rang her friend.

Chapter Twenty-Seven

Hearing Fran's voice was a comfort Ellie hadn't expected it to be. Perhaps speaking to someone from outside of the family, someone she knew wouldn't judge her, was precisely what she needed at the moment. Before really thinking it through, she'd admitted to feeling somewhat depressed and accepted Fran's offer to come over for the evening.

Living at home gave rise to the uncomfortable feeling of being a teenager again and needing to ask permission to have friends round, absurd really as her parents would never complain, but Ellie asked anyway. 'Mum, I've been speaking to Fran on the phone and she's coming over for an hour. Is that okay?'

'You don't have to ask, love. You know that.' Grace had made little comment about Ellie's renewed friendship with Fran. She was always one to keep her own counsel.

'We'll go up to my room, don't feel you and Dad need to make yourselves scarce.'

'Oh, okay, if you're sure. We're going to watch that new series on the BBC at 9pm so we'll leave you to it.'

Fran arrived within the hour and Ellie took her straight upstairs to her bedroom.

'Gosh, it's like going back in time, isn't it? Remember all those winter weekends when the three of us played our music up here?' Fran grinned at the memory. 'Your parents were the only ones who'd put up with us. I always envied you that. My mum wouldn't allow me to invite friends home very often – said she couldn't stand the noise.'

'Rosie emailed me today. She sent a picture of the three of us from sixth-form days, look.' Ellie pulled up the picture on her laptop.

'Wow, look how chubby Rosie was then, and my hair, goodness, whatever did I look like?'

'Look at Rosie now though.' Ellie opened the second image where Rosie smiled up at them, so beautiful and content.

'Well, she's certainly bagged herself a pretty hot man there, but fancy having twins to cope with, ugh!' Fran screwed her face up and pushed the laptop away. 'Now, am I right in detecting that things aren't quite all lovey-dovey with you and Phil at the moment?'

Ellie sighed. 'Perhaps I shouldn't have said anything, Fran, but it's good of you to come round.'

'Never a problem, would talking about it help?' Fran's expression oozed concern and Ellie suddenly found herself spilling out everything about Dave, his claims of an affair with her and his apparent desire to continue it. She confided how rotten she'd been feeling with the knowledge that she might have been unfaithful to Phil.

'So, you see, it's not something he's done which is troubling me but the fact that I might have been such a stupid idiot. I was beginning to think Phil and I could make a go of things too; we were getting on so well until this awful Dave came on the scene.' Ellie looked pale and drawn – admitting this to Fran brought back the terrible feelings of self-loathing and guilt she'd been struggling with.

'Wow, that's some predicament. What are you going to do about it, have you decided?' Fran asked.

'Well, I've managed to avoid Dave so far but as for any decisions, I honestly haven't a clue. I'd love to tell him to go away and leave me alone, but he's already made it clear that's not an option. The last time we met in the park, he was so awful and insisted we continue the relationship. That's when I ran to the doctor. I felt like a complete idiot but she was brilliant and helped me look at the situation more objectively. So far though, I've done nothing about it, which sadly isn't a long-term solution.'

'You'll have to decide sometime. It sounds as if this bloke's not going to go away easily?'

'Oh, Fran, I'm such a coward. I've been hiding my head in the sand, which is quite disheartening and not in the least productive.'

'Do you know what you really want?'

'Yes, I want this bloody awful man out of my life and my husband and son back again! The only sensible way forward is to tell Phil, but I don't think I could bear it if it's true. What on earth will he think of me, and will he still want me?'

'There is another option.' Fran had a smile on her face now, which completely threw Ellie. 'You could carry on with this affair. If Phil hasn't found out so far, chances are you could get away with it again and then you could keep both men happy, a win-win situation!'

Ellie was stunned and stared at her friend in disbelief.

'Are you saying you believe I did have an affair with this man? That's unthinkable, Fran. I'm not that sort of person... am I?' Even as she spoke the words Ellie remained unsure. The only certainty was that she didn't know anything for sure, and this wasn't what she'd expected to hear from her friend.

'Why shouldn't you have your cake and eat it? You work bloody hard to look after Phil's son and the house for him too – you deserve a bit of fun, so go ahead and take it while the offer's still there. You're only young once you know, and life's all about taking risks.'

'But that's not what I want, and Sam's my son too. I want to look after him, and it's not for Phil!'

'Bloody hell, he's certainly got you brainwashed, hasn't he? Look, Ellie, I didn't want to tell you this but you have a right to know. Phil's not the perfect husband you think he is. He's got a wandering eye himself, and hands as well!'

'No! Why are you saying all this, Fran? It's not true!' Tears were welling in her eyes, tears of anger as well as distress. If Fran had come round to help her, she was successfully doing precisely the opposite.

'Oh, come on, Els, get real, we're not kids anymore! This is how the world works. You get your fun where you can and as long as no one knows, who cares? Phil's a player, and I should know. He tried it on with me just a couple of weeks before your wedding and I'm pretty sure I'm not the first, either. Why do you think he doesn't want you seeing me again?' Fran paused, a look of uncertainty flashed across her face, but she continued, 'Well, it's too late now, I've told you.'

There was an uncomfortable silence as the two women stared at each other, Ellie stunned and speechless and Fran wondering how much more she should say. She was the first to break the silence.

'This isn't why I came round, but it's only right you should know. I told you before that Phil was controlling, but he also plays around himself, so why shouldn't you? Perhaps knowing the full facts will help you decide what to do about your lover.' Fran had said enough and the look on Ellie's face must surely have told her how unwelcome her words were. 'Sometimes the truth is hard to take, Els, but you know now. Look, it's probably best if I go, give you some space to think things through, I'll see myself out.'

As soon as her friend left the room, Ellie threw herself onto the bed and sobbed bitterly. Fran's words were sharp, painful to the point of being unbearable, but were they true? How on earth could she find out? Living under the threat of Dave's ultimatums appeared to be the worst thing ever since the amnesia. Not knowing what she might have done was unbearable. But now the whole sorry situation had gone downhill, plunging to a new low which she'd not thought possible. Had she had an affair with Dave? And was Phil some kind of womaniser as Fran suggested?

Ellie sobbed for what seemed to be hours, thankful her parents were engrossed in their television drama and unaware of her crisis. How was she to know what to do when there was absolutely no way of establishing the truth? Her instinct was to run away, to go somewhere to hide and lick her wounds, but even that was impossible; there was Sam, her son whom she loved, the only bright spark in her bewildering frightening life. Ellie knew she couldn't leave Sam. But then she thought of Rosie.

Chapter Twenty-Eight

'I didn't hear Fran go last night, Ellie, and when I looked into your room later, you were fast asleep. Is everything all right?'

'As all right as it can be, Mum. Listen, I've decided to go away for a few days to Cromer to stay with Rosie. She's invited me, and perhaps some sea air will do me good.'

Grace's eyebrows shot up. 'But what about Phil and Sam? And don't you have an appointment with the doctor?'

'The appointment can easily be cancelled and I'm going to take Sam with me. Rosie has two little boys about the same age and he'll enjoy a little holiday by the sea. Phil won't mind, I'm sure. It'll give him the chance to catch up with some work. I'm just going to finish packing, and then I'll go round to pick Sam up.' Ellie ran upstairs before her mother could think of any more obstacles to thwart her plan.

Ellie had fired off a quick email to Rosie late the previous night before climbing into bed, hearing her mother check in on her later but feigning sleep to avoid conversation. The encounter with Fran, and her unexpected revelations, cut deep and left a bitter taste in her mouth. Not only was she unsure of her own character, but now Phil's too was in doubt. Would this nightmare never end?

Rosie's reply was waiting for her when she awoke, telling her she'd be more than welcome and she couldn't wait to see Sam, confident they'd have a wonderful time together. If Rosie wondered about the suddenness of Ellie's decision, she didn't express it. Good old reliable Rosie, she was always the solid one of the three friends, dependable, faithful Rosie.

Ellie finished packing, unsure what or how much to take as presently she had no idea of how long her trip would be. The principal hurdle would be to persuade Phil to allow her to take their son away with her. She hoped her husband would understand, yet explaining why her greatest need at the moment was to get as far away as possible to collect her thoughts, was going to be a challenging task.

After a hasty goodbye to her parents, Ellie drove to Phil's, her mind still reeling from Fran's revelations of the night before and her opinion of her husband now coloured by this new insight. Phil had proved so considerate and caring since her accident but was it all an act to lull her into trusting him again? And if he'd been bold enough to attempt to seduce one of her friends, then what else was her husband capable of? Part of her wished Fran had never told her yet the sensible part accepted she should know the truth to enable her to make the right decision for her future. If only her thoughts could be switched off, for these horrid images to leave her mind. Ellie was becoming increasingly desperate to get away.

'Oh no, Ellie, you can't go away. You're not well enough yet!' Phil's reaction was no more than she expected but perhaps not laced with the anger it might have held.

'Don't you see, that's the point. I know I'm not well, so a few days away will do me good and it'll be a little holiday for Sam too with Rosie's boys to play with – and remember, Tom's a doctor. I couldn't be staying with more suitable friends.' Ellie found it difficult to look her husband in the eyes. Fran's words still echoed in her mind, and those images…

Phil picked up their son and balanced him on his hip. 'It's such a long drive too. Are you up to that yet?'

Could he be considering saying yes, she wondered, but then, did she need his permission? Sam was her son too, and she would be entirely within her rights to take him away. It wasn't as if they were leaving the country.

'I'm quite confident about driving and there's the satnav to direct me. Some time on your own will give you the chance to catch up on the work you've neglected of late and we'll Skype you every day.' Ellie would keep her promise. She knew how much Phil would miss Sam. They had such a strong bond, particularly as he'd been their son's primary carer during her time in hospital. Her husband looked dejected and she felt a pang of guilt until she reminded herself of Fran's revelations.

'I don't need time to catch up. My work's up to date now. If you want to go away maybe I can come with you, we could go to my parents if you like, you love it there. They have a pretty little villa with a pool which Sam would enjoy and Mum and Dad would be so pleased to see you too.'

Ellie's heart sank but she remained resolute. 'No, Phil, I need to go alone, just with Sam, please?' Something in her husband's eyes seemed to die and he looked at her with such pain etched on his face that her resolve nearly crumbled.

'Okay, but please be careful – you two are very precious to me. I'll miss you, Ellie.'

She turned away, embarrassed at the emotion and doubting if it was genuine. 'I'll pack his bag this morning and be off when we're ready. Don't worry, Phil, I'll ring as soon as we arrive and I'll have my phone with me at all times.'

Phil insisted on helping her pack for their son even though she longed for him to go, to leave her alone to effect her escape as swiftly and painlessly as possible. There were tears in her husband's eyes when he kissed Sam goodbye, and for a moment, Ellie thought he might kiss her too but he thought better of it, and then he was gone.

It was late morning, so Ellie thought it prudent to give Sam something to eat before setting off. Scrambled eggs would suffice with soft, buttered white bread, and she ate a good helping herself even though she didn't feel in the least bit hungry. After tidying the kitchen and making a couple of sandwiches, carefully cutting the crusts off Sam's cheese and tomato ones, Ellie put the supplies into a freezer bag and stowed them with the case into the boot of her Mini, alongside her suitcase. Her son's essentials took up far more space than her belongings, she thought, heaving the buggy into the footwell of the passenger seat.

If she'd been candid with Phil, Ellie would have admitted to being nervous about driving to Cromer. As far as she was aware, Norfolk wasn't a county she'd visited before. Her parents' preferred holiday destinations were further south, usually Cornwall or Devon. A hundred and eighty miles was a long journey to embark upon so soon after her accident, especially with Sam to entertain, but she would stop as often as necessary and hope he slept for much of the journey.

The little boy loved being in the car and gurgled happily as Ellie strapped him into his car seat in the back, chewing at his toy rabbit. For his birthday, his grandparents had bought him a toy steering wheel with knobs and a horn which fitted onto the back of the front passenger seat. He squealed when he saw it and patted his hand on the horn.

'Oh, Sam, you'll drive Mummy crazy if you do that all the way to Cromer.' She kissed her son and jumped into the driving seat to set off on their little adventure.

The first part of the journey passed quickly, the M18 being relatively quiet at that time of day. The plan hadn't particularly been to avoid the rush-hour traffic – Ellie just wanted to get away – but she was grateful for how it worked out. Sam nodded off soon after they entered the motorway, and they covered a good third of their journey before he woke, in need of food and a nappy change.

It was the first of only three stops, unhurried breaks which her son appeared to enjoy. Ellie bought a coffee and pastry for herself in the service station and a carton of juice for Sam, and they sat in a window seat, the little boy eagerly eating the sandwich she'd made earlier, followed by a strawberry yoghurt, his favourite, and slices of apple.

Singing nursery rhymes helped to pass the next stage of their journey, mother and son enthusiastically joining in with the words to his favourite CD, 'The Wheels on the Bus'.

Ellie found Norfolk to be enchanting, very green and flat, with the roads, although narrow in places, relatively easy to navigate, especially with help from her satnav. Sam slept again, causing her to wonder what kind of night she might suffer as a consequence of so much daytime napping but it was the least of her worries.

During their last stop, Ellie rang Rosie to update her on their progress and was relieved her friend still sounded enthusiastic about their visit. The thought crossed her mind that Rosie's invitation might have been issued on impulse and she might now regret it, but the excitement in her friend's voice reassured her otherwise.

Cromer itself was a delightful town and Ellie immediately felt drawn into its welcoming atmosphere. The charming brick-built Victorian houses gave the distinct impression of stepping back into the 1900s as she drove down MacDonald Road, heading towards the sea and Rosie's home. The salty tang in the air was refreshing after their long journey, and Ellie drove with the windows open, taking in welcome gulps of the energising air, her son relatively quiet now as he gazed from the window in awe of the unfamiliar surroundings.

'You're going to love it here, Sam. Auntie Rosie has two little boys for you to play with, and we can go to the beach every day!' As if he understood, Sam, who'd begun to grizzle during the last leg of their journey, suddenly smiled, kicked his legs and chattered away in his own unique language as at last they pulled up outside Rosie's home.

Chapter Twenty-Nine

R osie's Victorian terraced house was three storeys high, rendered and washed in a calm, cream paint with a magnificent bay window and a small forecourt crammed with an abundance of summer blooms. A hanging basket dripped with fuchsia, geraniums and surfinia, and two huge terracotta pots spilt their display of flowers on either side of the front door, providing a fragrant welcome for the two weary visitors.

Rosie was outside to greet them before Ellie managed to lift the cases from the boot, and the two women hugged warmly, the years since they'd met dissolving with the pleasure of being together again. She'd almost forgotten how much she'd always loved her quiet, gentle friend – Rosie's character was a complete contrast to the more outgoing and sometimes abrasive Fran, and it was so good to see her again.

'It's like moving house each time you go anywhere, isn't it?' Rosie laughed as she grabbed a case and several bags. 'Come in, come in!' The heartfelt pleasure in her voice brought welcome relief to Ellie – her friend wanted her there – it was going to be all right.

It was 7pm and Ellie was surprised to realise their journey

had taken nearly seven hours although frequent stops made it a more pleasant experience than she'd anticipated. After dumping the bags at the bottom of the staircase, she pulled out her phone and scrolled down to find Phil's number.

'Sorry about this, Rosie, but he'll worry if I don't let him know we're here safely.'

'Of course, I'll get the kettle on.' She tactfully moved away towards what must be the kitchen. Ellie kept the call brief, Sam chattered to his daddy more than she did, and with promises to Skype the next day, she ended the call and headed in the direction Rosie had disappeared. A delicious meaty aroma led her to the kitchen, one of many rooms in this delightful, rambling house. Sam appeared to be fascinated with his new surroundings, as was his mother; it was spacious and beautiful with period features, yet a contemporary feel everywhere. Rosie was pouring boiling water into a huge teapot.

'Tea all right?' she offered.

'Wonderful.'

'I put the boys to bed – thought it better to keep them in routine and we can get you two settled in before *the meeting of the toddlers!* Tom's at a partners' meeting but should be home by 9pm.' Rosie turned her attention to Sam and grinned at his solemn little face. 'Now then, young man, have you enjoyed your long ride in the car?'

Ellie, who'd flopped, exhausted onto a chair by the kitchen table, jiggled him on her knee, and he turned shyly into her shoulder. 'This is an imposter, Rosie – the real Sam is much more outgoing and somewhat mischievous at times, wait and see. I suppose he's tired. It's been a long day.'

'Well, whenever you're ready I'll show you to your room. Do you want that warming?'

Ellie had pulled out Sam's bedtime bottle and gratefully passed it to her friend to warm. Soon the baby was sucking happily away, his eyes fluttering as sleep slowly claimed him.

When he'd finished his bottle, they took him upstairs, where Ellie changed his nappy and his clothes as Rosie carried the rest of her things upstairs.

'What a beautiful room, oh, Rosie, I'm so happy to be here!' A spacious coastal-themed room was furnished with a double bed, a cot, prettily painted furniture and blue-and-white-striped curtains. Delicately patterned wallpaper completed the room with tiny sprigs of forget-me-nots, somewhat ironic, she thought. Rosie certainly possessed good taste. From the open window, the sea was visible, its saltiness refreshing and exciting.

'Thank you for inviting me, Rosie. It means a lot to be able to get away for a few days.' Her friend's kindness suddenly overcame Ellie, and as she lowered a sleepy Sam into the cot, there were tears in her eyes.

'Hey, I'm delighted you wanted to come – you're more than welcome, anytime.' Rosie gave her a warm hug before leading the way back downstairs, leaving Sam already snoring contentedly.

'Rosie, have I met Tom?' The question had been troubling her during the journey and once back in the kitchen she dared to ask.

'Oh, Ellie, yes, you have met him. You were my matron of honour when we married! I'm sorry, I hadn't fully appreciated just how difficult this must be for you, but you two got on like a house on fire. My husband has a rather quirky sense of humour and you both seemed to hit it off well.'

Ellie nodded, so it seemed she wasn't meeting Tom for the first time. 'And what about you? Tell me what you've been doing since sixth form.'

'Sixth form? Goodness, is that your last memory, you poor thing! Well, after A levels, I went to Norwich University Hospital to train as a nurse where I spent some of the happiest and most certainly the busiest years of my life. At the end of the course, I'd shed two stones and gained a husband, which is quite a bargain, I'd say! We were both in our final year when we met. Tom had been there for five years to my three. Almost from day one of meeting him I knew he was the one – yes, corny, I know!' Rosie paused and looked at Ellie, rolling her eyes. 'After that, I didn't return to York. Tom's family are all in Norfolk and I fell in love with the area, so when a GP vacancy came up in Cromer, it was a simple decision, and there've never been any regrets. This house was on the market when we were looking for a place to buy, it was a guest house then, hence all the en-suite bedrooms, and we've spent the intervening years making it our own. Tom's parents loaned us the money to buy it, we could never have afforded it ourselves, and since then, they've refused to let us pay a penny back.' Rosie smiled as Ellie's eyes widened. 'Yes, I felt a little guilty at first but honestly, they're loaded – pots of money, and as Tom's their only child, they convinced us he'd only inherit it one day, so why not now? Some gift, eh? It's meant we've been able to put all our money into getting the place just how we want it, a slow job at first as we were both working, and there are still things we'd like to do. The boys came along a year ago and now we live in happy chaos in our rambling old home.'

'Twins though, was it a surprise or are they in the family?'

'Neither, they're the product of IVF.'

'Oh, Rosie, sorry, I didn't mean to pry.' She instantly regretted her question, hoping she hadn't hit a raw nerve.

'It's fine and certainly no secret. But biologically, they're ours; my body just has problems conceiving naturally. The plan is to try IVF again in a year or two and pray it's only one baby next time!'

Their conversation was interrupted by the sound of the front door opening, and a minute later, Tom appeared in the kitchen doorway.

'Hi, Ellie!' The curve of his smile lit up his face, and his height filled the doorway. Ellie returned the greeting, instantly drawn to her friend's husband. Tom Appleby must have been all of six foot six tall and as thin as a rake. With high cheek-bones, a square jawline and mischievous green eyes, his bony, angular appearance fitted together well, and Tom had the air of someone who was totally at ease with himself. Oh, how Ellie envied that.

'What's for supper? I'm starving.' Tom kissed his wife on the cheek and nudged her gently towards the oven.

'Honestly, I don't know where you put all the food you eat. I only hope to goodness the boys don't grow up with an appetite like yours.' Rosie lifted a casserole dish from the oven and very soon the three of them were seated at the large kitchen table before plates of delicious beef and vegetables.

Ellie ate more than she'd managed in days. Her friends chatted about inconsequential things, including her in the conversation but not grilling her as to the accident or her condition since. It was precisely what she needed, no pressure. Inevitably their children became a topic for discussion, Sam being her favourite subject, and with their boys being so close in age, it was going to be fun watching how they would interact.

'At this time of year, we're at the beach almost every day, the boys absolutely love it, and as it's literally just at the end of the road, it's perfect. Perhaps we'll go tomorrow?' Rosie suggested.

'Great, I'm sure Sam will love it too, and he adores other children; we go to the park almost every day just so he can play with them.' Ellie yawned. 'Oh, excuse me, all that driving must be catching up with me.'

'If you'd like an early night, don't think you have to stay up and be sociable, we quite understand – we're not night owls ourselves. Tom has an early start on weekdays. We want your time here to be as relaxing as possible, so don't feel under any pressure whatsoever. You're here to rest and recuperate.' Rosie smiled at her friend, and Ellie was so pleased she was there.

Ellie did leave her friends alone after the meal. She was weary and also concerned that her son might wake in an unfamiliar room and become upset. There'd be plenty of time tomorrow to talk some more and for the boys to get to know each other.

Sam was still snoring softly, his rosebud lips parted and moist. His mother stood for several minutes gazing down into his cot, her mind a jumble of emotions. Had she been a coward to run away from the uncertainty of her life? Whatever the rights and wrongs of being in Cromer, she knew it was only a time of respite. Sooner or later, Ellie would need to go home and face up to reality, whatever that reality might be.

Chapter Thirty

To her great surprise, Ellie slept soundly, with her son sleeping through the night beside her. As she opened the curtains, the room was flooded with morning sunlight, it was another lovely day. She stretched languidly and peered into Sam's cot to smile at her little boy.

'Good morning, sleepyhead,' she greeted him. Sam chuckled, totally unperturbed at waking up in a different room, and playing contentedly with his toy rabbit. Waking beside her child was a new experience for Ellie, and she relished being with him from the outset of the day. Lifting him from the cot, she carried him into the en-suite bathroom, stripped off his night-clothes and gave him a good sponge down before dressing him in clean clothes. Popping a sweeter-smelling baby back into the cot with a few more toys, Ellie left the adjoining door open so her son could see her while she took a quick shower. Once dressed, they headed downstairs to where the noise told them the family were already up and about.

'Good morning, everyone.' Ellie smiled at the scene of domesticity before her. Two matching high chairs stood at one end of the table, holding two matching boys with Weetabix faces and huge grins. They were the image of their daddy, and both looked up to see who the interlopers were.

'Morning, Ellie, morning, Sam.' Rosie smiled. 'Meet Alex and Luke. Boys, this is Auntie Ellie and Sam.' There was a moment of silence as the three boys stared at each other, and then Sam made a bid to escape from his mother's arms, kicking his legs and reaching out to these new potential playmates. There were smiles all around as Rosie continued to spoon Weetabix into her sons' mouths, and Tom poured Ellie a mug of coffee.

'Being waited on won't last long. After breakfast you're one of the family so feel free to pour my coffee in future. It's every man for himself in the Appleby household, especially at mealtimes.' He offered toast which she accepted as she settled her son in the third high chair and pushed it near the twins.

'Hi, Alex, hi, Luke. This is Sam; he loves Weetabix too,' Ellie said. Luke very kindly reached over and offered him a fistful of the mushy cereal, a sign of happy times ahead.

'I'm afraid you'll have to butter your own toast; morning surgery starts at 8am, and I need to be on my way. Have a good day, ladies. I can't wait to hear all about it tonight.' With his trademark grin, Tom kissed Rosie and the twins, then left the women and children to it.

After a long lazy breakfast, Ellie helped to clear away then Rosie took her on the promised tour of the house. Exactly how much love and energy had been committed to making every space work for them was apparent. Originally the guest house boasted six double bedrooms with en suites and two singles. Tom had knocked two rooms together to make a fantastic master bedroom in which Rosie worked her magic with the décor. A different pastel colour adorned each of the rooms with pretty accessories completing each unique look. The second single room was now a study, and the boys occupied the room nearest to their parents, which still left masses of space for visitors.

'It's great to be able to have family and friends to stay whenever we want – we love having visitors,' Rosie enthused. 'And you're welcome to stay as long as you wish; we're going to have such fun.' Her confidence and positivity were infectious, making Ellie feel so welcome.

The rooms downstairs were equally spacious, the huge bay window at the front of the house fitted with a plush window seat where Ellie could imagine sitting, watching people of every description making their way to the beach and back. The whole of Cromer would possibly pass by this window at some time, not to mention the many visitors who swelled the population at holiday times.

A cosy playroom lit up Sam's eyes. He was keen to explore every inch and every toy but was watched warily by Luke and Alex. They moved back into the kitchen and sat again at the table, lowering their respective offspring onto the giant rug to play.

'The kitchen was perhaps the biggest project and the most expensive. It was a rather ugly utilitarian, stainless-steel affair when we moved in, no character, just pure business, so we made this our priority.' Rosie grinned. It was most certainly the heart of the home, a great space with modern units, a range and the obligatory family table. There was a large squashy sofa at the far end of the room with a bright rug in front of it and two boxes of toys, an ideal place for the twins to play while Rosie cooked. Two alcoves framed the far end of the room with large painted dressers fitted snugly into the recesses, housing collections of pretty china. Ellie felt completely comfortable, not only in such beautiful surroundings but also in her friend's welcoming presence. For the first time in days, her body and mind relaxed, as if her problems were being pushed aside and no longer greedily grabbing at her from every direction, consuming all her time and energy.

'The biggest compromise is the garden, or rather the lack of it.' Rosie continued her history of their occupancy. 'We'd have liked something bigger, but with the beach on our doorstep and oodles of space inside, it's not a major problem.' Ellie adored the little walled courtyard garden, again awash with colourful containers yet still with space for the boys to play. She could picture them in a few months' time pedalling around the paved courtyard on their tricycles. It was perfect. Rosie completed the grand tour and so obviously loved telling the story of their home.

'It's wonderful, Rosie. You must have worked so hard to bring it all to life and should be proud. I'd hate to have to clean it though!' She grinned at her friend.

'If it gets too much, I know a lovely lady who cleans at some of the B&Bs and is always up for a few extra hours. I'll happily admit to preferring to spend my time with the boys than doing housework. Talking of the boys, they seem to be getting on rather well now, don't you think?'

The three were bunched close together on the rug, each with a pile of toys from the boxes. As their mothers watched, Sam occasionally reached out to one of his new friends and touched his face, curiosity making him bold.

'I wonder if he's confused by how alike they are?' Rosie mused.

'Probably, do you ever get them muddled up, or can a mother always tell them apart?' Ellie asked, knowing she was going to struggle to fit the right name to the right boy.

'I'll admit to occasionally calling them the wrong name, but there's one difference, look, Alex has a freckle on his jawline just below his right ear.'

Ellie noticed when it was pointed out and the sight made her touch the nape of her neck, reminding her suddenly of her own birthmark – a shudder passed through her body as an unwelcome image of Dave entered her mind.

'Right, enough sitting around here; let's make a few sand-wiches and head for the beach, shall we?' Rosie claimed her attention once more and the thought was again pushed to the back of her mind.

'The forecast's good, and I'm longing to see Sam's reaction to the sea. My two rather take it all for granted now, so it's always a delight to watch other children splashing about. Can you start the sandwiches, Ellie? Alex needs his nappy changing.'

It was amazing to arrive at the beach within five minutes of leaving the front door. Rosie hadn't exaggerated, and if they'd forgotten anything, they could always pop back to get it. Slathered with sun cream and with hats on their heads, the three little boys were raring to go.

Ellie couldn't remember taking Sam to the seaside but was sure he must have been before. Perhaps they'd been on a day trip to Scarborough, a place she'd often been taken to as a child. It was something to ask Phil about when she Skyped him later, though conversations were surely going to be difficult now she was uncertain about her husband's character.

Rosie was good company and didn't attempt to press her friend to talk about anything more serious than what flavour ice cream she preferred. They chatted about their parents; Rosie's were still in the York area, retired and happily living in a bungalow with a huge garden to keep her dad from under her mother's feet. Rosie rarely went to visit – it was so much easier for her parents to come to them, which they did, frequently.

Ellie couldn't believe how satisfying digging in the sand could be, moulding perfect little sandcastles with the buckets, only for one of the boys to knock them down and laugh at the mock horror on her face. It was certainly therapeutic. Alex and

Luke were walking well on their own and ran in a wobbly fashion down to the water's edge every few minutes, jumping over the waves with a hop, skip, lurch and laughing with delight. A couple of months younger, Sam did his best to keep up but could only manage a few steps before resorting to crawling to catch up to his new friends.

At lunchtime, eating their picnic proved a messy job; the boys needed to be de-sanded before touching the food, and more of the picnic was lost to sand than they managed to eat, but it was all good fun. Ellie felt herself smiling more than she'd done for ages. The sea air and pleasant company were turning out to be beneficial, and it was only the first day. Watching Sam playing happily with the twins convinced her that coming to Cromer was the right move, even if her motives were somewhat cowardly.

Chapter Thirty-One

By 6pm, Ellie could procrastinate no longer and took a rapidly tiring Sam up to their room to Skype Phil. Her husband answered immediately.

'Ellie, are you both okay?' There was an element of panic in his voice.

'Yes, of course we are.'

'I thought you'd Skype sooner – or ring perhaps?'

Sam saved his mother from having to make excuses by almost pouncing onto the screen at the sight of his daddy, suddenly animated again as he patted his father's image with his chubby little fingers. Phil smiled and reached out his hand for a virtual high five.

'Hey, little chap, Daddy's missed you and Mummy so much!'

'We've spent much of the day on the beach.' Ellie wanted to get the report over with so she could finish the call and return to her new, more comfortable reality downstairs. 'Sam loved every minute and he gets on so well with Luke and Alex. Rosie and Tom are making us so welcome and we're planning on going to the zoo tomorrow.' Her false brightness sounded edgy even to herself.

'That's great. I've been thinking about you all day. You didn't say much on the phone last night?'

'We'd only just arrived, Phil and it'd been a long drive. Sam was tired too.' Once again, Ellie found it difficult to meet her husband's eyes, even on a screen and with so much distance between them. The man she'd thought he was, the Phil she'd been enjoying getting to know, was now a stranger for the second time. Unbidden images of him attempting to seduce Fran flashed behind her eyes. How could he have done such a thing and so close to their wedding? The heavy hint that Fran wasn't the only one was also hard to stomach. Phil, the man she'd loved enough to marry and create a child with, the man she was falling in love with all over again, was no better than their awful neighbour, Dave. But even as these images disturbed her, Ellie was also disgusted at herself. If Dave was telling the truth, she was as guilty as Phil. It took only a moment for these unsettling ruminations to cross her mind, and at the same time, thoughts of Rosie and Tom with their happy relationship prompted envy which shamed her.

Pulling her attention back to her husband, Ellie continued a bland dialogue, if only for their son's sake. Yes, Sam must be their priority; whatever they might or might not have done shouldn't affect his happiness, so for his sake, she forced herself to continue the inane conversation with Phil.

'The house used to be a guest house, so they've plenty of space, and we've got a lovely room with a sea view and an en suite.' After a few more minutes, Sam grew restless and Ellie used this as the excuse she needed to end the call.

'You will Skype tomorrow, won't you?' The anxiety was back in Phil's voice as she promised to do so before ending the call. No loving words, no expressions of regret at the miles between them, just a quick, clinical goodbye.

Ellie rang her parents next and a more relaxed conversation followed but one she also wished to keep brief. She extolled the virtues of her friend's home and Cromer itself, allowed Sam to burble into the handset and assured them they were both fit and well and already feeling the benefit of her break. Ellie hated deceiving her parents. They'd been so good to her but at this moment in time, her life was one huge enigma and there was virtually nothing she could say to assure them all was well; it so obviously wasn't.

Downstairs, Alex and Luke were bathed, in their pyjamas and playing happily on the rug with Tom, who'd just arrived home from work.

'Hi there, I've heard all about your fun-packed day on the beach. You look well for it.' He smiled. Ellie touched her face; she'd caught the sun and could feel the healthy glow on her usually pale complexion.

'It was wonderful. I think we all enjoyed it. You live in such a beautiful spot, Tom, I almost envy you.' She put Sam down for a final few minutes' play with his new friends and offered to help Rosie with their meal.

'All sorted, thanks. Just something from the freezer. I like to batch cook when I have time so we can eat what we want, when we want it. Feel free to bathe Sam and we'll eat when the boys are settled.'

'You're so super organised, Rosie.' On impulse, Ellie hugged her friend before scooping up a wriggling little boy and removing him to the bathroom.

Sea air is an amazing tonic for settling active toddlers, or so was the general consensus as the three adults ate a child-free meal nearly an hour later. The conversation was relaxed and amusing, with Tom regaling an incident at the surgery, obviously embellished, of a patient shouting out the personal nature of his complaint to a red-faced young receptionist after she'd asked him why he wanted an appointment. It had the desired effect of gaining him an emergency slot with no more probing questions. Tom quizzed them gently about their day, delighting in how well the boys had gelled as friends.

Tom and Rosie's company was relaxing and easy. They made no demands, asked no difficult questions and simply allowed her to 'be', which was precisely what she needed. For the following day a visit to the zoo was decided upon and as Rosie mentioned they had a great child-friendly café, Ellie offered to treat them to a meal to say thank you.

By 9.30pm, Ellie's eyes were closing; sea air was apparently good for adults too, and she excused herself and went upstairs for an early night. Thoughts of her conversation with Phil kept her awake for only a short while before she drifted off into the peace of a good night's sleep.

Chapter Thirty-Two

'I can't thank you enough for having us to stay, Rosie. We've only been here a couple of days, and I feel so much better already.' Ellie was keen for her friend to understand how much she appreciated her kindness. Amazonia Zoo proved to be the perfect destination for a family day out and a slightly cooler day added to the enjoyment. The two young mothers pushed their offspring around the winding paths, marvelling at the variety of nature in both the animals and the foliage on display.

'That's okay. I intend to order the most expensive thing on the menu so you'll be paying me back for sure! Seriously, it's lovely to see you too, and I thought you'd enjoy a visit to the zoo. Didn't you have aspirations to be a vet at one time, Ellie?' Rosie reminded her.

'I did at school, yes, but it was a bit of a pipe dream really. I'm not sure I'd have made the grade – and all those years of study. At uni, I apparently took a BA in arts and humanities but I remember nothing at all about it or even why I settled on that particular course.'

'You were always a creative thinker and interested in

people, so it certainly suited your personality. And you managed to get a great job in advertising afterwards, didn't you? Your degree must have helped.'

'Oh, Rosie, it appears you know more about my job than I do! Mum said I work for a company called Solutions but I haven't a clue who they are or what exactly I do there. It's a good job I'm on a career break. I'd be nothing short of useless to them now.' Ellie looked thoroughly dejected.

'Hey, don't dwell on all that now, you're on holiday! It's quite feasible your memory could return at any time and all the blanks will be filled in. Why not concentrate on Sam and enjoy your time here? Admittedly, I know virtually nothing about amnesia, but I do know being anxious won't help.' Rosie squeezed her friend's arm and Ellie attempted a smile.

'You're right. I don't want to waste our precious time together by worrying about the future.' Even as she formed the words, she knew it to be a tall order. She would have to return home at some point and face the mounting problems which her memory loss seemed to be constantly throwing up. 'Let's grab lunch now, remember, it's my treat!'

Rosie and her family were regular visitors to the small family-owned zoo which housed about 200 animals and after lunch, she guided them to the areas they'd so far not seen. Sam was amazed by the sight of so many animals and particularly taken with the spider monkeys, creatures Ellie fell for too, with their cute faces and bush-baby eyes. Alex and Luke favoured the big cats – jaguars, ocelots and pumas made them wide-eyed, and they growled at each other until they laughed. There was plenty of time to take everything in, even at a leisurely pace, and Ellie discovered watching the animals and their uncomplicated existence was therapeutic; if only life was so simple and straightforward for her.

The visit culminated in the obligatory stop at the play area where the children expended the last of their energy and enjoyed ice creams beneath the shade of a clump of trees.

The weary tourists arrived back in MacDonald Road late in the afternoon, hot and tired, with all three boys growing increasingly grizzly from too much excitement. None of them had slept during the day, and the lack of rest was catching up with them.

'Let's give the boys their tea and we'll settle for a quick pasta dish later when Tom comes home, shall we?' Rosie suggested.

'Fine by me. I'm not particularly hungry after the meal we ate at the zoo. It was delicious.'

'Yes, thanks, Ellie, I enjoyed it too.' Rosie scrambled eggs with cheese for the boys while Ellie buttered bread and sliced fruit. Soon their children were happily sitting in their high chairs, eating with their fingers and making a fine mess. Afterwards, all three went into the bath together, a novelty which gave rise to more fun and laughter.

Once the boys were settled in bed, their mothers breathed a sigh of relief which for Ellie was only short-lived when her phone rang.

'Gosh, it's Phil. I should have Skyped him with Sam!' A pang of guilt hit her hard; she'd completely forgotten to do as she'd promised! Answering her phone and ready with her excuses, she hoped he'd understand how tired their son had been. Phil, however, sounded subdued and not at all belligerent as she'd expected.

'Ellie, do you think you could come home?' He sounded weary, and low in spirits.

'But it's only been three days…'

'It's my dad. He died this afternoon.'

'Oh, no, I'm so sorry.' She could think of little more to say. With no recollection of Phil's parents, the news didn't touch her as much as it might otherwise have done.

'I have to go to Spain. Mum's in bits and things are rather complicated with him dying abroad, there'll be so much to arrange, and she needs me there. I thought perhaps you and Sam could come too. It would cheer her up to see you both?'

Ellie's heart felt suddenly heavy. It was the last thing she wanted at the moment – her relationship with Phil was strained enough, and meeting another 'family' member whom she couldn't remember was not what she needed. Although she experienced genuine sympathy for him, this didn't excuse what he'd done in the past, and she couldn't ignore the situation between them.

'I… I'm not sure it's a good idea. You'll need to spend time with your mother and we'd just be in the way.' There was silence for a few moments, and Ellie thought she heard a stifled sob. She was torn, but couldn't – really couldn't – go back to face him now and then to travel to Spain to stay with a stranger who'd just lost her husband – it was unthinkable. 'I'm so sorry, Phil, I don't think I can do that.'

'No, you're right – it was selfish of me to ask. It's probably no place for Sam either, even though I'd love to have you both with me. You're better off staying there. I'll book a flight for tomorrow and let you know what time I'll be leaving. Is Sam there? Can I speak to him?'

'He's in bed. I'm sorry, Phil but we've been to the zoo and he was exhausted. I'll Skype you first thing in the morning if it's okay, see how you're getting on?' She felt terrible, her heart ached for Phil's pain, but her priority must be whatever was best for her and Sam.

'That would be great, thanks, Ellie.' Phil ended the call; his voice was faint and weary, which served to pile on the guilt.

Rosie had tactfully left her friend alone to take the call and now Ellie went to find her to tell her the news.

'Poor Phil, he'll be so upset, and the distance will make life difficult. I wonder if his mother will want to return to England now she's alone?'

Rosie's comments set Ellie's mind off on a whole new train of thought. What if Josephine did want to move nearer to her son? Did they get on well, and what expectations would her mother-in-law have?

Unsurprisingly, Ellie was quiet and withdrawn during the evening but Tom and Rosie took her altered mood in their stride, their easy and undemanding company a balm to her confused state of mind.

When she eventually excused herself and went upstairs to bed, Ellie's thoughts kept her awake until the small hours. Natural empathy for Phil vied with the residual anger she still felt towards him, robbing her of the peace that this time away had so far brought her. She questioned whether she should return home or not, but what good would she be even if she did go to Spain with her husband? And it was August – it would be far too hot for Sam. He was better off here in this house of happiness, love and tranquillity, as was she. Or was it her selfishness talking? But no, even Phil seemed to see the sense of them not accompanying him. He'd probably only asked on impulse without really thinking through the practical-ities. Ellie would Skype him in the morning as promised, with Sam. It was the least she could do.

Chapter Thirty-Three

The Skype call to Phil the following morning was as arduous as Ellie expected. Seeing his face and hearing the weariness in his voice simply added more guilt, and she couldn't help but notice his eyes were ringed with red as if he'd been crying. Should she be with him? Duty and fidelity worked two ways, Ellie reminded herself. She would concentrate on their son, who thankfully possessed the power to distract his daddy.

Seeing Sam appeared to lift Phil's mood, but the little boy's concentration span was limited and when he heard his two new buddies clattering about in the kitchen, his daddy's time was cut short. Ellie lifted her son onto the floor and watched him crawl into the kitchen where Rosie greeted him warmly and scooped him up to carry him over to his friends.

'Please give my love to your mother.' Ellie went through the motions of sympathy and then listened to his travel plans.

'Will you stay until after the funeral?' she asked.

'I don't know when that will be yet. Mum toyed with the idea of bringing him home to York for the funeral, but I'm trying to persuade her to have a cremation in Spain and bring the ashes home afterwards for a memorial service. There's a huge expat community over there, and many of their friends would attend a cremation which would give them the chance to say goodbye. Even bringing the ashes home will be subject to bureaucracy, things are so different in Spain and we'll need permission. Not speaking the language adds to the complications. Mum's Spanish isn't too great either. Dad was the linguist.' Phil sounded weary before he'd even set off.

'Will you still be able to keep in touch? Sam loves to see you each day.'

'Yes, of course. I love to see him too, and you as well, Ellie.' He paused as if expecting or simply hoping for a response, but she couldn't say the words he longed to hear and felt simultaneously sad and guilty at the fact she could offer no comfort.

'Well, take care, Phil, we'll speak tomorrow.' She needed to finish this conversation.

'Right, and you too.' He responded in like manner, a catch in his voice, and the call was ended.

Taking a deep breath, Ellie entered the kitchen where her son was already eating a bowl of fruit. His face lit up when he saw her, and for the first time, she noticed how very like Phil he looked, his eyes and the expression of joy at seeing his mother almost took her breath away.

'How is he?' Rosie asked.

'Sad, but he's managed to get a flight to Spain later this morning. I think the language barrier will add to his burden and there'll be paperwork to sort out too. He's certainly going to have his hands full.'

'Poor Phil. Do you know if he was close to his dad?'

'No, not really.' Ellie could say no more as her eyes were brimming with tears. Was she handling this correctly, she wondered, but as ever, she didn't possess the answer to her own question.

'If the forecast for today's to be believed it's going to be very hot, possibly the hottest day of the year so far. I wondered if we should stay close to home, maybe an hour on the beach before it gets too warm and then let the boys play here, in the garden. There's plenty of shade out there after lunch. How does that sound to you?' Rosie turned to practicalities, shifting Ellie's thoughts to other things.

'Great, I think a good afternoon sleep might do Sam good too. I don't want him to get overtired and it's been such a busy couple of days.'

With breakfast cleared away, the little group gathered their belongings and headed for the beach. Sam wriggled to be allowed down onto the sand and soon kicked his legs and grasped at the warm grains with his fists, giggling as they trickled through his fingers. Alex and Luke used their spades to dig haphazardly with sand flying everywhere, and their mothers laughed at the excitement and pure joy such simple pleasures brought to their children. The shallow water was warm, and regular forays to the sea cooled their feet and calmed Ellie's spirit. Her son was now the most important person in her life and held her heart without knowing it. Her love for Sam was, at times, almost frightening.

As the sun rose higher in the sky, it quickly became too hot to stay on the beach, and the little party returned to the cool walls of the house, ready for a cold lunch and even colder drinks. Sam was happy to settle in his cot after lunch, and Rosie put Alex and Luke down for a nap too. Soon, the house settled into a peaceful stillness, the very walls seeming to sigh with the quietness. Rosie flopped onto the sofa, put up her bare feet and wriggled her toes.

'Much as I love my boys, time out is heaven!' She smiled, but on turning to her friend, Rosie's expression changed to one of concern. 'Ellie, love, I don't want to pry, but you seem to be carrying the weight of the world on your shoulders. Is there something wrong, other than the amnesia, of course?'

'Everything's wrong, Rosie, and I haven't a clue how to make it right.'

'Will talking about it help? I've often been told I'm a good listener.'

'The more I talk, the more complicated things seem to get. I tried talking to Fran before I came away, and after that conversation any hope I'd clung to of getting my life back was destroyed.' Ellie choked back the tears.

'Fran, you've seen Fran?' Rosie was surprised – she swung her feet to the floor and looked at Ellie with a frown on her face.

'Yes, a couple of times.' Ellie explained, 'I thought it would be good to meet up with someone I actually remembered, other than Mum and Dad. We went into the city one day for a drink and then she came round the evening before I came here. I rather wish she hadn't now, as Fran told me things I'd rather not have known.'

'Did she tell you you've barely been in touch since your wedding – and why?'

'If you mean the stripper thing, then yes, she did explain, but that's typical Fran, isn't it? She'd have thought it a good laugh even though it wouldn't be my idea of fun.'

'Yes, there was the stripper incident, but assuming you can't remember what happened, let me assure you nothing did. Karen and I sent him packing before he'd even removed his coat! I don't know what Fran was thinking of. Your mum was at the hen do and Phil's mum.' Rosie sounded quite irate, nothing like her usual self.

'But it was okay in the end, wasn't it? I didn't fall out with Fran over that, did I?'

'Not entirely, but it was utterly irresponsible of her. She knew you're not the sort of person to appreciate a stripper.' It seemed Rosie wasn't going to cut Fran any slack. Ellie found Rosie's faith in her character touching, but it brought a flush to her face as thoughts of Dave intruded into her mind, reminding her of the possibility she'd betrayed Phil. What on earth would Rosie think of her if she knew that little nugget of information?

'So, is there something else which soured our friendship?' she asked. Rosie was quiet for a moment as if deliberating whether to speak or not.

She looked Ellie in the eyes. 'Yes. Fran is quite simply not to be trusted. You probably never knew this, but she had a bit of a 'thing' for Phil before you were married – not that anything ever happened, but Fran told me she intended to seduce him. She was jealous of you, Ellie and I think she wanted him for herself. It happened a few weeks before your wedding and initially I thought she was joking; she said it would be a test, a kind of honey trap to see if Phil would be faithful to you. When I realised she was serious we had a big falling out over it. I eventually told her if she went anywhere near him, I'd expose her for the bitch she really was. Fran simply laughed it off and I assumed thought better of it, but a few days later, when a group of us were at a wine bar, I noticed Fran following Phil to the bar. She was so blatantly obvious I could have been sick, draping herself all over him and whispering something in his ear. I was tempted to intervene but it wasn't necessary. Phil turned on her pretty sharpish – I don't know what he said but the look of anger and disgust on his face was more than evident, and he physically pushed her away from him.

'Fran was pretty drunk but if I hadn't seen it with my own eyes, I wouldn't have believed she'd try it on with her best friend's fiancé. Phil wasn't impressed and sent her away with a flea in her ear, which was no more than she deserved! That's the point when my friendship with Fran ended, and apart from the wedding, I've not seen her since.' Rosie paused and looked at her friend with concern. 'I'm sorry, Ellie, but it's true,' she added and waited for a reaction.

After a thoughtful pause, Ellie decided to share precisely what Fran had told her. 'The version Fran told me was quite different. She claims Phil tried to seduce her just a few weeks before our wedding and hinted quite heavily that she wasn't the first one Phil had tried it on with. Surely, she wouldn't tell such an awful lie, would she?' Ellie was confused; why would Fran have deliberately misled her? Every instinct was crying out that Rosie must be right, yet how could Ellie know for sure?

'Oh, you poor thing! Please, Ellie, don't believe Fran's lies. For some warped reason, she gets her kicks from hurting other people.' Rosie appeared reluctant to say more, but after a pause continued. 'Do you remember Carl? He was in our year at sixth form?'

'Yes, the one who took the photo you sent me?'

'That's right, he wanted to be a professional photographer but I lost touch with him so I don't know if he made it or not. I had a huge crush on him then, well more than a crush really, but I made the mistake of telling Fran how much I liked him. The next thing I knew she was all over him, flirting and turning on her considerable charms. Carl was hooked, and I was suddenly out of the picture. I didn't stand a chance when she set her cap at him; beautiful, exciting Fran, I was just the fat friend who boys didn't notice. I tried hard to forgive her but she treated Carl so badly, leading him on and then dropping him like a hot brick when she grew bored with him. I watched her do it to other girls' boyfriends too. If someone has something which makes them happy, Fran goes all out to take it away from them or sour the situation, then she quietly gloats. Look, Ellie, I don't particularly enjoy telling you this, and I'm not one to speak out of turn, but you must believe me. Fran always has her own agenda and it's usually at someone else's expense. Please don't accept her twisted version of events without confirming them.' Rosie's face was troubled. 'It seems to me that Fran is up to her old tricks again. I hate speaking ill of anyone but it appears she's taken advantage of your illness to cause trouble again.'

Ellie was stunned but needed to know more. 'Fran told me Phil had a controlling personality – that he called all the shots in our marriage and I simply went along with what he wanted. She said you agreed with this and you were both concerned for me, even before my wedding.' Ellie wondered now if this too was a lie.

'What? That's absolute nonsense! How dare she! Phil's anything but controlling and I'd go as far as to say that yours is perhaps the happiest marriage I know, after Tom and me of course. I've never said anything of the kind and Fran has no right saying I did. Goodness, I don't know what game she's playing this time but I'd keep well away from her. She's poison!'

Rosie's revelations were astounding and Ellie was confused. She needed time to process what she'd learned. 'Would you mind if I went up to lie down while Sam's sleeping, Rosie? I need a little time to think about what you've said.'

'Ellie, I'm so sorry if this has upset you but you need to know the truth. Yes, please have a rest, it'll do you good and we can talk some more later if you like.'

Ellie retreated to her room, needing time to herself to calm down and process what Rosie had revealed about Fran. Hopefully, the boys would sleep a while longer so their mothers too could steal some quiet time to rest.

Chapter Thirty-Four

S am was snoring softly, blowing bubbles from his parted lips, and the sight of her son sleeping so peacefully filled Ellie's eyes with tears. She lay down on the bed, barely able to stand, and stared intently at the ceiling as if the answer to her predicament could be found there.

Rosie's revelations prompted a re-evaluation of what she'd understood to be true. It appeared Phil had been maligned by Fran, a woman who seemed to find enjoyment in causing pain to others. Her husband was a good man, as everyone was quick to tell her, but she'd treated him so badly of late, at a time when he needed her the most. Relief at finally knowing Phil's true character came with such mixed emotions – shame at how she'd withdrawn from him because of Fran's lies, and disgust at her actions. Phil deserved a better wife than she'd been – so, would it be better for him if she did not return to be his wife? He was clearly too good for her and Ellie couldn't bear the thought of him finding out she'd been unfaithful with Dave. Perhaps Phil would be better off without her – perhaps she could keep her shame to herself by not returning to him.

As her mind turned these thoughts over and over, assessing

them from all angles, Ellie did not come out well. The shame and guilt which hung so heavily inside her chest like a physical weight pressing down on her heart was well deserved. If only she could go back to the night of her date with Phil. If only Dave hadn't entered her life to crush the flower of hope which had begun to blossom within her. But *if only* was a dream, and Ellie was presently living in a nightmare.

Looking at the clock beside the bed, Ellie realised Phil would now be on his way to Spain to comfort his mother and oversee the obstacles of death in a foreign land, the final act of kindness he could perform for his father. How she wished she could remember his parents; they were, after all, Sam's grandparents and presumably her son was as precious to them as he was to Grace and Derek.

The only thing she could do for Phil now was to change her attitude towards him. She'd treated him shamefully, thinking the worst of him when he was completely innocent. But first, Ellie needed to know more about her in-laws, and a call to her mother was overdue. Moving into the en suite so as not to wake Sam, she rang her mother.

'Ellie, how lovely to hear you! How are things going?' Grace's voice was a welcome balm.

'We're fine, thanks, Mum. I presume you know about Phil's dad?'

'Yes, he rang to let us know. I'm so sorry, love. He'll be on his way now, won't he?'

'Yes, which is why I'm ringing. I can't remember anything about Phil's parents and was hoping you'd fill me in?'

'Yes, of course! We didn't know them too well, especially as they moved away, but Jim was a great man and Phil worshipped him, probably because he was an only child. He's going to miss him for sure. Josephine is rather quiet but lovely too in her way. I think she'll struggle to manage without Jim – he was the stronger of the partnership, but who knows, she'll have had to take more of a lead during his illness. Phil said even though they knew it was cancer the end came quite suddenly. They thought he had another year or so left. Did he not tell you about Jim's illness?'

'Not until recently. I don't think he wanted to worry me. How did I get on with them, Mum? I mean, did I like them, did we see much of them?'

'Oh, fine, no worries there, love. You went over a couple of times a year before Sam was born and thoroughly enjoyed yourselves. Sam only went once, I think, at the end of last year, but they doted on him. They were forever on the phone or that Skype thing. Do you know what'll happen about a funeral yet?'

'No, Phil said Josephine wanted to bring him back to York for the funeral but he thinks it'll be too complicated. He's hoping she'll agree to having a cremation in Spain and bringing his ashes home for a memorial service, but it's up to her I suppose.' Ellie wondered how long her husband would need to stay away.

'That sounds sensible and Josephine's the sort to listen to advice. She'll probably go along with what he suggests.'

'Was Jim old?' Ellie had no idea how old Phil's parents were.

'Not really, about seventy, I think. They had Phil later in life. Josephine was forty and had given up hope of ever conceiving so his arrival was a delightful surprise. They've always been a very active couple and latterly loved the life they'd carved out for themselves in Spain. I wonder if she'll want to stay there now?'

Grace imparted enough information for Ellie to form an idea of her in-laws. She was grateful their relationship had been a good one, for Phil's sake as well as her own.

'Phil told me he'd asked you to go to Spain with him,' Grace continued, 'but for what it's worth, I think you made the right decision in staying in Cromer. It's too soon for you to be thrust into another family crisis, and although Sam would be a comfort to Josephine, it's not a good time to have a baby around.'

'Thanks, Mum. I did feel awful about not going, but I'm glad you understand. I hope Phil will too.'

'Now, tell me how you both are. Are you having a good time?' There was an edge of concern to Grace's voice.

'We're fine, Sam's asleep at the moment, he's getting on like a house on fire with Rosie's boys and we're being made very welcome. We've already been to the beach a couple of times, it's just at the end of their street, and we visited the zoo yesterday. The weather's unbelievable, almost too hot today, so we're keeping out of it for a while.' Ellie hoped her answer would suffice and not wanting to get into a deeper conversation, she thanked her mother, sent love to her dad and ended the call.

Sam was waking when she came out of the bathroom and sounds of activity from downstairs drifted into her room. She lifted her son from his cot and went to join Rosie and the boys in the kitchen. Rosie was making a batch of scones while Alex and Luke played contentedly on the rug. Sam wriggled down, keen to join them.

'Hey, are you okay?' Rosie asked, enveloping her friend in a comforting hug.

'Yes, there's just so much to take in at times. It can become overwhelming.'

'It must be so hard, and we well-meaning friends don't always know what to do for the best. I'm never sure what to fill you in on or whether it's best to wait and see if you remember things for yourself.'

'What *things* are you thinking of, Rosie? Are there any more shocks in store for me?' Ellie sighed.

'No, don't worry, it's just the little things, like when we toured the house – I hoped you would remember it.'

'Why? Have I been here before?' Ellie was surprised. Cromer appeared to be new to her, yet was it?

'Yes, quite a few times, actually. The last time was before the twins were born and when you'd just found out you were pregnant too. You and Phil came for a long weekend, and the four of us talked babies non-stop! I was waddling like a beached whale by then and envious of your neat little bump, but we had a great time, eating out every day and staying in bed late each morning just because we could – because our lives were soon going to be changed by our respective babies.' Rosie smiled at the memory.

'So, Phil and I stayed here, together?'

'Yes, and you slept in the same room you're in now. You knew the twins were conceived by IVF but when I mentioned it earlier it was clearly something else you've forgotten.'

'Oh, Rosie, that's terrible and here was I thinking this was all new to me. I have absolutely no memories at all from the last ten years. It's not as if I remember some things and not others – there's simply nothing. But please do tell me about places I've been to before. I feel so stupid not remembering.'

'Hey, it isn't stupid at all. It is what it is, and there's nothing you can do about it. Now, you won't remember where the coffee is but that's not going to excuse you from making us a cup; it's in the cupboard over by the kettle.' Rosie smiled and as Ellie made coffee, she felt grateful for something practical to do.

'Thank you for being so candid earlier, Rosie. I know it wasn't easy to tell me about Fran and what she's like, but I needed to know. She's caused me so much pain and I've been so awful to Phil because of what she said, yet it seems he didn't deserve it. I'll have to make it up to him somehow.'

Later, as Ellie tried to sleep, her troubled mind played back the day's conversations with Rosie on a perpetual reel. Fran wasn't the friend she'd thought her to be and if Rosie hadn't been so honest, the damage she'd done could be irreparable, but then was her marriage beyond repair anyway? In that dreamy state of half awake, half asleep, her thoughts took her back to the time when she, Fran and Rosie were inseparable. They first met at school as gauche eleven-year-olds, leaving behind childhood years, yet far from being adults. Fran was the natural leader of the three from the beginning of their friendship, the daredevil whose audacious schemes both appealed to and occasionally daunted the other two.

Fran was the one to suggest skipping lessons to go into town or hanging out with the kind of boys their parents would disapprove of. She was the first to buy cigarettes and cider to try, encouraging them even when they were reluctant, her taunts ensuring their compliance. With a bold and enigmatic air about her, Fran drew others to her. She appeared so much older than her peers and maintained a popularity which Ellie secretly envied. Rosie was the quiet one – the one to hold back, to have doubts about that first swig of alcohol, the first cigarette. But Fran goaded her, and Rosie invariably capitulated, unwilling to be labelled a wimp.

Perhaps with hindsight, Ellie could see things with a clarity which was absent at the time. She remembered occasions when Fran treated Rosie badly, teased her beyond the acceptable, and a flush of shame swept over her because she'd never once stood up for her quieter, kinder friend.

The photograph Carl took of the three friends came to Ellie's mind and she remembered the day vividly. It was another of Fran's wild schemes but they were much older, at sixth-form college by then, and they should have been wiser. After registration, they left the college, unchallenged, Fran deciding for them all that they'd done enough revision and needed time out and as it was such a glorious hot June day, they'd taken less persuasion than usual to go along with her scheme.

A group of about six girls and six boys, Carl included, headed for the river, a local beauty spot where the water was perfect for swimming. Rosie and Carl appeared to be getting on well and Ellie, knowing now how Rosie had felt about him, remembered her friend's glowing face, which sadly wasn't to last for long.

None of them was prepared for swimming, they should have been in college studying but Fran didn't let that stop her and stripped down to her underwear, followed by some of the other girls and most of the boys. Rosie and Ellie declined to join in and sat a little away from the group who'd been drinking lager and were rather tipsy. The high jinks became a bit too high for their taste, especially when Fran removed her bra before jumping into the river, causing much giggling among the other girls and more than a bit of excitement among the boys who readily followed her into the water.

But that was Fran, embarrassing and yet beguiling in her unconventional ways. Looking back on the day, Ellie now recalled Rosie's sadness as Carl, besotted with Fran, followed her around like a lost puppy until she allowed him to become her boyfriend of the day. But Ellie hadn't known of Rosie's affection for Carl, or that Fran's interest in him was purely because she could take him from her friend. Looking back, it was clear – as clear as Fran's character was becoming, and Ellie wondered why it had taken her so long to see what was so plain, what had been staring her in the face all along.

Chapter Thirty-Five

There were several times over the next few days when Ellie's heart ached with the desire to pour her troubles out to Rosie, to confess her involvement with Dave and what he'd claimed they'd done, but shame kept the words bottled tightly inside her. Rosie was such a lovely person and Ellie couldn't bear for her to think badly of her, so she kept her torment to herself, attempting to push those ugly thoughts to the back of her mind.

By now, Ellie felt safe enough to assume Dave hadn't approached Phil as he'd threatened, and with her husband out of the country she was confident the two men would have no opportunity for contact. This gained her time, yet all the time in the world couldn't supply the answers she needed, and her mind reeled with the constant effort of searching for a solution to her predicament.

The days were bearable, even pleasant at times as Rosie and the children kept Ellie's mind occupied. But the monsters came at night when hateful thoughts filled her head and crowded her dreams – bitter, twisted scenarios playing out in glorious technicolour, none of which ended well. If she hadn't learned the truth about Phil from Rosie, it might have been easier to bear, but now she knew he was blameless and a good husband, her guilt tortured her constantly. She longed to be Phil's wife again, to own the happy marriage everyone assured her had been hers but the spectre of Dave overshadowed any chance of happiness and Ellie was still no wiser as to how to solve the dilemma.

Each day when Phil rang, Ellie was resolutely cheerful and supportive, helped immensely by Sam who could effortlessly bring a smile to his daddy's face, even in his darkest moments. Ellie even held a brief conversation with Josephine, a somewhat stilted few minutes, when neither woman knew quite what to say, but again Sam saved the day by demanding their attention.

As to the practicalities of death, Josephine agreed to her son's suggestion of cremation for her husband in Spain, which would be attended by the ex-pat community they were part of, a chance for their new friends to say goodbye. Jim's ashes would then be repatriated to England, and Phil was busy obtaining the various permissions. As things moved so much more swiftly in Spain, Jim was cremated within three days of his death.

Phil told Ellie he was returning to York within the week and bringing his mother with him. He was so visibly apprehensive as to her reaction and she immediately reassured him that whatever Josephine wanted was the right way forward. She would support him in whatever decision they made. Ellie also decided it was time to go home herself so she'd be there when he and his mother arrived and the relief in Phil's voice almost reduced her to tears.

Ellie and Sam's brief holiday with Rosie and her family was quickly drawing to a close. It had proved to be a welcome time of respite, but she knew there was no choice other than to return and face reality. In those dark, desperate moments during the nights, there'd been times when wild schemes of running away with her son invaded her mind. However, the morning light brought her to her senses and she knew in her heart it was impossible to hide away forever.

Another couple of lovely days were spent on the beach and they enjoyed one or two trips to local beauty spots, made all the better by the continuing excellent weather, but finally, Ellie's time in Cromer was at an end.

'Alex and Luke will miss you both so much when you go home.' Rosie was lamenting the fact her friend was leaving the following day. 'And I will too. It's been great having you stay. You will come back soon, won't you?'

'I'd love to, Rosie, and you've been so kind, but I honestly don't know what's going to happen. There are still decisions to be made and I'm not at all sure what the outcome will be.' Ellie's face clouded over as she spoke and Rosie looked puzzled but didn't pry.

'You know we're here for you, Ellie, anytime.'

The morning of departure arrived. Ellie woke early with a heavy heart, showered before Sam was awake and then tiptoed downstairs to have a few minutes to herself before the house burst into its usual hubbub of activity. She was not, however, alone. Tom was sitting at the kitchen table reading a novel, and he lifted his head, surprised to see her.

'Ah, you've discovered my guilty pleasure. It's the only time I have to indulge myself.' He lifted the novel from his lap to show her a David Baldacci thriller and gave a wry grin.

'Good for you. We all need a bit of escapism.' She smiled back. 'We're leaving today, Tom, and I want to thank you for all you've done for us. This break was exactly what we needed.'

'You've been very welcome, Ellie, but I've hardly done anything. Sadly, work occupies most of my time these days.'

'But you've shared your lovely home so generously and I'm grateful. It's been wonderful to escape here for a little while.'

'I'm glad it's helped.' Tom looked at her somewhat quizzically for a moment and then continued. 'Amnesia's a bloody awful condition and sadly no one can predict what will happen but I get the feeling there are things troubling you which go even deeper. Can I be so bold as to say don't feel so alone? Phil's a great chap and you can trust him. Talk to him, Ellie. He's hurting too.'

'Has Rosie been talking to you!' A flash of anger rose to burn Ellie's cheeks as she assumed her friend had betrayed her confidences.

'No, Rosie's said nothing. She wouldn't. It doesn't take a mind-reader to know you're troubled about something, and I've got to know Phil pretty well over the years. He's a great bloke and I know how much he loves you. You can talk to him – that's all I meant.'

'Oh gosh, I'm so sorry, Tom. I know Rosie wouldn't say anything. I'm just a bit wound up and being stupid, sorry.' Ellie instantly regretted her accusation; how could she assume such a thing after her friends had been so kind. And would it really have mattered if Rosie had shared her situation with Tom? They could both be trusted – she knew.

'Forget it. It's not important. I just want you to be happy, as you were before. I don't know what's preventing it but if we can help, just shout.' Tom stood up and put his book on the dresser. 'Now then, I'd better get ready for work and I think I can hear my sons gearing up for the day. We'll miss you, Ellie.' Tom stood and gave her a warm hug and a genuine smile before disappearing upstairs.

Well, I made a right mess of that, didn't I? she chided herself, then went back upstairs to see if Sam was awake.

Saying goodbye to Rosie and the boys was more emotional than Ellie had anticipated. She kissed the twins who beamed up at her ready for another day's fun and not understanding she was taking their new playmate away. Rosie's eyes were moist as the friends hugged and exchanged promises to keep in touch and visit again soon. Part of Ellie wanted to stay in hiding in her friend's warm and welcoming home, but it was impossible. It was time to leave. Perhaps she'd lost ten years of friendship with Rosie but the bond was still there and she knew they would remain friends forever.

Sam remained somewhat subdued on the journey home, obviously tired from his active week and sleeping on and off. A couple of lengthy stops broke their journey, and with quiet roads on their side, the time passed swiftly and uneventfully.

Ellie intended heading straight to her parents' home and spending the night there with Sam. Phil and Josephine were due back the following evening and she would use the day to get the house ready for their visitor and stock up on food in the fridge. It was a surprise to realise she was looking forward to seeing Phil again but as always, any positive emotions were tinged with a degree of unwelcome shame and fear.

Chapter Thirty-Six

G race and Derek welcomed Ellie home with enthusiasm, stirring pangs of guilt at her perceived selfishness in what had amounted to running away over the last week. Sam was as delighted to see his grandparents as they were him, and as Ellie so often did these days, she used her son to deflect awkward questions, chatting about the marvellous time he'd had and avoiding any serious conversation. Her avoidance tactics were perhaps unnecessary as it became apparent her parents would not push for a more serious discussion on her first day home, if at all.

The following morning, Grace offered to help Ellie prepare the house and do the shopping for Phil and Josephine. Ellie accepted gratefully having spent a few sleepless hours anticipating a confrontation with Dave and trying to decide how she would handle such a situation should it arise. *Was she hiding behind her mother's apron strings?*

Derek offered to join them and mow the lawn while the women 'pottered', as he called it. *Safety in numbers.* Ellie accepted gratefully.

With Phil having been away as well as his wife and son, their home needed very little attention. Ellie made up a bed in the second bedroom ready for her mother-in-law, opening the windows to allow the warm air to circulate, while Grace occupied Sam downstairs. Unable to resist looking across the road to number 40, Ellie thought a curtain moved, but the sight of Derek busily mowing the front lawn took away the frisson of fear she felt. Her dad's presence added a layer of protection of which he was completely ignorant. If Dave were at home, he would surely notice the activity and with the visible presence of her parents, she felt relatively safe. Surely, the man wouldn't dare to approach when she wasn't alone?

After a light lunch, Ellie put Sam in his cot to sleep and leaving Derek in charge, she and Grace went off to the supermarket to stock up on fresh food. She was still on edge, a fact which didn't go unnoticed by her mother.

'Ellie, love, I'm at a loss to know what's been troubling you lately and why you suddenly upped sticks and went to Cromer just when you and Phil were getting on so well. I don't mean to pry, and you don't have to tell me anything that happened between you but Phil needs your support now; he was close to his father and his passing won't be easy on him. Dad and I will do everything we can to help you, but the bottom line is, it's down to you.'

'Do you think I don't know?' Ellie snapped at her mother, instantly regretting it.

'Yes, of course you do, but hiding from a problem has never been your style. Whatever it is that's bugging you, it's time to face up to it. I have a feeling only you can sort this one out.' Grace's reply was firm and Ellie's response was to remain silent on their journey home.

When Ellie was a child and afraid of something, real or imaginary, she would run up to her bedroom and hide in the large walk-in wardrobe, wriggling behind the rack of clothes, confident her mother would come and find her and make everything right again. One day, she played with a large cut-glass bowl, a favourite of her mother's which held pride of place on the dining-room table. Turning it in her tiny hands to watch how the sun shone through it, making brilliant-coloured patterns on the table, the bowl slipped from her fingers and smashed into a million pieces on the wooden floor. Startled by the piercing noise and the certain knowledge she would be in trouble, Ellie ran to her safe place, squatting in the corner and hugging her knees while waiting for the inevitability of being found. Sure enough, it didn't take long for Grace to appear. As her mother quietly opened the wardrobe door, Ellie's tears flowed freely, convinced she was in the hottest water ever. Grace gently lifted her daughter from her hiding place and silently dried her tears.

'I'm sorry, Mummy, can you mend it?' the young Ellie sobbed bitterly.

'No, darling, it can't be mended but it's not important. I love you more than I loved that bowl and I dare say we can find something else to sit on the dining-room table.' Her mother couldn't fix that particular problem entirely but she did make everything okay again. How Ellie wished her mother could make everything right for her now but in her heart, she knew Grace was right. She was the only one with the power to solve her problems – no longer six years old, nor eighteen, she was twenty-eight and a mother herself. Her problem now was so much more complex than a broken crystal bowl, but the responsibility to make things right rested solely on Ellie's shoulders.

Sam was awake and playing in the garden with his grandfather when mother and daughter arrived back, and with only an hour to go until Phil would be home, Ellie started putting a meal together. Grace and Derek decided to leave, not wishing to overwhelm Josephine with company as soon as she arrived. They would visit later, perhaps the following day.

As soon as her parents left, an awful feeling of vulnerability descended as Ellie locked the door behind them and kept well away from the window in the hope that if Dave were around, he wouldn't decide to visit her. Thankfully, he didn't and it wasn't long before Phil's car pulled up outside. From the window she watched her husband help his mother from the passenger seat.

Josephine Graham was not quite what Ellie expected. They'd spoken briefly on Skype and the older woman's fine features and dark hair had surprised her as she was nothing like Phil. The lady who approached her now was barely five feet tall, small-boned and slim, with short dark hair framing a narrow face, tanned from living abroad. Elfin-like was perhaps the best way to describe her mother-in-law. Phil's fair hair and height must have been inherited from his father. Josephine appeared to be somewhat frail, an impression underlined by the sadness in her face; she was a grieving widow and her eyes held no spark of life, yet she attempted a smile when Ellie, holding Sam like a shield, greeted her at the door.

'My dear, how lovely to see you again.' Josephine spoke first.

'Hello, Josephine, I'm so sorry about Jim.' She faltered then, but her mother-in-law smiled a sad smile and turned her attention to Sam.

'Oh, you beautiful boy! You're the image of your daddy.' She reached out to take the child from his mother, and Sam happily allowed her to do so. Phil was close behind with two suitcases which he put down to reach out to Ellie.

'Hello, Ellie.' He searched her face, leaning close to kiss her cheek and clearly delighted when she didn't turn away. 'Sam!

My goodness, you've grown so much; it must be all that sea air!' The little boy wriggled from his grandmother's arms and reached out to Phil, beaming at the sight of his beloved daddy. It was such a poignant moment and Ellie felt suddenly mean at having taken him away from his daddy, even if it had been for only a week.

Ellie busied herself with making tea and coffee in the kitchen, unsure which her mother-in-law would prefer, while Phil took her cases up to the spare room.

'How are you doing, Ellie?' Josephine appeared in the kitchen, surprising Ellie, whose thoughts were miles away.

'Oh, I'm getting there, thanks.'

'It must be so strange for you, all these people who know you but who are strangers, myself included. But don't worry, I think I'm pretty easy-going and we've always got on well together. I'd like to thank you for letting me stay.'

'You don't need to thank me, Josephine, and you must stay as long as you like, really.' Ellie suddenly wondered if Josephine knew she wasn't living with Phil yet. 'I don't know if Phil's told you, but I'm staying with my parents for now.'

'Yes, he mentioned it, yet this is still your home and I'm grateful for being here.'

Phil joined them in the kitchen, followed closely by Sam, determinedly shadowing his daddy, not wanting to be parted from him again. They drank tea, and Ellie asked about their journey and told them a little of her time in Cromer, focusing mainly on their son, what he'd done and his excitement at making new friends.

Later, as they ate together, Phil and his mother discussed the arrangements for Jim's memorial service, which they'd managed to book for the following week at St Oswald's Church, Fulford, close to where Jim and Josephine lived for many years. Ellie didn't know Fulford was the area where her husband grew up, although she would have known before.

Concentrating on spooning chicken and mashed vegetables into Sam's mouth, she joined in the conversation only when necessary. Ellie wanted to be kind to Phil and Josephine, but being in their company gave rise to an awful feeling of not belonging, here or anywhere else, and she hadn't felt so alone since waking up in the hospital.

Chapter Thirty-Seven

Sitting in St Oswald's, Ellie experienced the strangest feeling – as if viewing the whole proceedings from above, floating, hovering over the congregation, seeing and hearing everything while wrapped in a cocoon of thought. She could see herself, sitting close to Phil and dressed in a black suit with a pale-pink blouse beneath, looking the part of the grieving daughter-in-law whilst not remembering the man whose life they were there to celebrate. Sam slept peacefully in his buggy beside her.

The beautiful Victorian church was bathed in sunlight, glorious shards of coloured light caressing the golden wood of the pews and the altar furniture. Flowers adorned every spare nook, from large arrangements to small posies, and their fragrance filled the vast space. Seated in the pews were about sixty people, most of whom were strangers to Ellie. The words of the elderly vicar resonated in her head as he extolled the virtues of her father-in-law, a man she apparently knew and loved but could not remember.

Josephine sat on the other side of her son sobbing silently into a large linen handkerchief, one of her husband's, Ellie presumed. Phil, ramrod straight, held his mother's hand, his chin set in the way she was beginning to recognise when he was attempting to keep his emotions in check. Her heart was filled with love for him, an overwhelming love which almost hurt at times.

Ellie wondered if she knew everything the vicar was saying about Jim and had simply forgotten it, or if his history was all new to her. It so often happened that you learned more about a person at their funeral than you ever did when they were alive.

A room was booked at a nearby hotel and the invitation extended to all those assembled to pay their respects. Ellie dreaded the gathering, and her fears were realised as a constant stream of people offered their condolences, not only to Josephine and Phil but to her too. She suppressed a sudden desire to reply, *'But I didn't know him.'* Phil divided his time between his wife and mother, although Ellie assured him she didn't need looking after, there were enough people there who she did know, well, her parents at least.

Sam again provided a screen for her to hide behind. She'd walked him around in his buggy before the service until he fell asleep, a state he maintained for the whole hour. On waking, he became a focus for the mourners, a reason to smile on such a sad occasion and even Josephine took her grandson to meet various old friends. The new generation – hope for the future – comfort in the knowledge that life goes on.

After refreshments were consumed and the platitudes acknowledged, they escaped back home to begin life without Jim Graham, no easy task for his wife and son. Ellie slipped away to the kitchen to make more tea, as if they hadn't drunk enough, leaving Phil and Josephine to mull over the service and comment on how so many of their old friends had changed.

'I'll be going home on Friday.' Josephine addressed her daughter-in-law when she brought the tray into the lounge. It had been two weeks since Jim's death, a week of which she'd spent in Spain with Phil and a week in York with the three of them.

'But you're welcome to stay longer.' Ellie's words were genuine; Josephine's presence hadn't been the stressful experience she'd expected it to be. 'Surely there's no reason to hurry back?'

'That's very kind, thank you, but I need to return to some kind of normality. It's too early to decide what I want to do in the long term, but for now, I need to go back to Spain, it's very much home and I think I'll feel closer to Jim there. Naturally, I'd love for you all to come and visit when things have settled down for you here.'

'We will, Mum, and we can always Skype.' Phil answered for them and the subject was closed but not before Ellie once again felt that guilty weight in her chest; everyone was waiting on her to sort herself out, but she was still procrastinating.

The two days until Josephine's flight home passed quickly. Phil returned to work and Ellie offered her car for Josephine's use to visit friends, an offer which was gratefully accepted. When the three of them were together at home, Sam, as ever, remained the focus, his grandmother delighting in his company and keen to help with his care as much as possible. Ellie found it increasingly hard to leave her son each night to return to her parents' home after being with him for twenty-four hours a day while in Cromer. She fell into a pattern of staying until Sam was bathed and in bed and then left with mixed feelings – relieved to escape from Phil and Josephine but aching with the separation from her son.

Phil took his mother to the airport on Friday morning. Ellie hugged her farewell with genuine affection. How could she not warm to her husband's mother, to this gentle lady who was grieving for her husband? The little boy, not fully understanding, accepted Josephine's hugs and kisses with his usual good-natured chuckles before moving on to the next toy to capture his attention.

The house felt eerily quiet when Sam went for his afternoon sleep and Ellie longed for Phil to come home. It was strange how she yearned for her husband's company yet felt almost frozen in his presence, unable to relax and converse easily for fear of what he might think if he learned of her darker side. Her frequent, furtive glances across the street to number 40 suggested no one was home, always a relief – but her luck would run out someday – she was bound to encounter Dave at some point.

When Phil arrived home, he was tired. They drank coffee in the conservatory while Sam played with his toys. Phil's mood was understandably pensive. He talked about his earliest memory of his father and some of the happy times they'd enjoyed as he was growing up. Jim was a great role model; it was no wonder Phil was such a brilliant dad.

This weekend, Ellie promised herself. *This weekend I'll tell him about Dave and throw myself on his mercy.* It sounded so dramatic inside her head, but neither she nor Phil could go on living this half-life. It was driving them both insane. She must find a way, find the words to say to her husband – be truthful and hope he could forgive her. If not, well, it didn't bear thinking about and Ellie refused to do so.

Chapter Thirty-Eight

For far too long, Ellie's every waking moment was consumed with her plight, and each night, her mind wrestled with it, preventing any release sleep might bring. Continuing this way would almost certainly make her ill, a possibility which in itself strengthened her resolve to talk to Phil. Ellie's relationship with her parents was also suffering, and although they'd stopped asking their daughter what was troubling her, their concerned looks and tactful avoidance only served to compound their daughter's feelings of guilt. But she would need to enlist her mother's help yet again to give her time alone with Phil, and so she asked Grace if she would look after Sam for a couple of hours the following afternoon. It was agreed she would take her grandson to the park to feed the ducks after lunch and then to the café for ice cream.

With her plan in place, Ellie set off to Phil's with mixed emotions and passed an uncomfortable morning vacillating over her decision to talk openly to her husband. On more than one occasion, she came close to picking up the phone to ring Grace and cancel their arrangement, yet refrained from doing so.

Almost as if his grandmother knew Sam was waking from his afternoon nap, Grace arrived to whisk her grandson away for a couple of hours and to spoil him thoroughly.

It was another beautiful day, not overly hot but bright enough to be comfortable in the garden. If Phil wondered at the reason he and Ellie were suddenly alone, he didn't ask.

'Shall we sit in the garden for a while?' he suggested, 'and perhaps… if there's any wine left?'

'I'll get it,' Ellie offered. Her hands trembled as she poured the wine into two large glasses and carried them into the garden, forcing a smile as she sat next to him on the bench. Perhaps it was the sadness behind her smile which prompted Phil to slide a protective arm around her shoulder.

He gently asked, 'What is it, love? Something's very wrong, and I'd like to help.' His tender concern unravelled her attempt at being brave and the tears, never far from spilling over, fell as Ellie let go of all the emotion she'd been holding inside for the last few weeks and wept bitterly.

It took several minutes to stem the flow of tears and regain some semblance of composure. Phil held his wife, stroking her hair, waiting patiently. Eventually, pulling away and taking a deep breath, Ellie turned to face him; the decision was made and she must tell him. Now. She would grasp the opportunity and face the consequences later. Unsure how to begin, Ellie decided to test the waters first, to see how much her husband knew.

'Do you know Dave who lives across the road?' Ellie watched as her husband suddenly stiffened, and his expression darkened.

'Why are you asking about him?' was the reply.

'He helped me to lift Sam's buggy in the other week.'

'Keep away from him, Ellie. He's bad news.' Phil scowled.

'What do you mean?'

'Just that. Dave Pearson is not a friend, that's all you need to know.'

'That sounds rather cryptic. Can't you tell me more?' Ellie was puzzled by this unexpected response.

'No, my love, just trust me on this, please.' Phil's face was set in a way she was beginning to recognise.

'But maybe I should know? I have no idea if Dave was a friend or not and I need to know about the neighbours if I'm going to come back here to live.'

Phil brightened instantly. 'You're coming home to live, really?' His sudden delight threw her, she'd let the subject be altered and now he was looking so hopeful.

'Well... I mean, eventually, I thought we'd agreed, no timescales?'

'Sorry, love, it's just I'm so anxious for things to get back to how they were before your accident.'

'And that's the point! I need to know how things were – concerning the neighbours, I mean. Were we friends with anyone in particular?'

'Well, you often had coffee with Christine from the corner house. She's been asking after you but said she wouldn't trouble you until you were feeling better.'

'And what about Dave?'

'Why him? Forget him, Ellie!' Phil sounded almost angry, but she needed to pursue the conversation now it had begun.

'Because he's said things, implied things...' Both their voices were rising. This wasn't the conversation she'd wanted to have.

'Oh no, Ellie! Tell me, you must tell me.' Phil turned to look directly at her and held her shoulders a little too tightly.

She'd done it now, told him part of the story, and there was no going back. 'Well, he's hinted that he and I were a little more than friends... I didn't know what to think. He's a horrible man who keeps pestering me, saying he's going to tell you things.'

'Oh, my poor darling, is this what's been worrying you? I am so sorry. I should have told you, warned you about him.' Phil pulled his wife close to him; she wanted and needed the comfort of his arms, but was unsure if she'd just driven a huge wedge between them.

'Told me what? Please, Phil, I don't know what to do. I've been terrified by what he said and thought I might lose you and Sam and I couldn't bear that. Have I done something to be ashamed of? If so, tell me – please!' Even though Ellie was distraught, her eyes were dry, all tears spent, her body screaming exhaustion, her mind grappling with fear. Had she had an affair with Dave – and did Phil already know?

'Tell me, please.' Her voice dropped to a trembling whisper. 'Phil?' Her eyes pleaded for an explanation of what his earlier words meant. Her head ached, and her whole body was tense. Phil took her hand in his own.

'There was an incident last year, just before Christmas.' He stared down at their joined hands, unable to look into her eyes.

'What kind of incident?' Ellie's voice was shaky.

'I don't know how to say it, he... he made a pass at you, groped you, whatever you want to call it.'

Ellie's free hand flew to her mouth as he continued.

'It was late afternoon. Dave came over on some pretext or other – he was always trying it on, so bloody transparent in the way he leered at you! At first, we laughed about his obsession but then he became a real nuisance. That afternoon you tried to keep him on the doorstep but he pushed his way in and forced himself on you. I arrived home early and found you in tears, trying to fight him off. As I came through the door, you'd just managed to knee him where it hurt; the situation was obvious and I'm afraid I lost my temper and lashed out at him. It sounds almost comical now, arriving home in the nick of time to defend your honour, but I really don't know how far he would have gone if I hadn't come home then.' Phil lifted his eyes to meet his wife's and saw the shock this information brought upon her.

'Were the police involved?' Ellie's mind was racing ahead, wondering how the situation had ended.

'No, we decided to let it drop. Perhaps we should have involved them. He might have thought twice about approaching you again, but to tell the truth, I hit him much harder than I should have done, and Dave left nursing a broken nose. My gallantry earned me a broken finger too, served me right I suppose. We decided it was unlikely he'd report it to the police as he was in the wrong, and concluded it would be better to let the whole incident drop and put it behind us. Dave never troubled you again. I don't know how he explained the broken nose to his wife, but neither of them has spoken to us since.'

'But he did seem to know things about me...'

'Like what?'

'Well, he mentioned the birthmark on the back of my neck. How could he have known about that?' Ellie was still unsure whether she was entirely blameless in this whole business and desperately needed reassurance to restore her peace of mind.

'Anyone could know. You often wore your hair up when it was longer, and the birthmark was quite visible.'

'But I never put my hair up; I've always been embarrassed by that mark!'

'Oh, Ellie, you got over it a long time ago. It was cooler and so much easier after Sam was born, and you look great with it tied up. You have nothing at all to reproach yourself for. I think Dave has, in some sick way, been trying to get revenge. Finding out about your amnesia gave him the opportunity he needed to stir things up between us. It must have seemed like a gift to him.'

'So, what do we do now?' Ellie looked to her husband for guidance.

'I'm going to go round to have a few words with Dave; he's gone too far this time.'

'No, Phil, don't! I can't bear the thought of you getting in some kind of fight. Please, let it drop.' She clung to his arm, fearful.

'We let it drop last time and look what happened. Dave needs to know he's been found out and he can't get away with treating you like this anymore.'

'If you're going to see him, I'm coming too.'

'No, please, let me handle it. I'll be very careful, but I want him to know if he comes near you again, we'll report him to the police for harassment.'

Ellie nodded her agreement, even managing a smile at the feeling of utter relief now flowing through her whole being. She hadn't betrayed Phil after all; this knowledge was all she needed to reclaim some of the happiness she'd felt before it was snatched away by that sad, bitter man and to regain some self-respect.

Ellie watched anxiously from the window as her husband marched across the street, his anger evident in his gait. She heard the hammering on the door as if it was on their own, and then a woman opened it, and after a brief moment, Phil pushed his way inside. Ellie panicked; should she have let him go alone? Yet the fact Dave's wife was in the house would probably have a restraining effect on Phil, and she hoped he wouldn't resort to violence. It wasn't in his nature.

It seemed an age until the door opened again and Phil came out alone, walking purposefully back to her, his shoulders more relaxed and some of the tension now gone from his body.

'What happened? Are you okay?' Ellie met him at the door and looked him over for signs of any injury, pulling him into the safety of their home, desperate to know what had transpired.

'Don't fret. I didn't touch the bastard. Come on through to the garden and I'll tell you all about it.'

'Well, what did he say?' Ellie's mouth was open as they sat again on the garden bench.

'Denied it at first, naturally, but then Angie was there, so he would, wouldn't he? Strangely though, it was Angie who told him he was lying; I think she's had her suspicions. I told him not to come within a mile of you ever again or I would personally make him regret it, and then I'd go to the police.'

'Oh, Phil, how awful.'

'He did admit it all then but the bloody idiot still tried to blame you which didn't go down well with Angie. She called him a coward for hiding behind a woman with amnesia and then actually offered me an apology on his behalf – poor woman! I doubt they'll manage to patch this up.' Phil smiled at Ellie as she laced her fingers through his, wondering with a sense of relief if this nightmare was finally coming to an end.

Chapter Thirty-Nine

A noise from inside the house distracted the couple. Grace was returning with Sam, and Ellie, still trembling from the horrendous events of the past hour, tried to compose herself as she followed Phil inside from the garden. Sam giggled, delighted to see his parents again, but his grandmother's face was a picture of consternation.

'Have you seen what's going on over the road?' Grace nodded in the direction of number 40. 'Just look, that woman's throwing clothes out of the bedroom window and yelling like a banshee. Not exactly the sort of behaviour you'd expect from round here.'

Sure enough, when they looked out of the window, they saw Angie Pearson angrily tossing her husband's belongings from the bedroom window, not caring who witnessed the scene – while Dave scrambled to gather them up, bundling them carelessly into his car. Grace was right. It wasn't the usual kind of behaviour for the estate, but Dave certainly deserved the humiliation and Phil at least couldn't resist a smile. Grace tutted loudly and moved Sam away from the window, as if the scene would scar him for life.

'We've had a lovely time feeding the ducks, haven't we, Sam?' She attempted to change the subject. 'But I must get back now... is everything okay with you?' Grace suddenly became aware of the difference in Ellie and Phil's demeanour and was puzzled as to what might have happened. She'd guessed her daughter was up to something when she asked her to look after Sam on a Saturday, it was unusual when they were both at home.

'Everything's fine, Mum. Actually, I won't be coming home tonight. I'm staying here with Phil.' Her words prompted a wide grin to cross her husband's face. Grace smiled too and nodded her approval before leaving them alone with their son.

Later that evening, when all was quiet again across the road and Sam was tucked up in bed, Phil and Ellie talked, really talked, as they sat holding hands on the sofa, enjoying their new-found closeness. They promised to tell each other every-thing in the future, no more secrets or attempts to protect the other; if they were going to make their relationship work, they needed to be on the same page. Ellie's continued memory loss was acknowledged as an unknown; perhaps the events of those lost years would remain unknown to her, but together they would cope and make new memories to treasure, to keep forever.

Ellie felt quite light-headed when they climbed the stairs to go to bed – from the wine or the events of the day, it was impossible to know. Finding a satin nightdress in one of her drawers, she slipped it on while her husband was in the bath-room. Was this how she'd felt the very first time they made love? Ellie had no way of telling, but was now nervous and a little shy. It seemed strange and unfair that this man knew her body intimately, yet she could remember nothing of his. Would she disappoint him? She hoped not.

As Ellie slid between the sheets, it felt strangely bizarre, yet exciting, and when Phil climbed in beside her, she turned to accept his kisses willingly, daring to touch his face and stroke the stubble on his chin. It was a face she'd grown to love. She weaved her fingers through his hair and as her husband buried his head into her soft neck, Ellie felt his tears on her skin, tears of joy and relief as he caressed her body and they became lost in rediscovering each other.

As Phil slept on in the dim light of early morning, Ellie gazed at her husband, smiling to herself and feeling like the luckiest woman on earth. How close she'd come to losing all this briefly crossed her mind; the very thought was painful and not one she wished to dwell on. But they were together now and even though she'd lost ten years' worth of memories, at that moment, she didn't care.

When Phil woke, he smiled lazily at Ellie and in the peaceful stillness of the early morning, they made love again, slowly and gently, enjoying the comfort they'd been denied for so long. Inevitably, happy sounds from Sam's nursery reached their ears and they slipped out of bed to fetch their son and enjoy the day ahead, Sunday, a family day to fill with nothing but good things.

Breakfast was the one meal Ellie had yet to make in her kitchen since the accident, and it became a long, lazy breakfast of eggs, bacon and toast. Pottering about the house in her nightclothes was another new experience and one she relished, now knowing without a doubt this was her home, the one place on earth she wanted to be, where she belonged. It pleased her to see how happy Phil was. For the first time in weeks, he appeared relaxed and hopeful for the future. Later they would go to Grace and Derek's to pick up Ellie's things. There would be no more dividing her time between the two houses. Neither she nor Phil was naïve enough to think life would be a bed of roses simply because they were together again. They accepted there were still obstacles to overcome but working together doubled their strength; they would face the future together.

Chapter Forty

On Monday morning, the glow of the weekend's events still lingered in Ellie's mind, feeling like a warm hug bringing comfort and the peace she had longed for of late. The new-found closeness to Phil, the relief of knowing Dave was nothing more than a troublemaker out for revenge, and once again living in her own home would certainly keep her smile in place for a long time.

The afternoon brought another appointment at the hospital to see Mr Samms, and Ellie rather relished the thought of telling him how much better she was, confident the doctor would be delighted for her. In anticipation of the appointment, she and Phil discussed the options over breakfast.

'You've never actually told me what Mr Samms offered by way of treatment, Ellie?'

'No, I didn't, did I? Sorry, love, but I was so confused and wanted to go it alone then.' Ellie smiled sadly, regretting the pain caused by her previous stubbornness.

'It doesn't matter. I'd just like to know what the options are.'

'Mr Samms said they could try hypnosis or something

called EMDR, Eye Movement Desensitisation and Reprocessing. It involves integrating the two hemispheres of the brain and sounds rather complicated, and I'd need to have several sessions.' She screwed her nose up at the thought.

'And how do you feel? Do you want to try either of them?'

'Quite honestly, no. I'm just getting my head around being your wife again and loving it!' Phil winked at Ellie and she laughed. 'The thought of someone messing with my head is even more unappealing now than it was at the beginning of all this. I think I still favour waiting, giving it more time. How about you?'

'Honestly, Ellie, whatever you decide is okay with me. You've been affected by the memory loss the most, but yes, I'd be happy to go along with leaving things to nature. We've got all the time in the world, haven't we?'

'We have, and it's no longer so important for me to remember, I don't need the last ten years now I have a future with you.'

Life was different since Ellie learned she could trust Phil implicitly – and more importantly she could trust herself. Her moral compass was no longer in doubt.

Phil kissed Ellie and Sam goodbye and left for work. Upstairs, the little boy played happily on the floor of the bedroom as his mother sorted out some of the items they'd brought from her parents' home the previous day. It was mainly clothing with a few cosmetics which wouldn't take long for her to organise in the lovely spacious room she shared with her husband.

Inevitably, a trace of that surreal feeling of living someone else's life hovered over her as Ellie looked through wardrobes and drawers which were filled with clothing she didn't recognise. As she worked, Ellie thought about her conversation with Phil and decided to refuse any offers of treatment from Mr Samms. Presently, things were ticking over so well, and she didn't want to risk tipping the balance again.

Her task took longer than expected as Ellie discovered items she couldn't remember buying or wearing, although they were clearly hers. Unable to resist trying some of them on, Ellie loved how they fitted – her clothes of today were of much better quality than those from her teenage years. With no other opinion available, Sam was asked what he thought of his mummy in various outfits, and his response was always positive, his huge smile and clapping hands reducing them both to laughter.

After lunch, Grace arrived to babysit while Ellie drove herself to the hospital. Becoming increasingly confident of driving in traffic, she chuckled, wondering if her father was right about 'muscle memory' taking over in such situations.

Mr Samms' office was filled with the bulk of his presence as Ellie sat opposite him, ready to answer his questions, this time in a much more positive way than before.

'How are you?' The doctor's face held genuine concern.

'Actually very well, thank you, although there's still no recollection of my missing ten years.' She smiled as he nodded thoughtfully.

'Do I detect that you're coping with this better than the last time we spoke?' he asked.

'You do, and yes, I am!' Ellie grinned. 'I'm living with Phil and Sam again, and things are going well. Clearly, amnesia is still causing problems. I can't even think about going back to work as I have no idea how to do my job, but I've started driving again, a skill which came back relatively easily and certainly helps with the practical side of life.'

'That's great news, Ellie, and it's good to see you so much more relaxed. Now you're feeling more like yourself, do you think it could be time to try some kind of treatment, EMDR perhaps, or hypnosis?'

Ellie didn't hesitate with her answer. 'Thank you, but I still don't think either option's right for me. When I first went home from the hospital to my parents' house, my mother made a suggestion which didn't work out then, but which I'd like to try now.' Ellie watched Mr Samms' puzzled expression with amusement, and explained. 'Mum suggested I forget about having amnesia and start to live from today onwards, embarking on a new life and not obsessing about the old.'

Mr Samms slapped both his hands down on his desk and roared with laughter, making her jump. 'Ha! That's a good one, very novel! I must say it's not something I've ever heard before, and I'm pretty certain it's not in any of the textbooks on amnesia either. But I love it! So, are you saying that even though your memory hasn't returned, you don't want to consider any treatment?'

'That's about it. When Mum made this suggestion, I tried it but things started to happen, making it impossible. However, now I think I'm ready to try her crazy idea; I'm living back at home and picking up the threads of my life – and I'm happy. I'm learning how to be Ellie again. It's not as if I've given up hope of remembering everything but it's somehow not as important as it was – no longer such a major issue. Maybe at a later date I might try some kind of treatment, but not yet. Is that all right with you?'

'Absolutely. I'd only want to pursue treatment if it was in your best interests and you were committed to doing so. If, as you say, you're happy with life as it is, then great! It's what we all want for you, Ellie. And please tell your mother I'd be interested in hearing about any other innovative ideas she may have; perhaps she could write a paper on her theory?' Mr Samms laughed. 'Seriously, though, I'm delighted things are looking up for you but I'd like to keep you on the books for a while longer. Shall we make your next appointment for six months, although if you need to see me before then just ring my secretary, okay?'

Ellie left the hospital with a much lighter heart than on previous visits. She called into the local supermarket to pick up a bottle of wine for later and a huge bouquet of flowers for her mother. Flowers could never repay Grace for all she and Derek had done but it was a simple token to say thank you. She also wanted to email Rosie to update her friend on what was happening in her life. Ellie could imagine the look of delight on Rosie's face on learning she was back at home with Phil again, and it was primarily thanks to her.

When she arrived home, Grace and Sam were still out at the park, so Ellie took out her laptop and wrote to her friend.

Hi Rosie,

Sorry it's taken so long to email but keep on reading and you'll see how manic things have been here, yet thankfully everything's so much better than when I arrived home from visiting you. We had such a fabulous week. Even a massive thank you seems inadequate to express how much I enjoyed and needed to be with you all.

I think you guessed there was something more than the amnesia troubling me and you were right, there was something far deeper, darker even… but thankfully it's gone! It's no longer an issue and I'm so happy I could sing and dance. It doesn't feel right to go into the details in an email but I promise to tell you all about it when we next meet, which I hope won't be too far into the future.

The best news is that I'm back living with Phil and Sam in our home — and yes, it does feel like home now too!

I can hardly describe the relief at being here and the hope we have for the future which is well and truly alive and kicking. Okay, so it's only been a couple of nights so far, wonderful nights in so many ways, but again — no details — Tom might be reading!

Of course, we accept that there's still a long way to go, whether my memory returns or not, but it's so much less daunting facing future uncertainties with Phil instead of on my own. I envied you and Tom your closeness when I was with you and despaired of ever having that again for myself, yet here I am, happy as a kid at Christmas!

Thanks again, Rosie, for all you've done for me, I'll write again soon.

Love to you, Tom and the boys,

Ellie xx

Almost as soon as Ellie hit the send button, a chirpy ding announced an incoming email. Clicking on the inbox, she gazed at the sender address, debating for a moment or two whether to open it. The sender was Fran.

Hi Ellie,
Well, I've just had a stinker of an

email from sweet little Rosie, my, how the worm's turned. She had the audacity to warn me off seeing you again — what a bloody cheek — as if I'd listen to anything she said! If I'd known you two were still in touch maybe I'd have been a bit more circumspect with my little games.

You always did have it all didn't you, and yet you never appreciated it. Great parents, a hunky, faithful husband who adores you — anyone else would value it but not you, taking it all for granted and still moaning as usual. Why shouldn't I have a little slice of your perfect life? You can't blame me for trying, can you?

So, you win again, you and your goody-goody husband, unless of course you haven't told him about your little extra-marital activities? Maybe Phil will be pleased to hear from me after all, and when he knows your little secrets, he might even need some comfort from a real woman, eh?

I suppose this is the end of a beautiful friendship, for the second time, Ellie. Who knows if we'll meet again, I rather hope not, a sentiment which I'm sure you'll share.

So goodbye, give my love to Phil.

Fran

Ellie was stunned; Fran truly was shameless, why on earth had she never realised it before? Her first instinct was to hit the delete button but on reflection she thought it might be prudent to let Phil read it first. Ellie wouldn't put it past Fran to try to cause more trouble. Rosie was right about her; she appeared to take pleasure in ruining other people's happiness. Keeping the email as new, Ellie would gladly delete it once her husband had seen it, after which she would also delete Fran from her life and not even dignify the email with a response. Her one-time friend didn't deserve it.

Chapter Forty-One

G race and Sam arrived home at the same time as the afternoon post, which brought two letters for Ellie; after thanking her mother for babysitting and hugging her son, she put the kettle on and sat down to open them.

'This one's from the CPS, Mum.' Her frown suggested she'd rather not have received this letter. Her mother took over making the tea, more interested than her daughter to learn what was inside. 'A date's been set for the sentencing of Trevor Simpson. That must be the name of the man who knocked me off my bike.' Ellie turned quite pale; the accident was something she'd prefer not to think about, the one event she didn't want to remember now her life was once more looking rosy.

'Are you expected to be there?' Grace asked.

'I'm not sure but they want me to write a victim impact statement for the judge to consider before sentencing.'

'What's a victim impact statement?'

'Probably just what it says, the impact the accident's had on me. There are some guidance notes here. I'll look at them later with Phil. I'm not sure this is something I want to do.' Ellie was confused, with no desire to dwell on negatives anymore, being obliged to think about the accident was an unwelcome intrusion. Putting the letter aside, she accepted the steaming mug of tea her mother offered before opening the second letter.

'Oh no, this one's from Solutions asking me to fix a time to see someone in human resources about returning to work. How on earth can I do that?' This letter was even more perplexing than the one from the CPS.

'The short answer is you can't. Talk to Phil about it later, love, he's probably been expecting this but with his dad dying and everything else it must have slipped his mind.'

Ellie nodded her agreement and put the letters aside to turn her attention to Sam. The little boy was beginning to grizzle, a sure sign he was ready for his tea.

Later that evening, Phil read both letters twice through.

'Do I have to do this victim impact thing?' Ellie asked after Sam was in bed and they were alone together.

'Of course you do! This idiot had been drinking – he could have killed you. The man deserves to have the book thrown at him.'

'The policeman who came to the hospital said he'd expressed remorse.'

'Huh, they all say that, their solicitors advise it in an attempt to get a more lenient sentence. If he hadn't been caught on camera, he'd probably have pleaded not guilty and then you would have been called to give evidence.' His expression was determined.

'But I can't give evidence if I can't remember anything about it!' Ellie was horrified at the thought of going to court.

'Don't worry, you don't have to, but you do need to make this statement. This Trevor Simpson's caused so much pain and he needs to know he can't get away with it.' Phil ran his fingers through his hair, a gesture Ellie noticed he often did when he was thinking.

'But what will I say?'

'Everything! You were in a coma for four weeks which impacted your family as well as you. We didn't know if you'd live or die. When you woke, you didn't even know who I was, or your son; think of the pain and anguish this has caused. And we nearly didn't make it as a couple, I mean, did we? It's the ripples in the pond effect and you need to write it all down. And it's not over yet, is it? There's no way you can return to work until your memory returns which will have financial implications too. You've lost relationships with friends you don't remember, and extended family – there's so much you can write about and it's still ongoing!' Phil was getting into his stride, and the more Ellie listened, the more she realised he was right. So, with his help and the guidance notes she would compose the statement.

Then they turned to the second letter. 'I'd completely forgotten your career break was due to come to an end. You should have returned before Sam's birthday when your twelve months were up but with the accident, they agreed to extend it for another three months. We have to decide on this one, Ellie, and let them know soon.'

'But I can hardly go back to work if I don't know how to do the job, can I?'

'True, but you'll need to talk to them and explain. They're apparently expecting you back, and quite soon.'

'Do we need the money, Phil? I mean, you mentioned financial implications and I have no idea how well off we are. Can we manage if I don't go out to work?'

'We'll manage somehow, love – we can always find a paper round for Sam.' Phil's expression was solemn but then he burst out laughing. 'Oh, Ellie, your face is a picture. The honest answer is yes, we can manage on my salary alone. Of course, it'll mean we don't have the same disposable income we're used to for luxuries like holidays and changing the car regularly, but after all we've been through lately, it doesn't bother me in the least. What's important is that you're happy here at home and I quite like knowing you'll be here when I get in from work. Sam loves having his mummy around full time too.'

'Did we have childcare plans for my return to work?' Ellie still felt awkward asking practical questions but needed to understand this side of their life, something she'd not considered before.

'Yes, we'd looked around a couple of day nurseries and put his name down at the one we particularly liked but only for three days a week. You intended working from home whenever possible and Grace offered to be a backup if we needed her.'

Ellie considered the problem. Having a career appealed to her, the best of both worlds, yet there was no way she could go back without a clue as to how to do her job.

'I'll ring Solutions tomorrow and make an appointment to call in and see someone. Perhaps the fairest thing would be to offer my resignation. They're probably obliged to take me back but to hold them to it would hardly be fair on them, would it? Was I any good at my job, Phil?' Ellie didn't even know the answer to that.

'Yes, you were, excellent, which is why they agreed to a career break. Solutions didn't want to lose you. But you're right, in fairness to them, you should offer to resign. If your memory comes back at a later date, you can consider returning to work then, but it isn't a major problem from a financial point of view, we're very fortunate in that respect. Now, are we eating at all tonight? I'm starving – but we can still afford a takeaway if you'd like?' Phil grinned.

'There's a lasagne in the fridge ready to warm up if that's okay?'

'Fantastic, and then you can tell me all about your visit to Mr Samms.'

Chapter Forty-Two

Two days later, Ellie left Sam with his grandma and drove to Rawcliffe on the outskirts of York city centre, to Tower Court, the business centre where Solutions was based. After receiving their letter, Ellie telephoned her employer and arranged an interview with Carly Jones, in human resources, for Tuesday morning. Unfortunately, the spell of glorious summer weather had finally broken and rain teemed down, lashing against the windscreen and making the Mini's wipers work furiously.

Parking in the centre's ample car park, Ellie stared up at the modern offices from inside the car. Being a few minutes early, she used the time to revise precisely what she was going to say. Having discussed this with Phil over the last couple of days, she was still undecided. The problem was that Ellie was still unsure what she wanted to do regarding her job. It was a relief to learn they didn't rely on her salary to live, although clearly their standard of living would be better if she could contribute to their finances, and if she was honest with herself, the thought of earning her own money appealed to her. The major obstacle, however, was that she hadn't a clue what her role at Solutions was. Ellie knew she was a graphic designer and according to Phil loved the work, yet she still had no idea what the job title entailed.

The rain eased a little, and, steadying her breathing, Ellie took the opportunity to dash to the office, where a logo of a question mark interwoven into the word Solutions informed her she needed to be on the second floor. Taking the stairs, she pushed open the swing doors at the top and entered a spacious lobby with a reception desk to the right.

'Ellie!' A young woman with frizzy red hair ran out from behind the desk and enveloped her in an enthusiastic bear hug. 'How great to see you. We've missed you!' The woman's grin was wide and her green eyes danced with delight as a somewhat perplexed Ellie took a step back. Unperturbed, the woman continued, 'Does this visit mean you're coming back to work? I do hope so – the office simply hasn't been the same without you. Why haven't you brought that lovely little boy with you? He must have grown so much since you last brought him in?'

Ellie gazed around the unfamiliar space, hoping someone might rescue her from this embarrassing situation but there was no one else there; she would have to extricate herself from this dilemma.

'I'm sorry, but do I know you?' She spoke apologetically, not wanting to offend.

'Ellie, you're joking!' The woman laughed, then on seeing her solemn expression appeared to realise her mistake. 'Oh, my goodness, you're not joking, are you?'

'No, I'm sorry but, you see, I'm suffering from amnesia and if I should know you, then I apologise but I can't remember.' She was unused to having to explain things herself. Her parents or Phil generally shielded her from such situations and most people Ellie had come into contact with since the accident knew of her amnesia.

'Not to worry.' The red-haired woman looked flustered; her face flushed with embarrassment. 'I'm Sally, the receptionist and Girl Friday of this crazy operation. I knew you had an appointment but the news of your, er… condition hadn't reached me. We're quite good friends, you and I, but don't worry, we can catch up another time. You're here to see Carly, I believe. Come on, I'll take you to her room.' Sally soon composed herself and Ellie dutifully followed through more glass doors and past several small offices which accommodated two or three people, most of whom had their heads bent over computer screens.

'It might sound a silly question,' Ellie ventured, 'but do I know Carly Jones?'

'Oh, you poor dear, how difficult this must be for you, but no, Carly's new to the company. She only joined us a couple of months ago and can be a bit stuffy at times but generally she's okay; hers is the kind of role which makes it difficult to be one of the guys, you know? But Carly's fair and sympathetic, so you've nothing to worry about.' Sally had stopped walking while they talked.

'And is it a big company?' Ellie wanted to know so much and Sally appeared friendly and willing to talk.

'About thirty employees in all, although most of them aren't here now, clearly. The type of work we do lends itself nicely to home-working, which you often did, particularly in the latter stages of your pregnancy. Oh my gosh, this feels so strange, telling you things about yourself. I honestly had no idea.'

'Don't worry about it. I find it rather odd myself but I appreciate the heads-up.'

Sally moved on to a room at the end of the corridor where a shiny silver plaque announced the occupant's name as Carly Jones. She knocked and opened the door without waiting for an answer.

'Hi, Carly, Ellie Graham to see you.' Sally left the room with an encouraging squeeze on Ellie's shoulder, and Carly Jones stood to greet her visitor. She was a slim woman, about Ellie's height but older, maybe in her forties, with a friendly face and shining blonde hair tied back in a tight bun with a few wisps escaping to soften the effect.

'Hello, pleased to meet you.' Her green, twinkling eyes peered at Ellie from behind a pair of rimless glasses. 'Take a seat and don't look so worried. This isn't the dentist!' Her words and ready smile put Ellie at ease as she sat opposite Carly and took a deep breath, trying to relax. Solutions was a whole new world to her, but, she reminded herself, there was nothing to worry about; Ellie didn't need this job, and intended to offer her resignation to this woman as she'd discussed with Phil over the weekend.

'I've been reading your file, Ellie, and it appears you're due to return to work after an extended career break. Unfortunately there was some kind of accident wasn't there, which delayed your return? Are you fully recovered now?'

'That's right. I was knocked off my bike and left in a coma for four weeks. Physically, I was fortunate not to suffer any broken bones, so I've healed well in some respects. But a head injury has left me with amnesia which is still causing problems, and as yet, there's no sign of my memory coming back.'

'Oh, my goodness, that's awful! How much of your memory have you lost? Sorry, that sounds totally intrusive and you don't have to tell me anything – it's just I'll need to know some details regarding your job.' Before Ellie had a chance to reply, there was a knock on the door and a man stepped inside.

'Sorry to interrupt, Carly, but Sally said Ellie was here and I wanted to say hello.' A warm smile split his long thin face. 'I'm Jeremy Bland, the CEO?' Then, when there was no sign of recognition, he continued, 'Sally explained you have no recollection of working here. I'm truly sorry, Ellie, I didn't realise. The last update we had was when Phil rang to say you were out of the coma and making progress. He did mention some memory problems but I didn't know it was so bad and still ongoing. How are you coping?' The look of genuine concern on this man's face made Ellie warm to him; although she had no recollection of him, it appeared she'd known him once and it seemed he was her boss.

'I take things a day at a time but as for work… well, this is all new to me. I'd hoped coming here might jog a memory, but it hasn't, I'm afraid.'

'Carly, do you mind?' Jeremy Bland pulled up a seat beside her. 'I don't want to take over but this is quite an unusual situation.'

'No, please, Jeremy, I think we need your input here.' Carly sounded relieved to share this unprecedented problem with her boss.

'As I have no idea what my role here is, I thought the fairest thing would be for me to offer my resignation,' Ellie continued.

'Is that what you really want?' Jeremy looked surprised.

'I don't think there's a choice. With no recollection of how to do my job, it would be impossible to return. I'd be a spare part which is something no business needs. So, look, here's my letter of resignation, I'm sorry but there's not a viable alternative.'

'Your concern for the company is appreciated, but we'll certainly miss you. Would you leave your letter with Carly and come with me for a few minutes? There's something I'd like to show you?' Jeremy stood and Ellie followed him from the room into another larger space, possibly a conference room. One wall was lined with poster-sized images of advertisements – designs which it was reasonable to assume were produced at Solutions.

'These are some of our best designs, the most successful and admittedly the most lucrative too. Most of these are for our regular customers, companies who come back to us time and time again because they like our product, our innovative approach.' Jeremy was clearly proud of the images displayed here, and Ellie could see why. She liked them too. They were modern, vibrant designs with exceptional use of colour. The images themselves were attractive and the slogans sharp, concise and to the point; it was obvious why the company was successful.

'Do *you* like them?' Jeremy asked.

'Very much, they're eye-catching without being in your face. Modern but timeless. Yes, I do like them.'

'These are all your work, Ellie. You've been our top designer for years, and to be frank, we're missing you. Our customers are missing you.' Jeremy's words stunned her; had she really designed these amazing images? He continued, 'We have other talented designers too, but none of them quite match your flair. Now you can see why we'll be sorry to let you go, but I fully understand the situation. It's an impossible one for us all. I can't help but think your skill must still be in there somewhere, and it's probably just a matter of recalling the technical side of the job. What I'd like to ask is if you'll seriously consider returning to work for us when your memory returns. Will you do that for me please?'

Still unable to believe she'd produced such fantastic work, Ellie nodded her agreement. 'I'm afraid it's a question of if my memory returns rather than when but yes, I'll certainly think seriously about coming back. I'd actually love to be able to come back.'

'Great! Now, Carly will process your letter of resignation and email you very soon. Keep in touch, Ellie, and please let me know how you get on. I hope your memory does return and not just for the sake of the company.' Jeremy walked her to the door where she said goodbye to him and a rather tearful Sally.

Driving home after being confronted with a part of her life which was utterly alien to her, Ellie was in a dream. She possessed a talent she couldn't remember, yet the evidence of which she'd seen with her own eyes, yet another thing on the list of things which were lost to her. Not for the first time she wondered how a whole chunk of her life could be so completely wiped from her conscious mind, and how many more surprises were in store for her in the future.

Chapter Forty-Three

September mellowed into October, the leaves turning into rich golds, reds and orange, a season which Ellie had always loved. It was as if the heat and frenzy of summer had dissipated, and as the weather outside settled into a cool, comfortable temperature, so did Ellie's emotions. She remained contentedly at home, focused on Sam and Phil and trying her best to 'forget' the amnesia which continued to raise its unwelcome head to frustrate and confuse her on occasions.

The autumn months also brought welcome closure with the sentencing of Trevor Simpson. Ellie had dutifully completed the victim impact statement for the CPS, a painful experience which hammered home to her exactly how much she'd lost along with her memory. The family decided not to attend the hearing but heard afterwards from the police that Simpson was given a three-year custodial sentence for causing serious injury by driving while under the influence of alcohol. He was also banned from driving for two years and fined £2,500. Phil grumbled that it wasn't enough, arguing Ellie's sentence was far greater and still ongoing but generally they were happy to put the accident behind them. Life was too good to allow recriminations to fester and breed unwelcome bitterness.

Trips to the park with Sam were so very different in the autumn, perhaps even more of a delight than in the heat of summer and undoubtedly less stressful with the spectre of Dave now banished for good. Knowing she'd done nothing to be ashamed of was a huge relief, indescribably so, and Ellie was once again free to laugh and enjoy her life in the present.

Sam was growing rapidly and becoming quite sturdy on his chunky little legs. He loved nothing more than crunching the dry leaves underfoot with his wellington boots, kicking them into swirls and laughing as they blew away from him on windy days.

It was after one of her and Sam's autumn walks that an unexpected visitor arrived in the form of Angie Pearson, Dave's wife. The anxious-looking woman was waiting on the doorstep as Ellie approached her home, a willowy figure of about the same age as her and quite pretty, except for the permanently worried expression on her face.

'Hello.' Angie spoke softly. 'Sorry to call unannounced but I wanted to see you before I left the area.' Ellie and Phil had welcomed the appearance of a 'for sale' sign at number 40 as good news, and the conclusion of a time they would rather forget.

'Won't you come in?' Ellie asked, not expecting the offer to be accepted, but Angie smiled and nodded. Once inside the house with Sam settled with his toys, Ellie offered coffee which was again accepted. The women settled somewhat uneasily in the lounge, Angie concentrating on hugging the mug in her hands, chewing on her bottom lip, unsure what to say.

'I've come to apologise… for Dave's despicable behaviour,' she blurted out.

'It's not for you to apologise, you didn't know what he was doing and you've been just as badly hurt by his actions as I have.' Ellie felt a rush of sympathy for this woman. 'Were we ever friends, Angie?' she asked.

'No, not really, acquaintances maybe? We'd pass the time of day, but as I've worked practically every hour God sends, there was never the chance for a friendship to develop. Dave was the one who was around more than me – and it appears he took advantage of it. I'm so sorry, Ellie – as if you don't have enough problems to cope with.' Angie shook her head sadly.

'Really, there's no need for you to apologise. You did nothing wrong. But tell me, did you know about the incident before – the time Phil broke Dave's nose?' Ellie was curious.

'No way! He told me he'd fallen down the stairs and as there was no way of knowing otherwise – well, you believe your husband, don't you? It's a kind of default setting, or perhaps I just wanted to believe him. Dave was always one to admire other women but I thought he was only window shopping – if I'd had any idea he was pestering you...' Angie chewed on her bottom lip and Ellie's heart went out to this woman.

'It's history now, and you don't have to apologise for his behaviour. So, what's next for you, Angie? I noticed the house is up for sale.'

'It is, and we've got a buyer. I'm moving out tomorrow, which is why I wanted to come over today. I've rented a flat near the hospital where I work and now the shock of the split's over, I'm quite looking forward to starting a new life. Dave and I married when we were both twenty, it was too young, and so I've decided to live a bit and enjoy the single life.'

'I'm sorry things have worked out badly for you, Angie.' A twinge of guilt nudged Ellie, although she knew it was ridiculous, she wasn't to blame.

'Well I'm not. We were talking about starting a family but thank goodness it never happened. It's a shame you had to suffer Dave's attention for me to find out what a bloody pig he really is, but quite honestly, I feel more relieved than upset. This has done me a huge favour.' A hint of a smile crossed Angie's face. She left after a few more minutes, and Ellie wished her well; a broken marriage isn't easy but Angie appeared to be moving on swiftly.

'Guess who came to visit today?' she asked Phil later.

'Obviously someone you didn't expect, so go on, tell me?'

'Angie Pearson.' Ellie grinned.

'Not to cause any trouble, I hope?' His expression suddenly changed to one of concern.

'No, just to say sorry, and goodbye. She's leaving tomorrow. They've got a buyer for the house and Angie's renting a flat, she seems keen to move on. I felt quite sorry for her – none of this was her fault – she just picked the wrong kind of man to marry.'

Ellie later reflected on how fortunate she was to have met and married Phil. Angie's visit served to put a full stop at the end of the Dave saga, a nightmare she wouldn't wish on anyone. There were still problems for Ellie and Phil to face in the future, but they would do so together, knowing the door was now firmly closed on the ugly chapter they'd suffered due to Dave Pearson.

Chapter Forty-Four

Autumn passed in happy domesticity and Ellie found herself anticipating the joys of a family Christmas, taking Sam to meet Father Christmas, the decorations and the presents. Unable to remember her son's first Christmas, she consoled herself with thinking he'd been only a few months old and wouldn't have understood the excitement of the festivities. However, this year he would certainly be more aware and his parents were determined to make it the best celebration ever.

By mid-November, Ellie had compiled lists for every aspect of Christmas and was firmly set on being super-organised well before the big event. A trip to York Designer Outlet at Fulford was planned with Grace, a girls' day out, so Phil would be left in charge of their son. It was a day to purchase presents, to put a tick beside many names on her list, and Ellie was intent on enjoying every moment.

The centre was amazing, already decked out for Christmas with giant baubles sparkling from the high ceilings, an enormous tree and a grotto, ready and waiting for the big man himself, who was not yet in residence. Fairy lights adorned every pillar, creating a bright and sparkling magical setting, the mood designed to enchant and encourage shoppers to part with their money.

Their first stop was for coffee and a good chat to catch up with Grace. Now that Ellie was settled at home, they didn't see each other quite as regularly as before, so there was always much to talk about.

'Has Josephine decided if she's coming for Christmas?' Grace inquired.

'She has, yes, and I'm delighted. I know things were strained at first but I really like her, Mum, and am so looking forward to seeing her again.'

'And has she had any thoughts about staying in Spain or coming home?'

'She's staying in Spain, at least for the foreseeable future. Josephine's been remarkably prudent in her decisions and is taking her time over them. For now, her life is in Spain, she and Jim made so many friends, and naturally she's reluctant to leave them. It could be she'll change her mind in the future, but Josephine's still relatively young, very fit, and certainly enjoys the lifestyle over there. We've promised to go over in February, which is something to look forward to after Christmas and we often speak on Skype. It's so important for Sam to know his other grandma.'

'I'm glad you're getting on well, you always did, you know, and with Jim too. He was a lovely man, Josephine must miss him dreadfully. But come on, we can't spend the day gossiping. There are presents to buy and your dad's credit card's burning a hole in my pocket!' Grace laughed and they set off to begin the serious task of shopping.

Even for a Wednesday, the stores were busy; it appeared everyone was intent on getting a head start on their Christmas shopping. Of course, the big temptation for both women was to look at toys and clothes for Sam, but Ellie was determined not to spend too much on him, he wanted for nothing, and she was conscious of having only one salary coming into the house. Grace didn't wish to spoil her grandson either but couldn't resist some cute dungarees and a matching shirt.

'Oh, they make such lovely things for children these days!' she exclaimed, hiding the price tag from her daughter. Ellie smiled; her mother would buy what she wanted; protesting was futile. Grace joined the queue at the checkout to pay for the dungarees on which she'd set her heart. While Ellie waited, she browsed some more practical items which her son needed, pyjamas and vests, he was growing so quickly and clothes didn't seem to fit him for very long. As she compared sizes, her attention was caught by a commotion near the till. Turning to see what was happening, Ellie was horrified to see Grace sprawled full length on the floor, unconscious.

'Mum!' She ran to the till and knelt beside her mother. 'Do you have a first-aider?' she asked the assistant who was standing with her mouth open. A supervisor appeared and took charge, checking Grace's pulse and asking what had happened. Ellie could tell her nothing but the lady who'd been next to her in the queue told them she just appeared to faint.

'Call an ambulance,' the supervisor instructed the till girl, who finally jumped into action. Grace moaned and opened her eyes.

'What happened?' she asked.

'You fainted, Mum,' Ellie answered, 'Are you hurt?'

'No, I don't think so. Where are we?' she asked, puzzled at all the fuss. Ellie looked at the supervisor, silently asking her opinion.

'I think we need the paramedics; your mum was out for more than a couple of minutes and seems a little confused. What's her name?'

'Grace.' Ellie felt useless and was trembling with shock.

'Grace, do you think you can stand up and we'll find you a chair somewhere a little less crowded?'

'I don't need a chair. Where's Derek?' she said, really scaring her daughter then. Finally, a chair was found in a changing room which offered a degree of privacy. The supervisor, a competent lady, stayed with them until the paramedics arrived twenty minutes later. Grace's confusion was a concern, but the calm way the paramedics assessed the situation and took over reassured Ellie.

'Can you tell me where you live, Grace?' the younger paramedic, who introduced herself as Jane, asked.

'In Spain, of course, but where am I now?'

Jane looked at Ellie who shook her head briefly. 'And who's this with you, love?'

Grace studied her daughter for a moment before smiling and saying, 'It's my daughter!'

Ellie breathed a sigh of relief to hear her mother say those words. She waited anxiously for Jane and her colleague, Gavin, to finish their assessment. It seemed to take an age.

'I think we need to take her to hospital for a few tests. We can do an ECG in the ambulance and the results will go straight through to A&E. Do you want to come with her in the ambulance?' Gavin asked.

'Yes, of course.' Ellie thought of her car, but knew she could get Phil to run her back later to pick it up. She had no intention of leaving her mother's side.

The patient was lifted onto a wheeled chair and pushed, protesting, through the shopping centre and out to the car park. Once inside the ambulance, the paramedics examined Grace more thoroughly and prepared an ECG as promised.

'What do you think it is?' Ellie hardly dared to ask.

'Too early to say, love, but not to worry, she seems to be perking up already.' It was true, colour was returning to

Grace's cheeks, and she managed to smile, pulling a face as if it was all a lot of fuss about nothing. Then, in about fifteen minutes, they set off to the hospital, a place Ellie wasn't keen to see again, but there was no way she was going to leave her mother's side.

Chapter Forty-Five

Being back in the York hospital was an unpleasant experience for Ellie. Although she'd visited Mr Samms as an outpatient twice since her accident, the very atmosphere took her back to the confusion and upset of her time as an in-patient. Worry about her mother, however, provided a focus other than those memories. As the paramedics handed over care to the A&E staff, Ellie tried to comfort Grace, assuring her all was well.

'Are you a relative?' a triage nurse asked.

'Yes, I'm her daughter.'

'And can you tell me exactly what happened?'

Ellie could only repeat what she'd told the paramedics – that her mother seemed fine before appearing to faint and had remained unconscious for about three minutes, coming round to a degree of confusion. After a brief physical check, the nurse smiled and said there was no apparent damage from the fall, but the doctor would still need to see her and probably want to do tests to discover why she lost consciousness and was confused. By this time, Grace was dozing, so the nurse again addressed Ellie.

'Has your mother any medical problems we should be aware of; heart disease, diabetes, or any recent surgeries?'

'She had a pacemaker fitted about six years ago. Actually, when I think about it, she had similar symptoms to this around that time, fainting fits and confusion afterwards. Could it be connected?'

'It could, yes, but we'll leave the doctor to decide. It might be some time before she's seen, as we're rather busy and it's not life-threatening so you may have to wait.' The nurse smiled an apology and left the cubicle. Ellie thought it was time to ring her father and Phil to let them know what had happened.

Derek, concerned at the news, left home immediately to get to the hospital. However, Phil had Sam to consider and wouldn't be of any use, so they decided he'd stay at home and she would keep him updated as to any change in her mother's condition.

'Who are you ringing?' Grace asked sleepily.

'Dad, of course, he's coming straight away, and I've rung Phil, but he's got Sam to look after.'

'You shouldn't have bothered them; they'll only worry and I'm feeling fine now. Can I not just go home; a cup of tea and a couple of paracetamols and I'll be as right as rain.'

'No, Mum, the doctor's coming to see you but we might have to wait. You were very confused when you came round and told the paramedic you lived in Spain.'

'Did I? How silly, it must have been because we were talking about Josephine, but I'll be okay now and the doctor must have more seriously ill people to attend to.'

'Well, you're staying here until the doctor's seen you. Your symptoms are similar to the time they discovered your irregular heartbeat and you had the pacemaker fitted. So perhaps it's something to do with that. Maybe an adjustment is needed or something but you gave me quite a fright.' Ellie noticed her mother looking at her strangely.

'Are you feeling ill again, Mum? Shall I call a nurse?'

'No.' Grace smiled at her daughter. 'What did you just say about the pacemaker?'

'Just that you seem to have the same symptoms as you did then, why?'

'Ellie, do you know when I had the pacemaker fitted?'

'About six years ago... oh my goodness, Mum, I can remember!' Ellie looked suddenly paler than her mother and flopped down on the high-backed chair beside the bed, feeling quite light-headed herself.

'What do you remember?' Grace's face was a picture of anticipation and wonder.

'You suffered a few fainting fits and periods of dizziness. It was in the summer because initially, we put it down to the hot weather. But, I remember, Mum, I can remember!'

'Can you remember anything else?'

Ellie closed her eyes. A strange feeling of seeing things as if through clouds almost made her dizzy. Memories were coming towards her, unclear and only in snatches. But the fog in her mind was lifting and the images were becoming clearer. Phil was there, smiling, and she was holding a baby and crying with joy.

'Are you all right, love?' Grace was concerned for her daughter but excited too. 'Tell me, sweetheart, what can you remember?' But Ellie remained silent for several minutes. Her head swam with images, snapshots of memories jumbled together and bouncing off the inside of her head.

'Shall I get the nurse for you?' Grace offered, swinging her legs over the side of the bed to sit up.

'No, I'm fine, honestly, Mum.' A starburst of fractured images swirled around the inside of her mind, her own personal light show. 'I can remember – my wedding, university, Australia, it's all there, Mum, it's coming back to me!' Ellie was crying and laughing at the same time. 'I know now who I am, I remember!'

Derek Watson entered the cubicle at that precise moment to find his wife and daughter in an unprecedented emotional state. He looked from one to the other, unable to comprehend the strange cocktail of laughter and tears.

'Grace, are you okay?' he asked, grabbing his wife's arm. 'What's going on? What's happened?'

'It's Ellie. She can remember, Derek, her memory's returned!' A garbled explanation followed and the couple watched their daughter as tears rolled down her face.

The family of three remained cosseted in the cubicle of the A&E department as if in their own micro-world. In other areas of the hospital, other dramas played out starring other people, but nothing could surpass the delight of the Watson family. Even the fears for Grace's health melted into the background as Ellie, unable to get her words out quickly enough, related everything she could remember, the memories which were assaulting her mind with remarkable speed and clarity. Admittedly, the chronology of events was somewhat chaotic, but she didn't care, confident that everything would come back to her in time.

It was almost an hour before a doctor arrived to examine Grace. 'Mrs Watson, tell me how you're feeling.'

'Absolutely fine!' she replied to the doctor's surprise.

'I believe you had a pacemaker fitted several years ago?'

'Six years to be exact.' Ellie laughed as she spoke. *She remembered!* The doctor, ignoring the strange behaviours, explained that the most likely cause of this recent episode was a battery failure in the pacemaker.

'So, will I have to come back to have it replaced?' Grace asked.

'No, we'll do it today. There are risks to allowing you to go home. You could black out at anytime, anywhere, so we'll admit you to the ward, do a few tests and replace the pace-maker as soon as a theatre is available.' The severity with which the doctor spoke brought them all down to earth. Grace required urgent care.

'Mum, I think perhaps I should get home. You'll be okay now Dad's here, won't you?'

'Of course, love. Wait till you tell Phil, he's going to be amazed! Your dad can run you home if you like. I'll be fine here on my own for a while, I'm ready for a little nap.'

'If you're sure? I could easily grab a taxi.'

'No, no. It's not far and he'll be back in no time. Now go on and tell that husband of yours the good news!'

Ellie kissed her mother goodbye and allowed her father to drive her home, anticipating the excitement her revelation would cause.

Chapter Forty-Six

Although less than twenty minutes, the drive home seemed like an eternity as Ellie's excitement bubbled over; she could hardly wait to see Phil and Sam. Unsurprisingly, her head was beginning to throb and felt like an overstuffed cushion, full of memories which had previously been lost to her. It was like witnessing a shattered pane of glass in reverse, the shards sliding into place to form a complete, clear pane once more.

Ellie remained silent for most of the journey, marvelling at what was happening to her, and Derek was content to be quiet too, aware of his daughter's need for space to assimilate her thoughts, and concerned for Grace, anxious to return to her side. He dropped Ellie outside her home and promised to let her know how her mother fared with the procedure she was to undergo.

Phil and Sam were playing with Sam's favourite toy of the moment, a train set, and his lips were pursed in concentration as he made sloppy chugging noises, encouraged by his daddy.

'How is she?' Phil jumped up to enquire after Grace,

concerned for her and Ellie. 'It must have been quite a shock for you?'

'It was, but she's going to be fine. The pacemaker needs a new battery, a minor procedure, but they're keeping her in to do it immediately. All being well, she should be home tomorrow.'

'Oh, that's good news, and how are you, love?'

'Never been better!' Ellie smiled at her husband, enjoying the moment, cherishing her secret for a few seconds more and anticipating his reaction. Her eyes danced as she looked at him and her son. Sam had crawled over to greet his mummy, and she scooped him up and kissed his cheek.

'Phil, I remembered when Mum had the pacemaker fitted. It was me who told the nurse.'

Her husband looked puzzled until it dawned on him exactly what she was saying. 'But that was five or six years ago, surely…'

'Yes, it was!' Ellie grinned, relishing the moment. 'Can you remember when you used the juicer for the first time and didn't put the lid on firmly enough?' She laughed out loud at her husband's expression.

'I can, but can you?' Phil was astounded.

'And I filmed you and threatened to post it on Facebook?'

'Sweetheart, can you remember?' He sounded desperate so she stopped teasing.

'Yes, yes, I can remember!'

Phil picked her up and swung her around, laughing. 'And what else can you remember?' he asked, holding his breath. Ellie turned to a somewhat bemused little boy who was again sitting on the floor surrounded by toys but more interested in his parents and their strangely animated conversation.

'I can remember when you were born, little man.' She addressed her son. 'The excruciating pain, the agony and the joy… bittersweet!' Ellie tickled Sam's ribs and he rolled on his back, chuckling as if he understood the significance of her happiness. 'And you, Phil, eating a meat pie while I was struggling with contractions and begging for gas and air!'

'But I was hungry!' He mirrored her grin. 'What else do you remember? Tell me, please?'

'Our wedding day when you promised we'd always be as happy. And we are, Phil, aren't we?' Ellie's eyes sparkled with tears – tears of joy, of relief.

'Yes, we are.' He lifted Sam from the floor and held his wife and his son in a long embrace. When he released her, she moved to the bookcase where photographs of their wedding held pride of place. Her memories were no longer flat, lifeless images. Instead, they were suddenly vibrant, three-dimensional, solid memories. It was as if the final pieces of the jigsaw puzzle of her life were falling into place, and she was no longer afraid of who she was; Ellie knew, she was complete once more.

Later, when Sam was in bed, Ellie described what had transpired with Grace, and the shock of seeing her mother unconscious.

'Perhaps the shock was the catalyst for your memory returning?' Phil wondered.

'Maybe,' she agreed and told him of her surprise when she realised she'd told the nurse how Grace had been fitted with a pacemaker. 'I didn't know I was remembering at first!' She laughed at the peculiarity of the situation. Not everything was clear yet, but images still flashed into her mind of past events, people and places. 'I'd like to look at the photos of Australia now I remember it, but not tonight. There'll be time later. I remember your dad, Phil, and I loved him dearly; his warmth and whacky sense of humour. He was such a lovely man – we laughed all the time when he was around, didn't we? I'm so sorry he's gone. I miss him too.'

Phil nodded, overwhelmed to finally have his wife back, all

of his wife. There was so much to discuss and plan for, but for the present, he simply wanted to take her into his arms, to hold her close.

A phone call from the hospital later that evening reassured them Grace was fine. The procedure was successful, and Derek would be able to take her home the following morning. Naturally, Grace was unconcerned with her own health and wanted to know how her daughter was. Derek had a list of questions from his wife which he dutifully asked and Ellie answered, confident her mother would want to grill her more thoroughly in person the following day.

'Tell Mum we'll come and see her tomorrow when she gets home.' She eventually ended the call. They'd all waited so long for this moment; they could wait another day to celebrate it.

As they lay in bed that night, wrapped in each other's arms, Ellie turned to look at Phil. 'You didn't tell me about the miscarriages before Sam, did you?'

'No, my love, I didn't. Sometimes it's better not to remember everything, and they were difficult times; we've certainly had our fair share of those during our marriage. But we have Sam now, and each other, it's enough.'

'Do you want more children, Phil?'

'Yes, we always wanted a little girl to complete our family, but there's plenty of time and I only want to try again when you're ready. You may even want to go back to work?'

'Oh, yes, I love work, and I've missed it. But I'd love another baby too.' She smiled at Phil and snuggled closer.

'There's no reason why you can't have both. You are your own woman, Ellie. You always have been; strong and determined, which is one of the many things I love about you.'

'About these miscarriages, it's still a little blurry; is there any reason why we can't have more children?'

'Absolutely none. The doctor said you should be fine now you've carried one baby to full term.'

In the darkened room, Phil's fingers touched Ellie's under the warmth of the duvet and she could almost hear the smile on his face.

Long after Phil drifted off to sleep, Ellie lay awake, remembering. Now she knew who Ellie Graham was, she could finally step into the future with confidence. Nothing in life is ever certain and there are no guarantees, but knowing herself and Phil was all Ellie needed. She smiled and closed her eyes. Sleep came much easier these days.

THE END

Also by Gillian Jackson

The Pharmacist

The Victim

The Deception

Abduction

Snatched

The Accident

The Shape of Truth

The Charcoal House

The Dead Husband

Author's notes

Thank you for reading *Remembering Ellie*. I hope you enjoyed her journey of discovery. When telling Ellie's story, it was impossible not to empathise with her situation – losing ten years of memories must be frightening – people, places and events vanished as if they had never happened. The more I considered it, the more I realised how terrifying it must be; amnesia is more than forgetting things. It's losing part of your life and even your unique identity.

To chart Ellie's story, I looked at the people in her life and asked the questions she would have asked of herself. Who are my real friends? Are those around me to be trusted? Is my marriage as perfect as I'm being told? But as well as questioning others, Ellie questioned herself. To be unsure of your character and trustworthiness and not knowing what you are capable of is probably far worse than being unsure of others.

Acknowledgements

My thanks, as always, to the team at Bloodhound Books for their incredible help in getting this book out into the world. Each book is a collaboration – I get to do the good bits of inventing characters and weaving plots, and they work on polishing and presenting my work to be the best it can be. I truly appreciate their guidance, dedication and professionalism throughout the process.

Thanks also for the support of my wonderful family, particularly my husband of fifty years, Derek, who selflessly watches endless football matches to give me the time and space I need to create my fantasy world.

A note from the publisher

Thank you for reading this book. If you enjoyed it please do consider leaving a review on Amazon to help others find it too.

We hate typos. All of our books have been rigorously edited and proofread, but sometimes mistakes do slip through. If you have spotted a typo, please do let us know and we can get it amended within hours.

info@bloodhoundbooks.com

Milton Keynes UK
Ingram Content Group UK Ltd.
UKHW022116280224
438615UK00007B/128

9 781916 978577